MW01199484

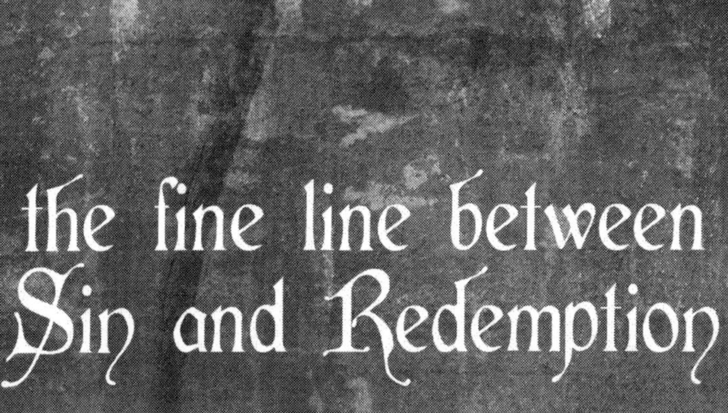

the fine line between
Sin and Redemption

7

By

Casey L. Bond
Jo Michaels
Tia Silverthorne Bach
Kelly Risser
N. L. Greene

First Edition
Published January 7, 2016
ISBN 10 - 1518846718
ISBN 13 - 978-1518846717

Cover design by Jo Michaels
Edited by Tia Silverthorne Bach and Jo Michaels of INDIE Books Gone Wild
Proofread by Kelly Risser

Acknowledgements

Casey:

I give all thanks to God for his amazing blessings in my life. Those blessings runneth over and He has given me a family who loves and supports me, friends who are more precious than gold and everything I need to survive and thrive in this beautiful world He has created.

I'm thankful to have found the amazing co-writers of this novel. They are beautiful, intelligent and classy and I'm proud to call them some of my closest friends. I have to credit Janet Wallace, founder of Utopia, for her vision. She created a conference in which creativity thrives and this book is one of the many examples of that vision come to life.

A huge thank you to Jo Michaels, Tia Silverthorne Bach, Kelly Risser and Nichole Greene for their hard work on this project and for taking a chance on me and my writing. It means the world to me.

Jo:

When we started this project, I wasn't sure we'd be able to out-do *Fractured Glass*. That book broke tons of "writing rules," yet it went on to win two awards. This one is just as good—if not better—and I know it's because of the women *in* this group. Thank you all for being so *amazingly* talented and fun to work with. I hope we're all friends forevermore. Thanks to my husband—I love you so friggin' much!—without whom none of this would've been possible, and to the awesome that's Janet Wallace for creating UTOPiAcon—the conference that changed our lives, and the place this novel was brainstormed.

Tia:

I am overwhelmed with gratitude for my writing sisters—Jo, Kelly, Nichole, and Casey. I adore each of you, and I'm grateful for your friendship, shared knowledge, and unwavering support. A huge thank you to Janet Wallace for the amazing conference, Utopia, which brings together those who love the written word, allowing us to form lifelong bonds.

Many thanks to my husband of 20 years and our three beautiful girls. They are more than I ever thought I'd have, and I thank God every day for them and my many blessings.

For all the readers who invite us into their lives by loving our words, thank you! We hope you love our latest tale.

Acknowledgements

A special shout out to my writing buddies, friends, and family who support me. You know who you are, and I hope I tell you often what you mean to me.

Kelly:

"Any time women come together with a collective intention, it's a powerful thing. Whether it's sitting down making a quilt, in a kitchen preparing a meal, in a club reading the same book, or around the table playing cards, or planning a birthday party, when women come together with a collective intention, magic happens."

~ Phylicia Rashad

To that I say, "Amen!" This book was truly a labor of love, one that we poured our hearts and souls into, and I can honestly say it would not have achieved this level of magic without input and effort from all these amazingly talented ladies that I am proud to call friends. Thank you, Casey, Jo, Nichole, and Tia, for sharing your time, talent and creativity. I love collaborating with you and can't wait until the next project! Although, really, I can't wait to see your faces again and give you big hugs!

As readers will discover, at its heart, 7 is about five amazing, gifted and loving women. I am fortunate to be surrounded by many women of this caliber in my life—for that, a shout out to my mom, sister, cousins, aunts, daughter, and girlfriends for always being there. I'd also like to give a big round of applause to the readers and bloggers who fall in love with our stories and proceed to tell us about it. Your enthusiasm for Fractured Glass is what led us to 7.

N. L.:

No matter how many books we write, Jo, Kelly, Casey, and Tia, you ladies will always be affectionately known to me as my FG girls! I am so honored to call all of you my friend and will forever treasure the time we've spent creating these worlds together. You four are not only fun to work with and extremely inspiring but I love that we laugh together, share our family's moments, and even our problems. That is true friendship and so rare, which makes me even more fortunate to be experiencing it with you ladies. I love you all to the moon and beyond! I can't wait to continue our journey together, writing stories and making memories until we're all old and grey! XOXO

Contents

Five.
The daughters.
Always sent to guide.

They stood in the white place and lifted their palms to the center of the circle. "So it has been done; so it shall begin."

As though a star went supernova, an epicenter formed at the joining of hands and radiated outward. When the light dimmed once again, the daughters were gone.

Their journey had begun.

Casey L. Bond

Part One

Rome, August 1, 64 AD
3:33am

Thomitus

For Thomitus, rest was a myth. Sleep was the most exhausting part of his day; it was also the most intense. Night terrors had plagued him since he had been old enough to remember them. The scene played out the same way every time, starting in the same place and ending with Thomitus screaming and thrashing against the figments haunting his imagination. That night was no different.

The sour stench of my own sweat mixes with the smell of sweet figs, dates, and citrus. Gusts of wind thrash my tunic about. The air is dry, so dry my throat feels like the sand piling between my toes, finding its way into the crevices of the leather sandals strapped to my feet. Where had they come from? What was I wearing? My long hair twists into my face before being blown back again.

A scene unfolds before me. A man is being led away in shackles and chains. Soldiers shove him forward, and he stumbles, cutting his knees apart on the rocky path. He pushes himself back to his feet and hangs his head. A soldier shoves the prisoner again, but he stays upright. If I were in his shoes, I would lash out. What more does he have to lose?

But the prisoner does not protest, just follows peacefully, as though nothing in the world is wrong with their behavior. Everything inside me roils violently, in stark contrast to this man's demeanor.

With the hilt of a sword, one of the soldiers strikes the man in the temple and he falls. His chin hits the ground, and the sound of his upper teeth colliding with his lower fills the air. It's much more difficult for him to rise back up this time, though I will it with all that is within me.

Churning. Something is wrong. But, what? A roar, more thunderous than the booming from overhead, fills the air. I had made that guttural sound. I run to him, shoving the soldiers away. The tips of my fingers tingled to find the cold metal clamped to his hands, to release him. I was the guilty one. Not him.

"No!" I cry out. "Do not arrest him! Take me!"

My pleas are swallowed by the blustery wind howling through the fields. My feet stick as if I am wading through waist-deep mud. I cannot make them move. The world seems off somehow. My feet are stone. They keep me prisoner.

The soldiers, the man, they don't seem affected by it at all. They move freely. Again, I call out, begging. "Please, take me instead! It is me that you want!"

They ignore me, acting as if I am not even there. I try to scream again, but I cannot.

Desperation squeezes my throat, choking off the very air I breathe. Molten lead flows through my veins, burning, cooling, and solidifying all at the same time. My muscles stiffen like stone.

I cannot move.

I cannot speak.

I cannot scream.

Josephine

Josephine, careful to avoid the hands of her lover striking out against something she could not even begin to wrap her mind around, gently tucked herself behind the unsettled man in the bed beside her. She whispered calming words, combed her fingers through his hair, and held him in her arms until he stopped beating the air in front of him, struggling against the blankets tangled around his limbs. She kept a tight grip on him, telling him he was okay, that all was right, that he was home. Josephine was one of the few people, including his parents and the soldiers who had fought beside him, that knew of his nightly battles. And she was the only one who had ever been able to calm him down during one of them.

Thomitus let out a groan that echoed across the low ceiling of their cubiculum. Shielding his eyes with his arm, ripples of taut muscle tensed and then relaxed again, concealing the steel beneath the soft skin that had been scraped clean the previous day at the baths. Josephine sat up beside him, clutching the linens close to her chest. She drank him in as she did every morning.

Through the villa's windows, the earliest rays of the sun filtered into the room, slowly caressing his bronzed skin like the hands of a lover. For a moment, she became jealous of the pale yellow light. Grinning as she thought of the previous night, she bit her thumb and watched him fight to stay asleep. He shifted positions from his left side to his right, fluffed his pillow, and squeezed his eyes closed. When that failed, he covered his face with it.

It was all she could do to rein in her mirth, knowing her giggles would make him aware he was being watched.

In the end, Thomitus gave in. He always did. There was much work to be done, and idleness, though tolerated within their higher class, was not something Josephine was accustomed to partaking in. Even as a small child, she recalled her father's words: Anyone with a mind could find something with which to busy themselves. Idleness only led to trouble.

When the skin of her bare feet met the tesserae, she shivered. That day was to be hot, but the air of the morning still provided a cooling breeze. August had been nearly unbearable, and the Great Fire had made it doubly so. She washed her face and toweled off, quickly arranged her dark blue stola, and affixed the golden brooch that ensured the garment stayed in place.

More rustling sounds came from the bed while Josephine sat at her small wooden table and combed through her long, silky strands of dark brown hair. As one particular knot gave in to her ministrations, Thomitus groaned, acquiescing to the time of day. Through the mirror, she watched him rise and dress, proud of him for accomplishing so much at such a young age. He had been a warrior for Rome, fighting bravely to extend the boundaries of the Empire, and soon, he would be a Senator. Of course, that fact would have to be kept secret for a while.

Instead of the customary purple stripe adorning his toga, he wore one that was devoid of color. She imagined him wearing the true colors of the title he would soon hold: Senator.

Josephine was proud of his accomplishments. He wanted to be more, to work hard and make Rome better for everyone who lived within her boundaries. Josephine would not care if they both lived in hovels and wore burlap, because she loved Thomitus with her entire heart. Most marriages were arranged for the family's benefit, to secure an upgrade in class or to gain land and privilege. But Thomitus and Josephine's story was different. Both had belonged to the same social class and were born to wealthy families.

7

They had taken notice of each other during their final year of education. When Thomitus pursued her publicly, her family had not protested, but welcomed him as one of their own. The pair was well suited and made each other genuinely happy.

She pinned a portion of her hair up with the golden laurel twig Thomitus had given her the previous month, allowing the rest of the ringlets to cascade down the length of her back. It was how he preferred it, and she wished to please him.

Looking in the mirror again, she started. He stood behind her, quiet as a mouse, but much more deadly. Thomitus, her warrior husband, whose skin bore the remnants of wounds from nearly forty battles, gently eased a necklace over her head and fastened it. He worked his calloused thumb up and down the slender column of her neck, making her melt into him as if she were no more than a piece of glowing-hot metal under the control of a skilled blacksmith.

The breeze entering their villa still carried the remnants of acrid smoke and ravaged hope. Gray soot dirtied white linen curtains that danced happily in the wind, unaware of the tragedy that lay beyond the sill. Her gaze went to the fabric as it moved, and her eyebrows pulled together.

"You worry too much about things beyond your control, my sweet." His deep voice usually had a soothing effect on her, but not that day.

"As do you. Your dreams were violent last night. At one point, I had to leave the bed because you were thrashing about so fiercely. You kept screaming not to take him, to take you. Who is he—the one you dream of so often?"

Thomitus's thumb stilled, and he rested his hands on her shoulders as if weary to the bone. "I am not certain. I experience it every night, as you know, but as far as I can recall, I have never seen the man in real life, never been in a similar situation in all of my battles. It is—"

She searched his face for an answer, and when she did not find it in the mirror, she stood and clung tightly to him until he found it for himself.

"It is as if I am not just fighting a simple battle, but a war for my soul. I can feel the implications of the outcome resonate through me, down to the marrow. I just cannot understand why the dreams will not leave me. But, I suppose they cannot last forever." His lips tilted in a smile that was probably meant to reassure her, but it betrayed the fact that he had not fully believed in his own words.

Josephine did not understand why he was plagued with such horrifying subconscious thoughts. Had he experienced trauma in battle, in losing friends before his eyes? He never let on and never shared those intimate details.

"Better to leave the past where it belongs. It is content there, and I prefer to dwell in the present," he would say. And she would not argue with him, because she would never want to cause him more pain by forcing him to relive what were certainly horrific memories.

“Why are there only two silver bars on your necklace, Jo?” Thomitus raked the scruff of his jaw against the smooth skin of her cheek, and she loved it.

She dug her fingers into his back, urging him closer. And he gave in to what she was asking. “They represent me and my beloved—you.”

“You had them before we met. How do you know that they were meant to represent us?”

Josephine fingered the cool metal. Two bars hung from a delicate silver string, one slightly longer than the other. Most of her jewelry was made of gold, but that silver was special to her. “I’ve always had them. I remember toying with them as a small child. As far as their representation of us? I just know it. In here.” She placed her hand over her heart and smiled up at him. “Please, be careful. You are fearless in battle,” she began, only to be cut short by his snort of derision. “No, listen to me, Thomitus. I know that you are brave; your valiance is legendary and is one of the many reasons I fell in love with you. But this is a different kind of battle. The stakes are equally as high, but you will be in unfamiliar territory with Nero. And I have heard that he tends to go mad. I do worry for you, for us. I realize what must be done, especially with the rumors coursing through the city, but I cannot help my feeling of unease.

You are everything to me, and I am terrified I will lose you."

With his fingers and thumb, Thomitus tipped her chin, making her look into his eyes. His dark hair was short, in the fashion of a soldier. He would always be one, though his battles had changed over the years. His hazel eyes churned brown, green, and golden. Nostrils flared, he breathed her in. With his knuckles, he brushed her cheek, tucking an errant strand of hair behind her ear. "And you are everything to me. You know the circumstances. If I can get close to him, learn his secrets, we can end this insanity. All of Rome will be free of him."

She swallowed the thick truth down like bile. "I know. And I will keep you with me until you return. Here—" she moved their clasped hands to her chest "—in my heart. Just do not forget yourself in this ruse; I would not survive losing you in any capacity."

He kissed her, passion pouring from his soul to hers. "I will return as soon as I am able. And *you* will also be with me." Thomitus placed her small hand over his heart and held it there.

She could feel the thundering, as if the beats were stamping her palm with affirmation.

It would be months before she laid eyes on her husband again, and she cringed at the thought of him being so far away.

He assured her the plan was falling into place, and that he had begun to work his way into Nero's inner circle. Thomitus told her he would uncover the secrets the Emperor held, and her husband vowed to relay any and all information to the Senate, as was their plan, swearing to keep Rome's best interests at the forefront of his mind. Equally as important, he promised to keep her in his heart. Always.

But sometimes, people lost sight of what was most important to them. Even more perilous was when the line they straddled, which was once very clear, blurred.

ROME, October 19, 67 AD

Thomitus

Nero was on a tangent—leaving all of those in his path scrambling to duck their heads for fear of losing them. Three years had passed since the Great Fire leveled three of the fourteen districts in the heart of Rome. In place of those charred homes and businesses, Nero's great palace complex in Domus Aurea was nearly complete. And, truly, it was a sight to behold.

Short and portly, with bird-like legs and pockmarked skin from head to toe, Nero's yellow-blond hair writhed with every jerk of his head and point of his finger. Spittle flew from his mouth as he raged at the artisans. His weak, blue eyes bulged from his red-splotched face when he glared.

Thomitus stood back, trying to sink into the wall. He'd seen Nero's fury unleashed many times in the past three years and knew there was absolutely no reasoning with him when he was in such a state.

Taking it all in, Thomitus blocked out the ranting and gazed at the beauty. To him, it was perfection and exactly what a palace should look like. More than three hundred rooms, none of them appointed with beds, but all with lavish furniture, statues, and artwork. Nero said it was no place to sleep, only to live. And the

Emperor and his men lived well. The frescoes alone were so impressively lifelike it felt as if a person could simply walk into them and dwell inside.

Fountains of fresh water from underground springs were scattered around the property, playing their watery tunes. Some of the fountains were fashioned in the form of great fishes, spouting into pools below. Others were chiseled likenesses of the gods and goddesses, each pouring their good fortunes upon all of Rome. It made him miss the impluvium in his own home. The water there had always brought him peace. He could sit for hours listening to the bubbling.

Josephine would love to see the grandeur. Despite having been absent from her for over a year, Thomitus thought about her often. In the beginning, he'd been able to sneak home much more often, but Nero wanted him close now, too close. Through it all, Thomitus had kept his promise to her and held her memory close to his heart. Most days, it felt as though he were with his regiment, readying for a great battle, all the while thinking of the comforts of home. But there were no hardships of battle to be found. Servants brought his food and poured his wine. He was bathed every day, and his body was anointed with the most expensive and lusciously scented oils Rome could import. He had no responsibilities beyond being a sounding board for the ramblings of the insane Emperor. No one would die from a command

Thomitus issued. He would not have to tell a widow that her husband had perished while expanding the Empire's borders.

No, Thomitus had it good. After years of serving his empire, his empire was serving him. He'd fought hard for Rome. He had come to see that Rome owed him the lavish treatment. He deserved to be pampered, to be served. He deserved fine food and entertainment, even more so than Nero—who had never stepped foot on a battlefield.

And, the next day, Thomitus would see home and his Josephine again. Nero had given Thomitus leave—after such a long time. He just hoped the spoiled man's sour mood would lighten, and he would keep his word. After Thomitus saw his wife, he would make arrangements to meet with the Senators. He had much to tell them—for the right price.

But he could not let the Emperor learn of the betrayal. Nero already had delusions someone was trying to poison him. Every man in Nero's circle was required to drink from his cup and take a bite from his plate before he would. "If I die, you will all die with me," he would say.

That was only a small example of the insanity that plagued the Emperor. He'd had Christians burned for practicing cannibalism within the Empire, saying they drank the blood and ate the flesh of their Christ in strange ceremonies. He had men flogged for looking at him in what he called a "suspicious manner." And no woman who caught his eye, married or not, was safe. He took anything he wanted. His power often went unchecked and unquestioned.

Because he had angered so many, it was possible the fears of retaliation were not unfounded. Still, it was good to be in the presence of the Emperor. Life was comfortable.

The two artisans who were plastering the ceilings and inlaying them with rubies, sapphires, and emeralds had gotten the pattern wrong in that particular room. Nero wanted the stones to form the outline of a sun. They had made the pattern of the moon and stars at night.

Thomitus sighed and leaned back against the wall. It would take hours at that pace, and he was eager to be on his way.

§

His sandals clapped on the freshly-cured concrete road. A pebble wedged itself beneath the crease of his middle toe, and he hopped for a second to free it, afraid to lose momentum. The warm evening sunlight cast a golden glow over the land, the great monuments. Lovers walked slowly along the promenades, arm in arm, sharing secrets and laughter. He envied them, but his resentment would not last for long. Soon, the entire land would be jealous of him and Josephine, not only for their great love rekindled, but also for the riches that might come from his plan.

As he rounded the corner, he could see the curtains of his villa flowing inward as if reaching for his lover, trying to keep her to themselves. Damn those curtains. Josephine was his, and he would remind her of that in only a few more long minutes.

He quietly climbed the stairs and eased the door of their home open. She was busy preparing the evening meal for herself. The pair had slaves to attend them, but cooking was one of Josephine's talents and her second love. She insisted on preparing all their food with her own hands. And he watched those hands form loaves of bread, kneading and pounding, punching and twisting. It made him imagine her fingers on his skin, trailing up and down his back, as they lost themselves in one another.

Flyaway strands of her dark hair flirted with her neck, and he longed to place a kiss just there, to erase the touch with his own. He could never have his fill of her. He had too long been denied her touch.

Josephine hummed a familiar tune, one she had learned just before their joining, one she said reminded her of him. So busy with her chores and engrossed in the song, she did not realize he was in the room until he reached around from behind her and brushed her cheek.

Her skin was silken, as it had always been, as he had imagined it was every night he was away. Her hair smelled like sunshine. His pulse quickened, and his groin tightened uncomfortably as he inhaled. It had been far too long.

Startled, she turned around, poised to strike out. Her eyes widened, and she choked out a strangled sound. "Thomitus?" Josephine felt the contours of his face. They had changed since she last saw him, he knew. Would she still want him, still long for him though he was different?

Josephine

She had been lost in a sweet daydream, one she called upon often in his absence. Walking hand in hand with Thomitus through their special vineyard. It was where they met in secret after their studies, and at any other free moment, to steal precious time until they were wed. The vineyard's grapes were ripe, the succulent globes nearly bursting, and their sweet scent filled the night air. Twinkling stars smiled down upon the couple as the gods blessed their intentions.

But the touch that fell upon her cheek, the strand of hair that always ran wild to attract his hands, was neither imagined nor expected. When she turned to find Thomitus standing in her kitchen, cloaked in the light blue toga reserved for Nero's closest advisers, she burst into tears and threw her arms around him.

She barely recognized him. The last time Thomitus left their home, left her behind, was more than a year before. She had counted the days: three hundred eighty-six. His dark, brown-black hair was longer, grazing his shoulders, and strands of silver had crept in along the sides. His face was still shaven but was no longer contoured. It had filled in. Pressing her body against his, she could feel that his stomach was soft, having given up the flat and muscled middle she remembered. Josephine did not care. He was home. He had come home to her.

He clutched the back of her head, holding her tightly against him, and whispered, "You never left my heart. I have held you close for so long... so long. And I have missed you." She could feel his tears seep into her hair, and hers soaked the cloth on his chest. Sobs wracked them both, the pair shedding the previous year of pent-up frustration, sadness, joy, and overwhelming relief, but mostly of love.

They kissed, held each other tight, and made love until well after the sun rose, their dinner long forgotten.

Lying in their bed, Thomitus's thumb rubbed up and down her arm as he held her. "I need to speak with you about certain things, things that could endanger us both. Do you want to hear them, or would you rather not know?"

7

Josephine cleared her throat. “I want to know everything.”

So, he told her. In great detail, he explained Nero: the man, the paranoia he experienced, and the danger he had been in. Josephine could not fathom how any person could be so entitled and frighteningly unstable at the same time. It had resulted in a volatile situation that threatened both her husband and homeland. A shiver passed over her as the implications clarified.

Something had to be done, and Thomitus had the opportunity to help end the reign of a tyrant. But something was holding her husband back. He would not meet her eyes when he told her he had never reported to the Senate.

“Why do you wait? Why not run to the Senate right now and be done with it? This is more information than they would ever need to unseat that mad man and save what little dignity Rome has managed to retain.”

Thomitus was quiet, seemingly pondering her question. “It is a delicate situation, one that involves our future. I do not wish to rush into things. I have information that the Senate needs. I have placed myself and my wife, home, and our lives in danger. A man should be compensated for sticking his neck out in such a way.”

He eased his arm from around her and quickly dressed as if to hide his body from her sight, but she was not sure why. “I fear that being in the company of the Emperor has been bad for my health. I have let myself go," he admitted.

She dressed as well and met him in the kitchen to prepare their midday meal. "It must be something to behold: the parties and extravagance, the lavishness."

Thomitus snorted. "You have no idea. The man has rubies in his sandals and had the workmen place gemstones of every color in the grout between the tiles on the floor. He has commissioned a statue of his likeness so enormous that a new addition must be made to the palace complex just to house it. He just mandated another coin with his visage be produced. It is strange, but I think the man is in love with his own face."

Josephine giggled and asked him to tell her more.

"The Emperor hosts parties every day. There is food in every room, entertainment in the form of dancers, magicians, handlers of exotic animals, so much abundance."

Josephine stiffened hearing how Thomitus had spent his days. She wondered how he had spent his nights. "And women aplenty, I assume?" Her eyes carefully watched his reaction. She wanted to claw his beautiful face, wanted to drown him in a fountain of the wine in which he had been imbibing. The thought of her Thomitus with another woman set her afire. It was common practice in Rome for a man to bed several women, but Josephine had made her thoughts on that particular tendency very clear when she first met Thomitus. Back then, he had agreed with her. She only hoped he had remained steadfast, because she was not sure what she might do.

Thomitus nodded, keeping his eyes affixed to hers. “Nero has his share of willing women. Though some in his circle shared in those festivities, I did not. I swear it to you, on my life. My position has not changed.”

She swallowed, hoping he was telling the truth. The gluttonous, slothful lifestyle to which he had grown accustomed had changed him, and Josephine was not sure it was for the better. He had information the Senate needed to bring the Emperor to his knees. The Thomitus she married would have given it to them freely, proud to have helped right a great wrong. The man before her wanted riches in exchange.

Disappointment and anger coursed through her veins. Part of her wanted to keep him in her sights, for fear of him leaving and never returning. The other part wanted him gone. The truth was she wanted her husband back, the brave soldier she loved, and the man who clearly knew right from wrong. She did not want the man who had been around the Emperor so long that feelings of wealth and entitlement corrupted the soul, one who used servants like slaves and would not lift a finger to help someone in need. Perhaps, though, she could remind Thomitus of the great man he once was. Perhaps she could show him how to work with his hands and use the muscles in his body for more than just serving the Emperor. She longed to show her husband how to use his many talents on her once again.

§

For two weeks, she had him back. And they had put the awkwardness of his absence behind them; they had moved forward again, as though their life together had no Emperor-sized wedge stuck in it.

Josephine had heard all good things come to an end at some point. Their fourteen-day respite came to an abrupt halt with two sharp knocks at their villa door.

Thomitus placed his finger over his lips, creeping toward the door. Shadows of the feet of the person on the other side shifted back and forth, blocking rays of sunshine. When he eased the door open, a wide smile formed on his lips. Thomitus flung the door open and embraced the person on the other side. When he released the visitor, Josephine could see it was none other than Beritus Augustus—Thomitus's best friend.

The two had grown up in the city of Rome together, playing chase and picking on the prettiest girls. Being born in the same month, they entered the Roman military at the same time, were assigned to the same regiment, and fought great battles back to back, keeping one another safe from harm.

She rushed forward to usher Beritus inside, urging him to join them for dinner. And he did. Over the evening's meal of freshly caught eel, ripe tomatoes, cheese, loaves of fresh bread, and bottles of their best wine, the evening passed quickly. The old friends spoke of Beritus's wife Aena and their newborn son, of sleepless nights, and long, fall days. Unease fell over the trio when Beritus's disposition changed from jovial to one of grave concern.

He cleared his throat. "I wish I could say that I was just here to visit and reminisce, but alas, I am here because of a very troubling matter."

"What is it?" Thomitus asked, quirking his left brow—the one that had been split in battle.

Josephine knew he could always speak freely with Beritus, as one might a sibling, a brother. She was anxious to hear what might be said between the friends. Mindlessly, she played with her necklace, as she often did when worried.

"The Emperor would like for you to return immediately," he said before swallowing the last gulp of sweet wine. His gaze dropped to the table. "And he would like Josephine to accompany you."

The room was still, save for a fly buzzing about the remnants of their meal. The silence was broken when Thomitus, with one strong swoop of his hand, cleared the table. Glass and pottery shattered. Their ministerium —fine, silver utensils her parents had given the couple when they married—made ringing noises as they clattered across the floor. And Thomitus let out a roar the entire city of Rome must have heard. It probably reached the ears of Nero himself.

"No!" Thomitus thundered, jumping up from his seat. "He will not have her."

Holding both hands out in an effort to calm him, Beritus nodded. "I truly think he just wants to meet your wife. He is… unsteady, and I cannot be certain, but that is the way it seemed when he dispatched me to find you both."

Thomitus would have nothing to do with reason. He paced the floors, raking both hands through the long hair on his head, muttering things about madness and greed.

Josephine's stomach filled with dread, churning and boiling with a feeling she could not place. She stood, staring blankly at the mess strewn dangerously across the floor. Why had Thomitus reacted in such a violent manner? He had never struck out before, never been quick to anger. If anything, she had once been impressed by his ability to maintain his cool poise and use his intellect to find a suitable answer to any problem.

It was not her Thomitus in that room. While the previous couple of weeks had been amazing with him, it was apparent his daily habits and thought processes had drastically changed. But she was determined to remind him of who he had been before he had set his eyes on the Emperor. They had worked in the garden and repaired their home together, though Thomitus had needed to take frequent respites from the work and chugged so much water they had nearly run out. She made healthy, light meals, and discouraged his habit of drinking wine throughout the day, only offering it to him at meals and hiding the bottles until he groaned with frustration and gave up the search for libations.

Beritus, after much coaxing, was able to calm his friend. "Let us talk about this, but quickly. He is expecting your arrival and will be displeased to wait."

"Fine. But I do not trust this. We need to keep her safe at all costs, Beritus. Swear it now."

Beritus looked Thomitus straight in the eye. "I swear it, both to you and to her." He nodded to Josephine, who quickly busied herself with cleaning up the mess her husband had so unthoughtfully made.

The three plotted and planned. In the end, they decided to present Josephine to the Emperor, per his request, as they could find no way to avoid bending to his will. But, they would lie. They would say that she had felt ill, tell him that his health was at risk by being around her.

Nero was ever paranoid about his wellbeing. He would send her home—or so they hoped.

Thomitus

Anger, when coursing through a man's veins, is not crimson, as most would believe. It is white, he thought. *White hot and scorching, even to the soul.* Thomitus had never felt such anger as he did at Nero in the moment Beritus said the Emperor had requested Josephine return to the palace with her husband. It was one thing to call on him. He was in the inner circle. It was a completely different thing to call upon and involve his wife in any of the debauchery within that complex.

His wife had never seen the snake handlers or the whores who sought the pockets of their next conquests. She had never seen unadulterated insanity either. And Nero had crazy to spare.

Why? Why would he want to meet her? An unsettling thought crept into Thomitus's mind. For a flash of a moment, he considered that he might be becoming as delusional and paranoid as the Emperor himself. Pushing that thought aside, reason won the battle. Nero might have had a fiery temper, and his moods might have changed like the seasons, but he was smart and calculating. Rarely did he make a move that was not thought out beforehand. Nero had a plan, and his plan seemed to have changed to involve Josephine.

Thomitus was beside himself as he sat by the impluvium, asking the gods to grant some form of respite from the wicked request. Water usually calmed him, but he was beyond mortal help. If Nero requested it, whatever it was, it had to be done. If not, death would come swiftly.

Beritus dragged his friend from the pool's side and pushed him into his wife's waiting arms before granting the couple one hour to prepare themselves and their home before they would need to leave for the palace. In that time, he would run home to check on his Aena and their son, needing to make sure they would be safe.

Thomitus watched Josephine take out her best stola, deep emerald and embroidered along the edges with golden thread. He observed her delicate fingers slip the fabric over the curves of her body. She pinned the garment modestly, and fixed her hair in an intricate knot, adding the laurel leaf comb on the left side. Brushing some wine on her lips to stain them, she regarded herself in the mirror.

Josephine

She stared at her reflection, the lines that had settled around her eyes and outlined her mouth, wondering what the visit might mean for her and her love. She, too, had changed since Thomitus had taken on the burden of spying. Time had a tendency to do that: transform a person, inside and out. The vow she took to carry him with her still burned strong in her bosom. She would simply need to remind him of it and of the reason he took on the challenge. Rome needed him. She needed him.

Looking through the mirror, she marveled at the very sight of Thomitus, already donning his pale blue toga, lacing his sandals around his calves. "Is there anything in particular you can tell me about Nero? Anything I should know?"

Sighing, Thomitus bowed his head. "He is volatile at best. I tried to remain calm, to be a fly on the wall—anything to avoid being the focus of his rage. The damage of an earthquake is greatest at its epicenter."

She swallowed, affixing silver baubles to her ears and pulling at the high collar circling the column of her throat. Somehow, it felt more like a noose than an accessory to enhance a woman's beauty. She could feel it tightening around her. Her breathing became shallow and more desperate as she considered the trouble they faced.

Once more, Thomitus had slipped up behind her, staring at her reflection. He brushed his knuckles over her cheek as he turned her body around to face his. "You have heard the plan?" he rasped.

"Yes."

7

“Please, do not falter. You are ill.” With a brush of his thumbs, he removed the pinkened powder from her cheeks. With a kiss of his lips, he took away the stain of wine. She regarded herself in the mirror. Her complexion was changed. It was sallow, pale, and sickly. Perhaps it would even be believable. She certainly felt ill.

Beritus returned, and the trio left the villa, assuring the servants their masters would return within a few days.

The walk through the maze of Rome’s streets seemed to take an eternity. The sun had just tucked itself between two of the seven hills that kept watch over the great city. Josephine hoped those hills would also keep the three of them safe. Beritus walked more swiftly than his companions did. Perhaps he was eager to return to his wife and child. Maybe he was worried they had taken too long to return. Either way, she was convinced they were like flies walking into a spider’s intricate web.

As they neared the complex, Thomitus stopped, earning an exasperated look from Beritus. He put his hands up and slapped his thighs. “Why are you stopping? We really should hurry.”

Thomitus gnashed his teeth and grabbed Josephine’s elbows, pulling her tightly to him and kissing her roughly. Whispering in her ear sternly, he said, “You will only speak when necessary. Blend in and keep low. I will guard you.”

She nodded and drew a deep inhale to calm her racing heart.

Turning, he ordered. "You guard her with your life."

"What about you, my old friend?"

Thomitus shook his head. "Without her, there is no me, no point to life, or living it."

In silence, the three resumed a steadier pace, and before any of them wanted to, they had arrived at the palatial complex.

Beritus was dismissed by a guard near the entrance, but stayed with the couple, keeping his vow. Josephine's mouth gaped as she took it all in: the gold, the statues that stood taller than the ceiling in their villa, the colorful stones and tiles, and the intricate paintings along each wall. Every painting was different, but the themes were similar. Nero wanted to show the world he was important. One room depicted him leading the way during a difficult battle, soot smudged on his face, his sword pointing toward the enemy. Josephine was certain the Emperor had never stepped foot on a battlefield in his short life.

In another room, the scene's theme was dramatically different. Winged women, barely clothed, stretched in the air atop Nero, petting him and feeding him grapes by hand. It was hedonistic, and bile burned the back of her throat.

With each room, the scenes morphed: Nero taming wild beasts, Nero being dressed by his servants, the citizens of Rome bowing to him. Then, she saw a fresco depicting the gods and goddesses themselves bowing to Nero. Such a thing was unheard of. *Does the man consider himself a god?*

The scent of lush plants and their perfumed flowers filled the air along with the sound of trickling water. There were fountains everywhere. Peacocks strutted around the courtyard square, its foundation made of intricate tiling. The males squawked and revealed their plumage. The fowl ran toward the edges of the great square.

Josephine could hear the sweet sound of various instruments melting into melody in the warm, night air. If she had not been concerned for her life, she might have allowed herself to get lost in the beauty of such a place.

And she knew immediately that very beauty had been what tempted Thomitus, what kept him away from her so long. Bitterness and sadness roiled through her veins until the beautiful façade crumbled and she could see the opulence for what it truly was: a den of thieves.

It had become abundantly clear to her. The rumors that swirled through town like the acrid smoke after the Great Fire were true. Nero wanted a palace. There was no room for one to be built in the city, not for one of that size. He had leveled an enormous number of buildings to make room. Perhaps the fire was not lit by his hand, but it was certainly by his command.

Either way, men, women, and children had died to make room for his dream, a fantasy he had put before the lives and welfare of his own citizens.

Boisterous laughter and giggling came from a room on the other side of the square. Candles flickered in the window, illuminating those inside, all clustered around one man, a man Josephine was growing to hate with each passing moment. Nero.

The guard led them into the room where the women were barely dressed in sheer fabric, and the men, those Nero trusted the most, had access to the most powerful man in the Empire.

Josephine looked at him, really looked at him.

Her first impression was one of pity. He was so young, just seventeen when he rose to power, to have assumed such responsibility. "How old is he?" she whispered to her husband.

"Twenty-nine."

She nodded almost imperceptibly.

Beritus cleared his throat. "Emperor, I have fetched the couple, as you ordered."

Nero's eyes were like that of a hawk's. His mouth did not even flinch, but those eyes never missed anything, darting from person to person, taking in what their bodies said, beyond the words they spoke.

Josephine felt his scrutiny as though she were a bug beneath a thick glass.

Chuckling, Nero stood from his couch and approached with arms outstretched. "We have missed you, Thomitus. I feared you would not return, so I called for you. We have much to discuss."

Thomitus did not back down but smiled openly. "I apologize, Excellence. My wife and I have been apart for far too long and had some catching up to do." He grabbed Josephine's hand and gave it a quick, reassuring squeeze.

She returned it with one of her own, though she was not sure she could hold on much longer. Her palm was wet with perspiration from worry.

Nero simply laughed and clapped Thomitus on the shoulder. "This is the sweet Josephine?"

Thomitus stiffened beside her and clutched her hand so hard it hurt, but he would not let her go.

Nero looked her over from head to toe and back up again, a satisfied smirk on his face. "You have kept him away, have you?" he asked, biting his too-plump lip until it became purple and bulbous. Skin marred with pitted scars from the plague he battled at a young age was taut on his face. His hair was limp and greasy, and Josephine had to hold her breath to keep from smelling the sour body odor radiating from him. She simply smiled and lowered her head and eyes to the floor. She could feel the heat waft from him when he stepped in front of her.

When his pudgy fingers lifted her chin, she felt Thomitus stiffen again. *Will he assault the*

Emperor for me? Maybe there is hope left for the man.

"Look at me, Josephine," Nero ordered sternly. "Are you ill? You are very pale."

"I-I have been lately, Emperor. But the physicians say that the malady will pass."

"Good, good," he said as if pondering whether her recovery would be a blessing or curse.

She swallowed and met his eyes with her own.

"You are quite a beauty. Have you ever been with child?"

Josephine felt gutted. It had always been her dream to have children of her own, but Thomitus's life as a soldier, and of late as Nero's plaything, had pushed those dreams aside. "No, Emperor. We have not conceived."

Thomitus opened his mouth, and she worried what might fly out, so she spoke again first. "However, we are working on remedying that situation. Right, husband?" She smiled up at Thomitus and squeezed his hand again.

With a sly smile, he straightened his spine. "Of course. I cannot wait to attempt the remedy again, wife."

Nero burst into a fit of laughter, enjoying the innuendo more than one ought to have. His laughs became forced, and then he stilled, strangely raking his eyes over the two of them. "There is someone feeding information to the

Senate about me, Thomitus. Would you know who that person is?"

Thomitus's dark brows knitted together. "I have no idea, my Emperor. But as my vow, I will find out who the traitor is." Releasing Josephine's hand, he placed his own over his heart, kneeling deeply.

Nero smiled, seemingly placated, but Josephine noticed the smile did not reach those dull blue eyes. "See that you do, or I will make sure that all of my men have a turn at trying to help your wife conceive the child she so desperately craves."

Her gasp filled the air just before Thomitus's pleas fell upon Nero's deaf ears.

Josephine was dragged away and locked in one of the palace's rooms, the Frescos within depicting a variety of vile sexual acts. The Emperor had surely chosen that room specifically to remind her of his threat. She was certain he would make good on his promise should Thomitus fail. A feeling of dread and despair filled her, exhausting her, and she fell asleep recalling the way Thomitus had pleaded for her freedom. "Please, Emperor. Allow her to return home. I swear that I will find the traitor, and that I will personally make him pay."

"You will make the traitor wish he were never born, Thomitus. Or I will make you wish the same," Nero had coolly responded before sauntering away with his entourage.

Thomitus

Nero had no right! He may be Emperor, but he had gone too far. *He certainly does not own Jo! She is my wife.* Beritus had been ordered to escort Thomitus to his own room and to stand guard outside it until further notice. Nero had even gone so far as to threaten Beritus's family if he failed in his duty.

Thomitus's sandals slapped against the smooth tiles along the floor of his room. There were few furnishings, only a lounger in the corner, a few plants potted in glazed or gilded urns, and the frescoes that Nero had become obsessed with. They depicted diverse scenes illuminating how amazing the Emperor was, and a small desk with parchment and a dry inkwell sitting atop it. Roaring deep inside, Thomitus cursed and raged for hours trying to figure out how to get Josephine out of the Emperor's grasp. They would have to flee the city of Rome, leave their home and belongings.

But, that would put Beritus and his family in danger. No. They must stay. Thomitus could not do that to his friend.

Thomitus rushed to the door, placing his palms against the cool wood. "Beritus?" he whispered.

"Yes?"

"Do you think you could somehow find some ink and a quill?"

Beritus shuffled beyond the door. "I will see what I can do, but can make no promises. And I will not risk my family."

"I would not ask if it was not important, but please, do not endanger yourself or the wellbeing of your loved ones."

"Very well," came the muffled reply.

Thomitus could not rest. He tossed and turned, unable to get comfortable or ease the thoughts rushing through his mind. When the night seemed darkest, he heard the faintest whisper. But it was not Beritus who called out. It was Josephine.

Through a tiny crack in the western wall of Thomitus's room, her voice came, tentative and trembling. "Thom?"

He rushed to the wall and knelt before it, searching the cold stone with his hands, just thankful she was on the other side. "Are you okay? Did they harm you in any way?" His voice broke on the last word. He squeezed his eyes closed and hoped she had been handled delicately and treated as a lady should be.

"I am unharmed, other than my confinement, that is. I did not speak sooner for fear of the guard outside my door, but I can hear his snoring now."

He smiled and thanked the gods for their mercy. Then he asked for their continued blessing, that she be kept safe, asking the he be sacrificed before her.

"I have a plan," he whispered. "It may take some time, but it also may work to our favor. I just need for you to stay strong no matter what."

"I can be strong," she answered, with enough strength in her words that his own resolve was made more rigid. "But I need you to also be strong, Thomitus, without hope of gain. You need to do the right thing. Though it is not always the easiest way, it is the path that should be taken."

Thomitus hung his head. He had been changed by that place, by the man who owned it. He had become just like Nero, slothful and gluttonous, not only gorging on food but upon power and wealth. The deadliest sins often overlapped. That palace was built upon lust, pride, and the wrath of an absolute mad man—a tyrant—who not only threatened the empire, but everything Thomitus held dear in life.

Vowing to speak again the following night, the couple kept quiet. For weeks, they met in secret, in the dark, clinging to one another through a small crack in the stone façade. He would fall into a fitful sleep, his head propped against that cool stone, and she would calm him, as she did at their home. Each dream was the same: He had done something wrong, something terrible, and was running for his life. When he tried to right the situation, it was too late. He would beg and plead to take the place of the one he had wronged. The feeling of dread and emptiness consumed his dreams, but his waking moments were filled with Josephine and determination.

Beritus had been able to slip a quill and a vat of fresh ink beneath the door. And with those simple gifts, locked in a room in a palace constructed of and for sin, Thomitus secured his place in history.

He was allowed out of his room during daylight hours, ordered to locate the traitor. And he did search diligently, questioning guards and even those who counted themselves among the inner circle. He made notes and scribbles of whereabouts and dates, of pertinent information. Knowing he was the spy Nero sought. During those interviews, Nero kept a close watch, his eyes searching for anything that might condemn Thomitus and his wife. He also learned of more secrets to which he had not previously been privy.

Some of them were damning. Nero had spies everywhere. He also had appetites no one seemed to be able to whet. If a married woman caught his eye, her husband would be enlisted in the military. If he was already a soldier, he would be sent to the front line. If the enemies did not tear him apart, Nero would order one of his trusted men to take care of the obstacle. Then, the Emperor would console the woman, luring her into bed. When he had his fill, he would toss her aside, penniless, into the streets.

His trusted men ran the city with iron fists. They took a district, and everything coming in or going out of the area was taxed. They were made rich on the backs of the poor. Those men took what they wanted—just like their Emperor. Those were only small examples of the corruption. Nero had senators in his pocket. No one was going to take his power.

Over the course of a few months, as the year 68 began, Nero's moods became increasingly sour. His paranoia found new victims at every corner, and Thomitus knew his time to produce a traitor was quickly running out. Nero was watching even closer than before. But Thomitus kept his mouth closed and his ears open, and locked in his room at night with his pen, sitting across the wall from his only love, he scribbled.

At the end of March, rumors of Senator Galba's plan to overthrow Nero and claim the role of Emperor became more than whispers. Galba had support. He had the majority of the Senate behind him, but more importantly, the man had won the heart of the people.

Things happened quickly after that.

7

March, 28, 68 AD

Josephine

She could hear the sound of footsteps outside her door, shuffling against the wood, and iron keys in the lock. The vile room had been her prison, one she was most willing to escape if it was not for leaving Thomitus behind. He had never left her. Every night, he met her, and every night, he reassured her. Those words had lost their power. The soldiers approached.

Will Nero make good on his promise? Is Thomitus still alive? Her heart pounded as she backed into the farthest corner of the room. The wooden door swung open, ricocheting off the fresco behind it, tiny chips of plaster and paint trickling to the ground in a small pile.

Guards escorted her from the palace. Before the sunlight could assault her eyes, a musky-smelling sack was placed over her head. She could hear the gossip swirling around her. The Emperor had been run off. Senator Galba was Rome's new Emperor, quickly making good on the promises to rid the city of the filth that was associated with Nero and his reign. She panted with fear. They thought her to be part of the filth.

Nero had run like a coward and gone into hiding. The persons concealing him had been put to death when the Emperor was found. But he was not found alive. He had heard their approach and took the dishonorable way out, before they could find him, seize him, and bring him to justice. The only one left in his circle, Epuphroditos, had been the one charged with running Nero through, as he lacked the bravery to fall upon his own sword.

Josephine was shoved into a wall, or that was how it felt. With trembling fingers, she removed the moldy sack from her head after the door slammed closed behind her and took in her surroundings. Surrounded by four close walls and a low ceiling, she was in a cell. The door was wooden, thick, and only a tiny square of the timber had been cut away to make a window her upper arm would not even fit through. Her throat was dry as the Roman soil.

For days, they kept her there. No food. No water. No facilities other than a corner of the room, but she did not even need that corner after a couple of days. Having consumed nothing, she had nothing to expel. Mice scurried through the few tiny piles of hay that littered the floor. They were too quick for her to catch, especially in her weakened state. She felt as though her arms were leaden. And she was cold.

So cold.

Curling into a ball, she tried to keep warm, her thoughts traveling to Thomitus and his uncertain fate. She was alone. She was hungry, tired, frightened.

She cried.

She yelled.

She slept.

She starved.

Hour by hour, she weakened. Her muscles became as tired as her mind. She had considered every scenario and none, save Thomitus riding in on a white horse and taking her away from that awful place, seemed to be remotely positive. And that possibility was non-existent. If Thomitus were coming, he would have already shown up.

Thomitus

Guards appeared while Thomitus was crossing the palace pavilion. *There are too many of them for Nero have sanctioned this*, he thought. They marched determinedly toward the Emperor's known quarters. Thomitus tried to hurry away, but two seized him by the arms, wrestling his thickened body to the ground. Heavy punches landed on his lower back, on his kidneys, and he had no choice but to submit—it was a move he had once taught those under his command.

Thick shackles clamped onto his wrists, and the men hauled him upright. He was spat upon, kicked, gagged, and then a thick sack was placed over his head. The beating continued as they shoved him along.

"Nero's inner circle, huh?" They taunted.

"The Emperor has been found. The coward is dead, too frightened to fall upon his own sword, he had to have a friend run him through." They laughed. The story was more than likely true, but they did not know about Thomitus, what he had decided to do—to save Josephine.

They did not know about her. She had no affiliation with the late Emperor. She was innocent. "Josephine," he tried to say, the material of the gag distorting his words.

The sack was ripped from his head, the afternoon light blinding him. He tried to get his bearings, blinking through watery eyes.

"Aww, he's crying." One of the guards teased, his lip pursed.

"Josephine." Thomitus tried again.

He was in the city's center, approaching the gates of the Colosseum. He swallowed, knowing exactly what happened in that arena. But as they entered the gate and approached the center ring, he found no crowd, only a stone block streaming with fresh blood. A giant of a man awaited, holding the handle of a large ax.

That was it. That was how he would die. Frantically, Thomitus fought, using his last bit of strength, screaming Josephine's name through the gag until one of the guards tore it away. "Josephine!" He roared. "She's at the palace. She's innocent! I swear she's innocent. Nero was holding her prisoner."

The guards laughed at him. "There are no innocents in that place."

As they strapped him to the stone, smashing his cheek into the crevices of pooled blood, flies buzzed around his face. “She is innocent. Nero took her!”

One particularly nasty guard, with snarled, yellow teeth, and a scar that ran from his left tear duct to his jaw sneered and crouched down. “Josephine, you say?”

Thomitus tried to nod. “Yes. Please, save her.”

The guard smiled, looking from his friend back to Thomitus. “Oh, I will find her. I will take real good care of her, too.”

“No!” Thomitus roared. Their laughter echoed over the empty seats. His forehead was strapped to the rock. Flashes of Josephine entered his mind.

Her smiling.

Her laughing.

Her crying.

Her crouched in that awful room in the palace, beating her hands against the door, begging for release.

Soldiers making good on their promise.

Josephine.

He muttered her name, and a meaty fist connected with his jaw, snapping the bones apart at the hinge so he could speak no more. The last sound he heard was the whoosh of the ax blade through the air.

Josephine

Sharp pangs pinched her stomach from within. She curled into the fetal position to make it stop. It had been so long since anyone had brought food. Something was wrong. Or, perhaps they had forgotten her.

Thomitus was gone.

Everyone was gone.

They were going to leave her to rot in there, she was sure of it. *How long has it been?* She had not even needed to relieve herself in days. She rocked back and forth on the cold tile. Her body was too hot.

Where is Thomitus?

Has he told the Senate about Nero?

Will he come for me?

Time blurred.

Josephine's mind was a murky bog.

The sound of footsteps outside her door startled her awake. With difficulty, she pushed herself up to standing, legs quivering beneath her.

Thomitus was on the other side of the door. He had come for her at last.

Excitement washed over her as she stumbled toward the sounds. But when the door was wrenched open, it was not Thomitus's face she saw.

7

Four soldiers stood proudly, chests broad and grins wide.

Has he come through after all? A rush of excitement flooded her veins. Her mouth was a desert. "Did Thomitus send you?"

A vile-smelling man stepped through the doorway. "Are you Josephine?"

"Y-yes," she rasped.

"Thomitus told us all about you. I can see why he was so concerned," he said, circling her. His eyes raked over her body, and she trembled, not from weakness, but from fear. The other men stepped into the room.

Thomitus told them about me? He sent them for me? Her heart crumbled into a million dried-up pieces of flesh. She could almost feel the flecks sprinkling the skin of her feet, a light snow of heartbreak. The only one she had ever allowed herself to love had betrayed her. If she had tears, they would have flown like engorged rivers out of their banks. But she had nothing left to give.

When the men grabbed her wrists, she screamed and clawed. She kicked out at them. But she was far too weak. And the men were far too strong, too determined to break her.

And they did.

Again, and again, and again.

JO MICHAELS

Part Two

Date: September 24, 1584
Location: On the banks of the Thames near St. Paul's Cathedral

Sir Thomas sat on the bench in the garden and watched the barges float past. He was surrounded by roses; the smell helped his jangling nerves a bit, but the lapping noise of the water was what always incited true calm. As he leaned forwards, propped his elbows on his knees, and clasped his hands, he prayed for a favorable outcome. He whispered, "Amen," and a shrill scream split the air, causing him to leap to his feet and spin around.

One of his father's servants rushed from the back door of the manor and gestured wildly. "'Tis a girl, 'tis a girl! Come, Sir Thomas, and look. She is very handsome."

Relief spread through Thomas's chest. He lifted his eyes towards the sky in thanks before running for the house to see his wife and new daughter. He was made to wait, so he paced the hall and ran his fingers through his hair several times. In the moment before his annoyance at being summoned too early peaked, one of the chambermaids poked her head out. "They are ready, sir."

With his heart hammering in his chest, he pushed open the door to the bedchamber and put his head through the crack. "May I enter, my lady?"

7

His wife's sweet voice reached him. "Thomas, you certainly have a flair for the dramatic." She giggled. "Of course you may enter. Come, see our little daughter."

He opened the door the rest of the way and strode to stand beside his wife. Her face was suffused but radiant, and she exuded happiness as she presented the baby bundle to him. Before he took the child into his arms, he leaned down and kissed his wife soundly. "She is beautiful. I am so proud of you."

Lady Kelleigh squeezed his hand. "I love you. Now hold her so you may meet properly."

Warmth flooded his chest as he gazed at his wife's face. Tearing his eyes away, he focused instead on the wiggling bundle. He lifted his daughter slowly, being careful to cradle her head. Her eyes were wide open, and she stared at him as she suckled her fingers.

"She likes you already."

A smile split his face, and he was cooing at the child before he could stop himself.

His wife laughed. "It is good to see you so taken with her. I had a horror you would be disappointed she was not a son."

"Disappointed? I fear I am completely in love with her already, and she does not even have a name." He rubbed noses with the baby.

"A name! I quite forgot. Pray, what do you wish to call her?"

With a tilt of his head, he examined his daughter's face a long time before speaking. "Marian Elizabeth. After your mother and our sovereign Queen."

Kelleigh's face brightened. "Yes! It is perfect. My mother will be honored, as will your benefactor."

Thomas laid Marian in her mother's arms and kissed both ladies. "I shall step out so my loves may rest."

His feet took him straight to the tavern, and he ordered a round for all those in attendance. He lifted his pint of dagger ale. "To my new daughter, Marian."

Men clapped him on the back and shook his hand. Hearty rounds of "congratulations" came from all directions.

Rather than stay and accept another drink, he bid adieu to the other men and set off towards the palace to tend to his workshop. Another shipment of gold and copper was to arrive in a fortnight, and he needed to make room for it to be stored until he could use it. He also had some new ideas about how to set stones in the precious metal and was eager to see how it would look. So often, gems were simply wrapped; he intended to try to change the casements.

It was as exhilarating as it was dangerous. There was a chance the Queen would be displeased and would not name him royal goldsmith as she had hinted she might do.

7

His steps were light as he bid good day to the guards and went up the stairs to the tower. When he neared the door to his shop, he paused and tilted his head. Raised voices were coming from the interior, and he was sure he had locked the door before leaving the previous evening.

"I tell you he is hiding something! No man can change the colour of gold the way he has. We must find whatever witchcraft is being used and do away with it," one of the men said.

"Witchcraft?"

"It must be. Gold is yellow and too soft to endure long wear, yet his pieces are green, pink, and blue, and remain unblemished but for a few scratches. There are no breakages. It is as though he has cast a spell on them."

Anger flared in Thomas, and he kicked open the door to face his accusers. One he recognized right away as a goldsmith from Surrey who had been a most excellent ally in the past. "Guards!" Thomas yelled.

Both men gasped and dropped the precious metals and papers they were holding.

Queen Elizabeth handed out harsh punishment for those caught thieving—especially within the palace walls. The two men were certainly facing a long period in the stocks for their slights. They knew their outcome would not be favorable; men were executed for less. One fell to his knees and begged for mercy.

Harsh footfalls were followed by the visage of a member of the guard. "Yes, Sir Russell?"

"These men are robbing me. Arrest them!"

Another guard appeared, and they escorted the two would-be thieves away.

Thomas fell into a chair and dropped his head into his hands, feeling every bit like the apprentice again. Memories of the master goldsmith came to mind, and Thomas's stomach turned as he recalled the harsh words spoken to him. "You are a fool. There is no room in the Queen's court for a roustabout who believes he knows everything. Joining gold with silver and iron! You will be accused of witchcraft!" After that, he was beaten with a stick that left welts on his legs and back and a small scar in his right eyebrow, which his fingers moved to rub with the memory. Never again, while under the master's watchful eye, did Thomas dare to try anything new. A surge of queasiness had him bolting from his seat to vomit the dagger ale into a privy pot.

Shaking, he sat back down and put his head between his knees as he took deep breaths. *Witchcraft, it is not.*

It took a while to regain his countenance, but once steady again, he worked until the sun cast long rents of light through the room that made the floating dust motes sparkle in their chaotic dance. He lifted a dazzling article off the bench and held it in his palm, stretching out his arm to thrust the gem into a beam. When the light struck, it split into thousands of tiny dots that decorated the walls of the tower room.

Thomas smiled, turned the emerald this way and that, and laughed aloud at his accomplishment. He was certain the Queen would be filled with rapturous joy at his discovery, but he was not ready to reveal the piece yet. It would take several weeks of refinement before he dared to present the article to her. It had to be the most breathtaking thing she had ever seen.

Pulling the jewel from the light, he wrapped the piece in leather cloth and placed it in the lockbox. It would be safe there next to his notebook. He then threaded the key through a ribbon and tied it 'round his neck, letting it fall behind his doublet. Softly cursing himself for leaving the notebook out and the tiny key in the room—yet thankful the thieves had not found them—he gave his chest a pat, locked the tower door, and made his way towards home.

His stomach growled as he envisioned ladling stew into his mouth, its warm gravy flowing over his tongue and down his throat. So caught up in the fantasy, he almost fell when his foot caught on a form lying in the road. "Pardon," he muttered.

"Please, sir, might you have a coin?"

Thomas spun around, ready to give the beggar a word, until his eyes found the owner of the voice.

A monk, robes tattered and stained, crouched on the hard cobblestone with his hands up in supplication.

Thomas's words died on his lips as his tongue darted out in a futile attempt at carrying moisture to the parched skin. Pity flowed through him. Once proud members of society, there seemed to be an influx of godly men writhing in ditches and begging on streets amongst the common vagabonds. Monasteries were closing in rapid succession—as were convents—and the poor had flooded London in droves. It always made Thomas sick when he saw how the devout had fallen.

He fished out money, put his hand on the monk's shoulder, and handed over two farthings. "God bless you. Please, leave the road before you are caught and beaten for begging."

"God bless you, my son." A moment later, the monk disappeared.

As Thomas finished the walk home, he deliberated the plight of Catholic figures. There was no way to save them, but he felt good for doing what he could, even though he was a devout Anglican.

Venison. The odor struck his nose as he entered his childhood home, and he was eager whilst he ate, to hear how well his daughter had fared on her first day of life.

7

Date: November 26, 1584
Location: Palace of Whitehall, London

Thomas pulled at his shirt's frilly collar as he waited to see the Queen. He had not slept the night before, and his brain was clouded. His hand shook—not from the chill of the November air, but from the sheer mental weight of the item his fingers held. It had taken two months to perfect the pronged setting, but it was stunning. He hoped Her Majesty would agree.

To make it look the best it could, he'd placed the emerald on a swatch of red velvet in an ornamented box. His heel tapped repeatedly on the stone floor, and when Her Majesty's handmaiden summoned him, he leapt from his seat so quickly, she started and put a hand to her chest.

"Sorry," he mumbled.

"Right this way, Sir Thomas." She sniffed, lifted her face towards the sky, and spun around, her pinsons silent on the stone floor.

He hurried after her, hands trembling. Once he was shown into the Queen's rooms, he bowed deeply and kissed Elizabeth's ring in greeting.

"Sir Thomas. I hear you have something that may interest me?" Her question boomed through the enclosed space.

It was a moment before he found his voice. With a shaky hand, he lifted the lid of the box and held it out for her to examine. "I..." He licked his lips with a dry tongue as the words died.

There was no need to speak; she already had the necklace in her hand and was walking towards the window. "All this for a necklace?" She turned the emerald over in the light. "Oh, I see. Is this what those thieves were after?"

"I believe so, Your Grace." His voice squeaked.

She turned and lifted an eyebrow. "Did you know I allowed them to plead their case?"

He shook his head.

"They mentioned witchcraft."

He felt the blood drain from his face and his eyes widen.

"Do not look so pallid. Witchcraft! Indeed! Any fool knows good metallurgy when they see it." Again, her attention went to the item in her hand, and she turned it over several times. "You are a master of your craft, sir. I recognized it from the first piece of yours I saw. This is exquisite." Smiling, she turned back, her eyes dancing with mischief. "This is going to make you a very rich man. The way the light plays off the cuts of the gem when the back is left exposed so. Clever." She moved behind a huge desk and sat, resting her chin on her hand. "Pray tell, do you still reside with your father?"

"Yes, Your Majesty."

7

"Oh, do stop with all the formalities, and sit down." A laugh escaped her throat. "I tire of it all now and again. Besides, your family has been loyal to mine since my father was on the throne. I knighted you for your bravery on the battlefield. Surely you can see your way to using my name when we are closeted together as we now are. I give you leave to do so."

Thomas gingerly sat in a high-backed chair opposite the Queen's desk and cast his eyes to his shoes. Heart hammering, he tried to do as he was told. "Your... Elizabeth, forgive me, this will be difficult."

"Will it be easier if I command you?"

His head snapped up in alarm, only to find her smiling at him. He laughed nervously. "It may."

"Fine. Then I command thee, Sir Thomas, to refer to your sovereign Queen as Lizzy when there are no others present. Is that better?"

He felt ridiculous but nodded.

"At last." Elizabeth reached up and tugged at her hair, pulling her red wig off and exposing short, blonde fuzz. She scratched her scalp and sighed with pleasure. Once the hair was back in place, she leaned forwards. "Now, tell me why you and your lady wife are residing with your father."

"Since my mother passed, my father is in need of a woman to run his household."

"Ah, yes. That is all women are good for." She turned up the corner of her lip. "Tell me, do you believe your wife would enjoy life at court?"

Thomas's heart pounded. "I believe she would make a most excellent lady's maid to any of the fine women here at court."

Elizabeth laughed, the sound like jingling bells. "I do not wish her to be a handmaiden. Rather, my desire is to have women wait on her."

"I am not sure I grasp your meaning, Y... Lizzy."

"Thomas, this piece is exactly the sort of thing I have been searching for. It is exquisite! I must have you in my employment immediately, which means you and your wife will be appointed apartments here in the palace. She will be doted on. No more need to run a household." Her smile was dazzling, and the excitement in her person radiated through the room.

"You wish for me to become the royal goldsmith?"

"Yes. It is what you want." It was not a question. She knew what was in his heart before he had to say it. "I only ask that you keep your wares for my household alone. Is that agreeable?"

Struck dumb, he gaped and nodded.

"Please, do close your mouth. You look like a codfish." Laughter burst out of the Queen forcefully, and she wrapped her arms around her middle as though she were in pain.

It wasn't long before he was chuckling along with her. Once their mirth faded, he braved the question that had been on his mind since Elizabeth mentioned it. "Might I ask what became of the thieves caught in my workshop?"

She smiled. It wasn't warm, and her eyes were two pieces of rock in her face. "I had them hanged. No one steals in my kingdom and is allowed to keep their life." With a tilt of her head, she asked, "Is that not what you desired?"

"I have no mind to tell Your Majesty how to govern a kingdom. I was only curious."

"Then let it away from your mind. We have pleasantries to discuss. How soon might I be able to call upon you to ornament my dresses?"

Not wishing to appear rude, he tarried with Elizabeth until he knew it was time to take his leave. With a gracious bow and many thanks, he bade her good day, accepted the emerald with a promise to return it after copying the setting, and fled forthwith to his home. He could not wait to get there and tell Kelleigh they would be moving into the palace.

"Kelleigh!" He ran through the halls screaming.

She appeared from around a bend, her eyes wide and her hand over her heart.

"Kelleigh! Oh, thank God!" Pulling her into an embrace, he squeezed until she slapped his arms and pushed him back.

Concern was etched into her every feature. "Thomas? Is everything all right?"

He was sure elation exuded from every pound of his person, but she seemed distressed. Grabbing her and spinning in a circle, he whispered, "My prayers have been answered. We shall move into the palace in a fortnight!"

Eyes wide, she pushed him back and stared. "If you were planning humor at my expense, I dare say you have chosen most offensive words. Tell me you speak the truth, and I shall consider forgiving you for giving me such an awful fright when you arrived."

"I speak the truth, my love. Our lady Queen has appointed me royal goldsmith. She wants us to come to court, and she wants me to only create finery for her and her ladies."

Lady Kelleigh put her fingertips to her mouth, widened her eyes, and chuffed. "I cannot believe it is true! Husband, you have done it!"

Wailing echoed off the stone walls, sounding like a lamb being brought to slaughter.

Though the sound of Marian crying wiped the look from Kelleigh's face, Thomas's mood could not be soured. He placed his hand over his wife's. "I will retrieve her and bring her to you in our bedchamber."

7

When he turned to go, she caught hold of his arm, drawing him back to her. “I love you, husband. I am so proud of what you have done.”

After he kissed her soundly, he guided his fingers over her cheek and tucked a stray bit of hair behind her ear, bringing his palm back to cup her chin. “I love you, too. Now go.”

Her laughter followed him through the house as he sought out his daughter.

Marian was lying in her crib, making gurgling sounds. She looked positively angelic as she poked her fingers into the fleshy part of her face.

Being careful to keep his voice low and even, he kissed her on the head and whispered, “What have I here? Do my eyes deceive me, or is that an angel where my daughter is supposed to be?”

She blew a raspberry in his ear, and he chuckled, lifting her from the crib to take her to her mother for feeding.

Date: March 20, 1585
Location: Palace of Whitehall, London

Lady Kelleigh spun in a circle, her skirts swishing in a wide arc.

"You look lovely," Thomas said. "Did the Queen help you pick that colour?"

She nodded, her eyes sparkling.

"It suits you." His eyes drank her in.

Her dress was the deep green of a well-grown hedge, with wide slashes in the sleeves to allow snow-white satin to show through. But his gaze was locked on the bejeweled, square neckline. Her breasts were fuller since the birth of Marian, and they showed well in the low-cut gown, the silver necklace she always wore seeming to point to the deep cleft between the soft mounds.

He stood and pulled Kelleigh towards him, pushing his hands into her hair on either side, and bringing her lips to his own. Their bodies pressed flush against one another, and he felt the tingles of arousal tighten the fabric of his breeches. When he could stand it no longer, he released her lips and pressed his own to her neck below her ear. "We shall complete this task in the evening."

Releasing her, and noting how red her cheeks had become—making her all the more stunning—he blew her a little kiss before walking out the door. His ears picked up the sounds of her ladies giggling, and he smiled. *That ought to give them something to have a good bit of intrigue over.*

Whistling, he strode through the palace towards his new workshop. It was a fine place, undecorated but for the wooden tables, instruments, and smelting tools. A perfect hideaway to finish the piece he planned to present to the Queen at the ball in two days' time.

It was to be a grand event, and nobles from distant lands had been invited to take part in the festivities. He planned to honor and delight his benefactor for all to see.

Already, he had constructed fine settings for many pieces of jet and diamonds Her Majesty planned to wear for the portrait she had commissioned. All that was left was to set the stones and add the last ruby to the newest necklace.

As he stoked the flames to make molten gold, he smiled. Queen Elizabeth was sure to show him high regard.

He was in the midst of a delicate procedure, bending the soft metal to hold one of the diamonds in place, when someone knocked on the door and startled him. As the jewel tumbled to the tabletop and the metal cooled, he dropped his tools, sighed, rubbed his palms over his face, and said, "Enter!" It came out as harshly as he intended.

A red-faced, sweaty page entered, his eyes wide. “S… Sir Thomas!” He bowed. “My most humble apologies for disturbing you, sir.”

“I daresay this is important.” Thomas’s mind whirled through scenarios as he waited.

“’Tis your father, sir. He has fallen to the ague. I was told to bring you forthwith.”

Ague was a terrible illness, and it had a greater impact on those who were later in their years. He shuddered. His father would be five score and two soon. In a flash, Thomas was off his stool and making haste for the door. As his feet struck the cobblestones, he wondered how long the old man had been taken with chills before he summoned the doctor. Stubborn fool. Never did admit his weaknesses, and he never took no for an answer. King Henry VIII certainly saw something there; he made the man a lord at age twenty and gave him the house on the Thames. Thomas never discovered why, but he was sure it was related to the loyalty and stubbornness of his father. Stubborn… More like pride or… Thoughts were cut short when Thomas turned a bend near the house and saw a group of palace guards standing by the door.

He wondered why the Queen would be visiting. Unless… Legs flying furiously underneath his body carried him faster than he had ever run. By the time he approached the door, his chest was heaving, and he had slowed to a walk. No longer was he in a rush, because there could only be one reason she was there.

Several of the guards said hello as he passed, and he tarried by the strong slab of oak separating him from his father's corpse.

Sadness and fear settled into Thomas's heart when the familiar wood encountered his hand. After a deep breath, he pushed.

"You scoundrel!" Elizabeth shrieked.

Without a thought, he sprinted through the house towards the voice. But laughter pulled him up short of the doorway, and he paused to listen.

"I always said you were a bright child, Lizzy. His Highness loved you very much; he always spoke well of your intelligence and handsomeness."

"My dear Lord Russell, you do use such flattering words, but there is no need. I know my father's heart. He bewitched me at a young age with compliments." She sighed and sniffled. "Did you know he read to me no less than every fortnight?"

"I did not."

"He would change his voice to sound like a lady when the character demanded it of him. You know, these are the kinds of memories you shall leave with your own family. Thomas, just yesterday, said to—"

Thomas stepped around the corner and cleared his throat. He felt his face grow warm as he bowed to Elizabeth before turning to his father. "I was summoned by a page and made haste, but I see you have an amiable companion already."

Wrapped in a woolen blanket, the old man still shivered, his face coated with a sheen of sweat. But he chortled and smiled. "I do. Her Highness has been most delightful to converse with. I could ask for no better company." A sudden coughing fit had him retching.

Thomas wrung his hands, not knowing what to do. His eyes met Elizabeth's, and she gave a small shake of her head, her eyes wide with sadness.

After the hacking subsided, Lord Russell took a shaky breath. "Please, my most ardent apologies."

Elizabeth waved her hand. "You are ill. I shall send the doctor 'round again on the 'morrow." She stood, smoothed her skirts, and gave the Lord's fingers a light touch. "Be well, Lord Russell." Before she passed through the archway, she turned back and gestured. "Accompany me to the door, Sir Thomas."

Thomas walked in silence with her until they approached the exit; then, he met her gaze. "How much longer before he is consumed by the illness?"

"My doctor approximated no more than one week. Ague has riddled this place recently. We shall move to Windsor before Easter. Already I have missed my visit to Greenwich. We have tarried in London for too many months." She got a faraway look in her eyes at the mention of

Greenwich but quickly recovered. “I command you to stay by your father’s side until he is recovered or dead. You will join my household after whatever comes to pass, has.” With that, she swirled out of the house in a cloud of red velvet.

Jaw hanging, Thomas cursed silently. There would be no grand ball, no chance to receive accolades in the presence of innumerable nobles for his craftsmanship.

Date: May 2, 1585
Location: Windsor Castle

Despite every doctor condemning Lord Russell to the icy grip of Death, the old man survived. It was quite a struggle, but Thomas had tended to his duties as expected. If he never emptied another chamber pot filled with vomit, it would be quite all right with him.

He missed Easter at Windsor Castle, but his wife was full of intrigue by the time he arrived.

Rumors Lady Kelleigh had become a favorite of one of the lords at court were whispered, but Thomas could find no fault in her manners when she was near the subject of the gossip: Lord Hale. Watching from a corner during one of the balls, Thomas surmised it was the blatant flirting of Lord Hale that fanned the flames of imagination. But Kelleigh responded with grace and humility, no matter the reddening of her cheeks as he praised her openly.

Elizabeth leaned to Thomas's ear. "She is every bit the lady, and I approve of her mannerisms. I enjoy her company very much. A word of warning: Lord Hale is a beastly man. He will find a way to seize hold of what he desires. Do not leave her side, or I fear I will have to remove his head for spoiling your wife."

His insides churned. Surely, this man would take no liberties with another's wife if she were not willing. Rather than sit idly by, Thomas hastened across the room and swept

Kelleigh away for dancing. He held her close during the waltz. “Take care. Lord Hale is not to be trusted.”

“He is harmless. An insufferable flirt.” She cast her eyes to the floor.

“Tell me you have not had private audience with him.”

Her cheeks turned scarlet. “Of course not!”

“Do you wish to?”

“No.”

Their eyes met, and he gauged the truth in hers, finding them open, honest, and a bit angry.

He pulled her closer. “I am sorry. I shall never doubt your absolute devotion. I beg of you, do not find yourself alone with him.”

“You seem greatly troubled by it. I shall heed your warning, husband.”

His heart swelled with love and calmed its thunderous pace. They swirled around the floor with the music until their feet ached.

When the others departed the hall, Thomas took her by the hand and led her towards an exit. On the way, he caught the Queen’s eye.

She gave him a single nod and a small smile as her eyes followed the couple out.

Once he and Kelleigh arrived at their suite of rooms, he shooed her ladies out and bolted the door.

"Why did you send them anon? However will I remove myself from these lacings?" She put her fists on her hips and scowled.

They had not had occasion to be alone since he arrived two days prior. He had missed her, and his body betrayed his thoughts.

A giggle escaped her closed mouth, and she lifted the back of her hand to her lips. "Oh, I see."

"No, you do not. But you shall." It came out as a growl, and Thomas crossed the room in two strides. He pulled her body to his, moaning when her exquisite breasts encountered his chest. It had been too long since he had tasted of her.

Unable to hold back, he dipped his head and crushed their lips together. His hand moved from her waist to the laces on her bodice, and he pulled the ties, loosening the garment enough so it could be removed. Next, he attacked her skirts. Three layers were undone and cast to the floor before he could behold her.

He took a step back, never releasing her hand, and let his eyes drink her in.

Modest as she was, she tipped her head forward so her hair covered her nakedness, even as her free hand moved to cover her most secret spot.

"My lady, please, do not cover your beauty."

She sucked in her bottom lip and continued to stare at the floor. "But—"

"Shhhh... Hush, now. Please?"

It seemed she struggled with her own will, but eventually won. Her hands dropped, and slowly, inch by inch, her head rose until she looked directly at him.

Pride filled him at seeing his wife overcome her shyness, and he allowed his eyes to roam her flesh.

"Truly, husband, you do flatter me with your gaze," she whispered. "You make me feel beautiful."

"You are stunning." Quickly, he removed his breeches and shirt, casting them to the stone floor with her garments, and embraced her again. Their skin was as liquid fire, rolling and licking the flames of the other in their caress. Hotter and hotter it burned, until it seemed he could stand it no longer. Reason boiled away, and he allowed himself to be lost in her moans, her whimpers, and the touch of her fingers.

They fell to the bed and he was overcome with desire.

Time became a thing measured only by the hourglass and as insignificant as smoke lost on a breeze.

§

Thomas awoke with the first brilliant rays of sunlight streaming through the windows. Rolling over, he stared at his wife, thinking how lovely she looked as the light played through her brown hair, her face serene as she slept. He burned with an unsated inferno. "Good morning, my lady." He kissed her lips, jaw, and neck.

Her eyelids fluttered, she giggled, her arms snaked around, and her hands caught in his hair. She pulled him down into a spiral of oblivion once again.

She lay in his arms afterward, seeming content, her necklace picking up the rays of the sun and splitting the solid beams into several more. Carefully, he reached out and lifted it, remembering the time he had stolen it and tried to take a scraping to test. It had been impossible to damage. When he had asked her about it, she told him it had been with her since birth, and she knew not where it came from.

Never had he seen, or touched, silver so light and pure. It radiated something that connected to his heart, but he could never figure out what.

Kelleigh had been livid when she discovered it missing, and she had pouted over it for days. He never dared to try stealing it again.

A sigh left her, and she looked up at him with a mischievous twinkle in her eyes, distracting him from his musings of the past.

"Again, my love?" he whispered.

As answer, she brought her lips to his and wrapped her limbs around his body.

There was no hesitation in his body as it responded to her advances, and they were lost in the love of one another for several hours more.

When they finally arose, near midday, it was to trumpets blaring in the courtyard.

He dashed to the window and peered through the murky glass.

"What is it?" Kelleigh asked.

"It seems a monarch or great lord has announced their arrival. I must be off. We have tarried too long." With a mischievous grin, he spun around and caught hold of her waist, pulling her to him. His left hand held her in place against his hip while the right pushed the hair floating in her face behind her ear before cupping her jaw. "Though, I would tarry all day with you if I were allowed."

Their lips met as gently as a petal touches a pond.

When they parted, she sighed and embraced him, pressing her ear to his chest. "How I love thee."

"You know I love you, too." He grinned. "Tonight, we shall play with our daughter in the garden. But now I must go to work."

A new lightness in his step accompanied him as he readied and set off.

Date: May 15, 1585
Location: Windsor Castle

Thomas had completed the stone settings and was locking the jewels away when someone pounded on the door. Quickly, he stuffed the key down his shirt, placed the canvas over the new lockbox, and went to pull back the iron bar. When he yanked the wood back, he was met with his wife's ashen, tear-stained face. "Kelleigh! Whatever has you in such a state?" He caught her as she fainted and pulled her to the only chair in the room, propping her up carefully and fanning her face. "Sweetheart? Return to me."

She opened her eyes and blinked. Fresh tears sprang up when her eyes met his, cascading down her cheeks before dropping on her cloak. "Oh, husband..."

Upon closer inspection, he saw that one sleeve was torn free from the bodice and was hanging freely.

Her eyes tracked his own, and she gasped, pulling the cloak around herself more tightly.

Immediately, his thoughts ran to Lord Hale, sure the man had attacked and harmed Kelleigh in some way. Thomas's insides caught fire and pushed hot coals through his veins. He ground his teeth. "I shall do that pompous Lord bodily harm if he has but laid a finger on you!"

"'Twas not him," she whispered.

His eyes burned as the air assaulted them. “There is another!”

Nearly inaudible, her words carried out on a faint breath. “No. It is your father. He has passed.”

Rage faded as sorrow bled in on top of confusion. “But, your dress.”

She shrugged. “I caught it on a chair in my haste and ripped it.” Sadness dripped from her words.

Thomas knelt in front of her and rested his head in her lap as grief consumed him. It was a comfort having her hands on his hair, even as his beard scratched and picked at the delicate satin of her skirt when his body shook. Gently, she stroked his hair and the scar in his eyebrow, allowing calm to descend upon him after a while. When he had poured the last, salty tear, he rose and guided her to her feet and into an embrace.

“The Queen sent me. She would like an audience with you forthwith.”

Inhaling, he nodded. “We shall go to her.” He took Kelleigh by the hand and led her out, locking the door behind them.

Every now and again, as they made their way through the palace, he would press her fingers more tightly between his own. It helped having her nearby in such a trying time. They finally arrived at the Queen’s antechamber, and he knocked.

One of her maids opened the door. She had a deep scowl on her face. "Her Majesty has been waiting! In with you!"

Chastised, he pulled his wife along as he hurried inside.

Elizabeth was seated in a high-backed chair on a dais with all her ladies around her, here and there on brightly coloured cushions, applying themselves either in needlepoint or in the reading of small books. She smiled softly at the couple and rose to greet them. "Sir Thomas, Lady Kelleigh, I am wrought with grief at hearing of your father's death. It pains my heart greatly to know he has passed from this world."

"Thank you, Your Highness." Thomas bowed, took her hand, and kissed the fingers lightly. "I am aggrieved as well. I must return to London immediately."

She turned to Kelleigh, who repeated the show of respect and gave thanks for the condolences.

"I am ordering your lady wife to accompany you on your journey. Your child will remain in the care of her nanny until you return so you may go swiftly." Elizabeth snapped her fingers, and one of her ladies leapt up, handing over a box. "This is for your father's funeral."

Thomas received the box and bowed again. "Thank you, Your Grace."

"Now, you must be on your way. You know it is at least a half-day's ride back to London. I shall send for the horses to be made ready."

Kelleigh fell into a deep curtsey. "Thank you again, Your Highness. Your kindness knows no measure."

She and Thomas left, hands clasped once again. They ran for their apartments to pack and kiss their daughter goodbye.

Marian was carried in and put on the carpet. She crawled to her mother's leg and put two chubby hands in the air. "Mama!"

"There you are! My beautiful girl!" Kelleigh picked the baby up and snuggled her close, kissing her head. Tears formed. "How I shall miss you!" One drop escaped and landed on her curls.

"Mama!" Marian smiled and clapped her hands.

Thomas took her and kissed her cheek. "We love you. Be a good girl."

She gurgled at him, spraying baby slobber everywhere.

He laughed, dragged his hand down his face, and handed her back to her nurse. "Thank you. We shall only be away a fortnight."

"Bye-bye!" Marian chanted, her little fingers opening and closing.

Sniffling and waving, Kelleigh sobbed as she was led through the corridors toward the paddock.

"Wife, will it be so difficult?"

Through tears, she mumbled at him. "It is not as though I am away from her very often."

"Well, it is a good thing I am around to apply distractions!" With that, he stopped walking, dropped the bag he was carrying, pulled her close, and kissed her soundly.

When they parted, her face was flushed, and she was smiling.

"There! That is better. Now, let us be off. We have much to tend to."

They emerged to the courtyard and made their way to the stables where the Master of the Horse was waiting with two steeds.

"I cannot ride on that… thing!" Kelleigh said.

Thomas laughed. "If you would, please, fetch my lady a man's saddle. She cannot stay aloft like a proper woman should." He winked at her.

She blushed and dropped her head.

In a moment, the horse was outfitted with the new saddle, and the couple were on their way back to London.

7

Date: May 28, 1585
Location: On the banks of the Thames near St. Paul's Cathedral

Kelleigh rolled over and put her arms around her husband, resting her head on his chest. "I know your father's passing has been difficult, but what else is it that has been troubling you? You have spent many hours walking the Thames to listen to the water rushing. Where is your mind these last days?"

Thomas dropped his right arm from its position behind his head and pushed her hair behind her ear. He smiled, thinking how she always noticed when he was elsewhere. It was nice to be cared about. "I have something very special for the Queen, but I know not when I should present it. The decision troubles me greatly."

"Why? What do you suppose will come of it?"

"I do not know. My fear is that she will hate the sight of it, and I shall lose my employment."

She sat up, clutching the duvet to her chest. "After sending such a gracious amount for your father's interment, I do not think she will so quickly cast you out."

"He was a favorite of her father. It was her duty. My presentation could be seen as a move for power."

"Is that the truth of it?"

He sighed. "Yes. I have great pride in my work, and I want it to be seen by all, admired, and praised. I plan to make a gift publicly."

"Husband, pride is a mortal sin. You should not throw such words around loosely."

"And I struggle with it daily." His hand found hers, and he pulled her back into his arms. "I do not know what to do."

"I suggest you present her with the gift in her chambers."

Thomas smiled. "But that would be in contrast to my plan."

"You cannot risk everything you have worked for—the position of your family—for the sake of praise! It is as though I know not who you are. *My* Thomas would never put ambition before blood." With that, she stood, dressed in haste, and fled the bedchamber.

As he stared out the window, deeply in thought, he rubbed the scar in his eyebrow until it stung. She was right, but he knew not how to remove the ingrained desire for recognition. It was like the night sky's grasp on the stars; it had hold of his heart and refused to loosen the fingers holding him captive. He had worked his whole life to be recognized.

Frustrated, he donned his clothing and shoes and left to take a walk along the Thames so he could think clearly. They were to leave the next morning, and still he had not closed the house.

7

He kicked at rocks as he walked to the bench where he had sat the day Marian was born. Once seated, his thoughts ran roughshod as he considered how to breach the issue.

For the remainder of the day, Kelleigh did not speak to him. When they mounted the horses to return to Windsor the next day, he could no longer stand it.

“Wife, please accept my apologies. I fear I have grown too used to thinking only of myself.”

She glared at him. “Did you think on it, then?”

“I did.”

“And?”

“There is no need to present the piece publicly. I shall gift it to the Queen in private.” Even as the words left his lips, he wished to recall them. There was not a thing in the world he desired more than being renowned for his work.

After a moment of studying his face, she fixed her eyes forwards. “I do not accept your apology.”

“What? Why?”

“Because it is insincere.”

The remainder of their journey passed in silence as he tried to discern how she could have known and what he might have shown on his face.

They dismounted, turned the horses over to the groom, and stalked to their apartments.

When Kelleigh saw Marian, it seemed all the upset and arguments bled right out. Cooing and nuzzling one another commenced, and Thomas excused himself.

As he meandered the halls of the palace, he thought about his wife's perception and advice. Suddenly, he was faced with the door to his workshop. He unlocked it, went in, and closed it quietly before throwing the iron bar and letting out a huge whoosh of air.

Once he had pulled himself out of the dark place his mind was thrusting him, he fetched a pint and sat on the cot in the corner to drink and contemplate. It was not long before, weary from riding, he collapsed and allowed his eyes to close.

His thighs were burning as though he had been set to the stake. Something carried his sandal-clad feet forwards to the temple where the priests and teachers of the law resided. He knelt on the steps until summoned. Wind assaulted Thomas from all sides, sending his robes into a frenzy.

A man, seeming familiar, exited the temple and knelt on the sand. "You have come to give us what we desire."

Thomas woke and seized the privy pot, emptying the contents of his stomach. Bile burned in his throat a second time, and he heaved again. Shaking, he rolled off the cot and rushed through the palace to his apartments.

He leapt onto the bed and shook his wife awake. "I am sorry. I will not present the Queen with the trinket in front of the nobles." Several passes of ill swept through him, taking his breath quite away, until she sat up. His voice wavered. "I am sorry."

"Whatever has happened, husband? You look like the Reaper has come to claim you." She squinted and touched his hand.

Beads of sweat consumed him.

A rapid knock sounded at the door, followed by the nanny's voice. "My Lady, come quickly! 'Tis Marian!"

Kelleigh leapt from the bed and ran, Thomas close on her heels.

Marian was shivering and coated in perspiration. She was taken into her mother's arms but was unresponsive. Tears poured down Kelleigh's face, and her voice was barely above a whisper. "Please, do not succumb. I could not bear it if I lost you."

Thomas could not move. His feet had turned to stone as he gazed upon his sick child. He twisted towards the nanny. "Ague?"

She shrugged even as she wrung her hands. "I know not."

"Go. Fetch a doctor!"

"At once, sir."

While she was gone, he turned to comfort his wife.

"I do not know what to do. She is so quiet, but I know she is so ill." Kelleigh hiccupped and sniffled as she swayed to and fro.

He put his arms around the pair and moved with them, trying to provide all he could silently.

It was not long until the doctor arrived, still in his nightshirt, bag in hand. "I would like to examine her, if you please."

Kelleigh placed Marian in her crib and backed away.

The doctor moved in and turned her over. Right away, she retched and covered the duvet in thick, green vomit. He lifted her away from the putrid pile and put her on the rug. "Please, would someone remove the filth from the child's bed?"

Thomas put his hands on Kelleigh's. She had such a frightful grip on her fingers they had turned blue. "I love you. She will be fine."

Standing up and cradling Marian, the doctor moved to hand her back to her mother. Once the exchange was made, he cleared his throat. "I am afraid she has caught the ague."

"What shall we do?" She turned to her husband and gripped the front of his shirt with her free hand. "I cannot bear it." Her eyes were wet, and her hand trembled.

He answered, "We shall do whatever the doctor tells us to, and we shall pray."

Lips pressed together in a thin line, she nodded.

"Doctor, what is it that you suggest?" He never took his eyes off his wife.

"Keep watch on her. Try to make her comfortable. Do not let her choke when she must vomit. Use this—" the doctor passed over a small, smooth, wooden spoon "—when she has a shaking spell so she does not swallow her tongue."

Thomas said, "We owe you many thanks."

Kelleigh cradled her daughter and repeated the words, but they were without conviction.

§

A month later, Kelleigh still had not recovered from the ague fright, but Marian was improving by the day. She could not go far without her mother as a shadow. No more balls or fine dinners were attended; she just stayed with the baby.

Thomas was troubled by the change and often begged his wife to attend him. Most nights, she refused. He knew not what to do, so he went alone and sat by himself in a corner or at the Queen's table.

Her Majesty's gift had been completed, along with the special jewelry—a large piece of jet surrounded by three rubies, each held in a four-pronged setting—for the portrait she had commissioned William Segar to paint. While the painting was complete, and resplendent, Thomas had wavered on his previous notion to give the gift in private, so he had kept it locked away. Instead, he had presented the Queen with a new girdle book holder. It was embellished like none other, and he had discovered a method for making it lighter so it would not tug on her waist.

She had praised him repeatedly, and thus invited him to join the royal table on several occasions, but he knew he would never be satisfied until she praised him publicly. It weighed heavily on his mind.

A number of nobles were to arrive within the week, and Elizabeth had sanctioned another royal ball.

Indecision had kept him awake the previous two weeks, listening to the sounds of his wife's breathing as she slept. If she discovered his secret, there was no way to know what she might do.

7

Date: July 2, 1585
Location: Windsor Castle

Trumpets sounded, and Thomas leapt from his chair by the fire and ran to the window.

Henry IV, King of France, dismounted and strode to the castle steps with his shoulders back and his head high.

Thomas snorted. King indeed. With all the intrigue surrounding the man, 'twould be a wonder if he sat on the throne much longer. With a sigh, Thomas returned to his seat and gazed at the fire.

Seven times more, he fled to the window, but no one of equal importance to Queen Elizabeth arrived. It was the eighth time that was fruitful. King John III of Sweden arrived, leading his wife, Gunilla, an exceedingly handsome woman, along by the hand. He seemed an amiable sort, and he laughed each time his long beard moved with the blustery wind. On his coattails rode in Frederick II, King of Denmark, and his wife, Sophie.

Those were the nobles Thomas had been hoping would grace Her Majesty with their presence.

He paced, muttering, arguing with himself.

After the twentieth time across the floor, he threw his hands in the air. "I surrender!" With that, he hurried to his wardrobe to dress. As he tied the laces on his breeches, he thought about the pending celebration. All the nobles would be gifted precious articles with gemstones set by his hand. While each and every one was beautiful beyond belief, the one he had crafted for the Queen was stunning.

He made haste to his workshop and stuffed the key in the slot to open his strongbox. Once the article was checked over a final time, he breathed deeply, returned it, and fastened the latch. His feet were lighter as he made his way to greet the newly arrived nobles.

As he passed his apartments, he met Kelleigh in the hall. She caught him by the hand. "I am thinking I shall go with you this eve."

His heart thundered in his chest. If she attended, there was no way he could present the jewelry without her knowing. Trying to stay calm, his mind grew tangled with ways to convince her to change her mind. It seemed he waited a beat too long.

"What are you plotting?" Her eyes narrowed.

"Plotting? Nothing! I would be honored if you would accompany me to the ball." He hoped his face looked as sincere as he was trying to make it.

She pulled one side of her mouth back and lifted an eyebrow. "All right. I shall have my ladies attend me and be ready by supper."

Kissing her hand and giving a little nod of his head, he nearly fled down the halls, sure the roaring of his heart would give away the absolute horrified state he was in. Once he turned enough corners to be sure she would not see him if she had followed, he leaned his back against a wall and put his hands on his knees, trying to catch a breath.

"Sir Thomas Russell!" Lord Hale's voice boomed through the corridor like the echo of cannon fire.

Thomas jerked upright. "Lord Hale, it is always a pleasure making your acquaintance." It was the furthest thing from amiable, but he had to get rid of the portly lord, and pleasantries often worked to his advantage. "What brings you to this wing?" Hale's rooms were on the far side of the palace, and Thomas could not recall a reason the man should be where he was standing.

"I thought to take a turn in the gardens. Would you accompany me?"

"Nay. I must decline. I have an audience with the Queen. I was on my way to her when I came upon you."

Lord Hale's face split slowly, and his eyebrows lowered. "Were you not resting against that wall?"

Thinking quickly, Thomas answered, "Only for a moment. I had been running quite a ways before I turned this corner, and I paused to regain my breath."

"I see. Well, do not tarry here with me. Continue on, Sir Thomas."

"Thank you, my Lord." He bowed and turned away.

"Might I ask?"

Without turning around, he paused his forward motion. "Yes, my Lord?"

"Will your lady wife be accompanying you to the festivities this evening?"

"Yes, my Lord. She shall be." Fury propelled his legs as he stomped away. Lord Hale's implication could not have been missed. It took Thomas the length of the walk to return to a calm state. By the time he knocked on the Queen's receiving room door, he hoped his colour was back to its usual state.

A servant opened the door and ushered him in. When he was announced, the Queen glanced at him only a moment before returning her attention to King Frederick.

Thomas moved around the room, greeting those he knew, and allowing introductions to be made to those he did not. When he approached Elizabeth, her face held no warmth. He attempted to hide his shock, but he could not reason why she might be angry. An introduction was made, King Frederick stepped away for a moment, and Thomas dared ask. "Your Highness, have I angered you?"

"Where have you been?"

"Pardon?"

"I sent a page to fetch you hours ago." Her cheeks grew pink.

"My most ardent apologies, Your Majesty. I received no summons." Panic gripped him tightly around the edges of his heart. If her ire was risen, 'twould be worse later. He watched as the fine muscles around her face grew tight.

"No?"

"Of course not, Your Highness. I would have come forthwith."

Looking down her nose at him, she loosened her jaw. "Very well. Please do attend my guests. They have been admiring your work—" she gestured to the painting of herself where the fine craftsmanship of the pieces he had created were captured forevermore "—and expressed desire to make your acquaintance."

Ashamed, he bowed deeply. "Please, accept my most humble apology."

"I do. Now go."

He scurried away, terrified he had put the first dagger into the back of his grand scheme of recognition. For the remainder of the afternoon, he jolted whenever spoken to or touched, as though he were expecting to be carted to prison.

At long last, the gathering broke for supper, and he was able to fetch his wife. He walked slowly towards his apartments, half expecting her to breathe fire at him when he arrived. Carefully, he pushed his head inside the door.

Kelleigh was sitting on a stool and stood when she glanced up and saw him.

His mouth fell open.

On her head was a gold tiara, her reddish brown hair spilling down to graze the tops of her ears. Her dress was ivory and had a heavily bejeweled collar that dipped just low enough to draw his eyes away from her sapphire ones.

"You look stunning."

Her cheeks turned bright pink.

"Even more handsome when you blush."

They turned scarlet, and she lowered her eyes.

He moved to stand in front of her and lifted her chin. "Tonight, you do not look down unless in the presence of royalty. You will steal all their hearts."

She smiled and placed a chaste kiss on his lips. "Then we should be going. We cannot keep everyone waiting."

They moved to the hall, his hand in hers, but his mind returned to his workshop, thinking of the fine jewelry tucked away in the strongbox.

7

Date: July 2, 1585
Location: Windsor Castle

When Thomas and Kelleigh entered the ballroom, she gasped and put her hand to her mouth.

Candles were lit in every space, lighting the room like a sunny day in the glade. Golden cloth draped the tables, and candelabra in silver adored their tops, catching the light and reflecting it back.

He nodded. Her Highness would have it no other way. It was a night to be remembered.

Everyone ate and danced until well into the evening.

Just before midnight, Thomas excused himself and slipped out a side door. It did not take him long to retrieve the container of jewelry for the Queen, and he was back at Kelleigh's side, heart pounding, before he could reconsider.

Her eyes went to the box immediately. "Husband! What are you planning to do?" With wide eyes, she put her shaking hand on his arm. "I thought you had changed your mind!" She kept her voice low, but she hissed as she spoke, letting her anger have free reign.

"I have decided." His ire rose as she challenged him. He knew what was best for his family and his work, and he would do what he had settled upon—no matter the consequences.

A single tear escaped and rushed down her face to drip from her chin. Without another word, she rose, bade him goodnight, and left.

Anger fueled him as he stood and made his way to the Queen's table, where she sat with all the visiting nobles. He waited to be acknowledged.

"How good of you to join us, Sir Thomas. Pray, where is your wife? I did so want to introduce her."

"She was not feeling well, Your Majesty. She has retired for the evening, but she asked me to send you thanks for the honor of allowing us to attend this evening." He smiled and bowed. "I also have brought you a gift to honor you and give you my thanks for your generosity when my father passed." Carefully, he placed the box on the table and removed the lid.

Everyone at the table gasped.

A necklace and earrings sat inside, both adored with rubies, sapphires, jet, and pearls in the new, pronged setting style he had crafted.

His breath caught as he waited.

Gently, Elizabeth lifted the items from the box and held them up to the light. They sparkled and cast colours across the faces of the nobles seated nearby.

He watched her features, examining every turn of her eyes.

7

She dropped the jewelry back in the box and looked at him. Her face was a mask—completely unreadable. “Tell me, Sir Thomas, this gift you have presented me with…”

“Yes, Your Grace?”

“Did my royal coffers not fund it?”

His heart hit his feet and glued them to the floor. “Yes, Your Grace, they did.”

“Then how, do you suppose, have you gifted me anything at all?”

Tingles raced up and down his body, lighting his skin on fire. “I…”

Elizabeth rose from her chair, lifted the box, and dropped it in the lap of Queen Gunilla. “That, my boy, is a gift. What you have brought to me is nothing more than what I have commissioned.” The Queen slammed her hand on the table. “A gift indeed. Remove yourself from my sight, and do not return.” She leaned forwards so only he could hear. “I am not blind. Do not suppose you can make a name for yourself by using me. Be gone to London on the ‘morrow. Do not return. I never wish to look upon your face again.”

He fled.

Date: July 26, 1585
Location: On the banks of the Thames near St. Paul's Cathedral

Kelleigh gasped and pulled the woolen blanket more tightly around her shoulders. For three days, she had lain ill, sweating, vomiting, and seizing.

Running a hand through her hair, Thomas's heart broke while he watched her waste away as the ague consumed her body. Ashen skin made his brown hand look much darker as it contrasted when he brushed her cheek. "Do not leave me. Please."

Between chattering teeth, she managed to form three words. "Happy birthday, husband."

He gripped her hand. "I cannot go on in this life without you."

She squeezed his fingers in return. Suddenly, her body convulsed, and her eyes rolled back to show the whites.

"Nurse!" Over and over he screamed the word, praying the woman would make it before Kelleigh choked as he tried to hold her body to the bed.

After one last jolt, she lay still.

Pulling away, he kept his eyes pressed tightly closed and prayed. Slowly, he cracked one eye a small bit and followed it with the other.

7

Kelleigh did not move. Her chest was still, and her eyes gazed blankly. At her throat, her necklace lit, as though burning from within, and turned to ash, blowing away on the light breeze in the room. There was not even a mark to indicate the jewelry had ever been there.

He gasped and threw his body over hers, pressing himself to her, asking God to make a trade. She could not be gone. Never had he loved another as he had cared for her, and he vowed never to do so again. A guttural roar filled the halls as he loosed his grief and anger with himself.

"I can go back!" he screamed into the air. "I can repair the rent I have split in our lives! Please, give me one more chance to do right." As the sobs choked him, he prayed silently, shoulders shaking.

But Thomas knew it was too late. His heart split open his chest and fell from his body, along with a river of tears. "I love you. I love you. I could never say those words enough. To hear you speak them in return one more time... I would give my own life to hear it." Every muscle went limp. "I am sorry."

Tia Silverthorne Bach

Part Three

Date: May 12-13, 1863
Location: Wake County, North Carolina, Anderson Homestead

Walking up to the small white house nestled in a dense copse of pine trees, Thomas drew in a deep breath. He had almost everything he'd ever wanted, but not many miles away, hate and ego threatened to destroy everything.

He hadn't been home in months, and the sight of his beautiful wife on the front porch took his breath away. She was gliding back and forth on a broken down, old wooden swing, her belly swollen with his child. Seeing the deteriorated house—broken shutters, rotting wood, uneven steps—brought back familiar feelings of anger and determination. He couldn't let his child live in a shack while the well-maintained main house sat only half a mile away, barely used.

Of course, Cassandra didn't mind. She loved him with an intensity he'd never experienced before. Just one year prior, they'd lost their first child six months into the pregnancy. His wife didn't let it deter her dreams any more than living in squalor did. She always made the best out of everything, even being home for months by herself while he fought in the damned war. Although he felt obligated to fulfill his duty, his heart wasn't in it. He was back for only a few days to say goodbye to his father.

A man who might not even notice his middle son's presence.

Shaking off the thoughts swirling in his head, Thomas picked up his pace. His wife's gaze fell upon him, and her face lit up like a candle in a dark room. She pushed herself up from the swing and stood at the top of the steps. Covering the distance between them at a slight jog, Thomas wrapped her in his arms and swung her around. Loosening his embrace, he feathered kisses around her face before taking her mouth with his. His hands slipped to her belly, and as he bent to kiss it, he was rewarded with a strong kick.

Straightening, he smiled. "How's the little one doing?" Feeling the reminder of his growing child took some of the worries away. He couldn't wait to meet the baby and just wanted the little one to be born healthy and for his wife to make it through without complications. "Are you feeling okay?"

"Please, don't worry about me. Everything's going great. Doc Turner says the baby will be here in another month or so." Her hands joined his, and they made a circle of love around their child.

Thomas wanted to stay in the moment forever, but as much as he cherished every second with his wife, he needed to check on his father. "How's Dad?"

"His health issues are too extensive according to Doc, and there's no more he can do to help. I've been spending a lot of time with your father. He's fading. We should go see him."

"I know," Thomas said. Yet, he hesitated. "Nicholas is with him now."

Nicholas had gone straight to the main house when they arrived back home, while Thomas rushed to his wife's side. Seeing their father together never went well. Benjamin Thomas Anderson was a hard man, and he didn't bother to hide his preference for his eldest son. No matter what Thomas did, Nicholas was the favored first born. In their studies with private tutors, he was always at the top of his class. When he graduated, he went to Columbia University to study law and was one of the first students admitted into their program.

He was almost finished when Zebulon Baird Vance, the son of a man long trusted by their father, approached Benjamin and requested the boys sign up for the infantry and support the South's interest in the war. The elder Anderson initially joined in the war efforts, but a heart attack and a bullet wound sidelined him, and he was sent home. Two additional heart attacks left him on death's doorstep.

"You should both be with him."

Her suggestion brought Thomas back to the present, and he nodded.

"Come on." She took his hand. "Let's go check on him." She guided him toward their small barn.

His horse was there, but he needed to saddle one up for his wife for the short trip to the main house. Realizing he'd been gone too long, he redirected his thoughts, not wanting the danger of having his very pregnant wife on a horse.

As he was about to turn around and offer to walk with her, Nicholas came up on his horse, Duke, his prized stallion. He hopped down and clapped his brother on the back. "Just been to see Dad. You should head there."

Thomas didn't look up to see the smug look of importance on his brother's face. "That's the plan."

"And how's my favorite sister?" Nicholas asked, putting an arm around her. "I hear I'll be an uncle soon."

"Not long." She gave a half smile and eased out of his embrace, her eyes intent on her husband.

Thomas bristled at the contact, hating Nicholas's proximity.

"Why don't you two go visit with Dad for a while? I'll go check on Benji and see how he's doing out in the fields and then check on the staff."

Benji was the baby of the family. He constantly told his brothers how much he hated the nickname, but that only made Thomas use it more. It was a brother thing. Benji was only fifteen, but he loved the outdoors and found solace in the fields doing manual labor. Thomas knew his brother's heart because they were often together, working the fields and fulfilling the needs of their large family plantation, while Nicholas was off studying and handling the business side of things.

Or doing nothing.

Thomas and Benji had always been close. At eight years old, Thomas took on a big brother role for the first time. But thanks to the cruelty of fate, he also found himself a father figure. His mother, Delilah, had died giving birth to Benji, and their father had fallen apart and retreated to the solitude of loneliness and despair. Nicholas never attempted to step into the role of the eldest son. Unless it was to boss one of his brothers around.

"He came by here earlier with some vegetables for us," Cassandra said. "He said he'd be back in later tonight to check on me. We weren't sure when you two were coming in. Benji and I were going to have dinner with your father; it's something we've been doing every night."

"Does Benji spend all of his time in the fields?" Nicholas asked.

She looked at the ground.

Thomas knew his wife all too well—she would avoid conflict for the sake of peace—and he wouldn't let his brother treat her like a child. "Casey isn't Benji's keeper. And you and I both know Benji loves being out in the fields. It's in his blood."

"We shouldn't encourage him to be out in the fields all day. He needs to be back at the house doing his studies. Maude should be seeing to that." Nicholas mounted his horse.

Maude was the cook for the main house. She was an older slave woman who'd been on staff when the boys were young. When their mother died, their father put Maude in charge. She hired tutors for the boys and tended to their every need. Thomas loved her, but Benji had formed the tightest bond with the only mother he'd ever known.

"He's young. He needs to get some energy out," Thomas replied.

"I'll decide what's best for him. You have your own family now. Casey needs you. That should be *your* main concern. Anyway, I'm going to head out. Father's expecting you." After that final word, Nicholas turned his horse and galloped away.

Needing an outlet for anger and built up energy, Thomas kicked the wooden post in front of him. He hated how his brother tried to take control of everything. He didn't know the first thing about keeping up their land, nor did he care about Benji; instead, Nicholas focused on power and money. Thomas worked the land and managed their people, and he'd taught his youngest brother from an early age. But more than anything, Thomas hated when Nicholas used the nickname Casey. That was Thomas's name for her, and Nicholas damn well knew it.

"Do you mind if we walk? I could use the fresh air. You shouldn't be on a horse anyway."

She nodded and slipped her arm around his. "Benji's done great while you've been away. You'd be so proud. Your father's not easy on him—"

"Never has been. He thinks Benji's just a younger version of me." Thomas kicked at the dirt, seeing the face of his father and Nicholas, always the cohorts, in the dusty earth.

"Look at me."

Thomas hesitated, but she insisted, guiding his face back to her with a feathery touch.

She maneuvered his body into hers and put her hand on his chest. When she was concerned, she'd get a serious face like a teacher standing at the front of a room demanding her students' full attention. "Your father needs you; he doesn't always show it well, I know, but since you've been gone, I think he's realized how much you did around here."

"Maybe. But Nicholas is the one who figures out the money. That's all Dad really cares about."

She shook her head, but then her face softened. "He only has a few more days. Please, try to make your peace with him. And with your brother. Our child won't have any grandparents; I don't want him to lose any more family."

Staring into her green-blue eyes, he wondered how he deserved her. She was the best thing that had ever happened to him. From the moment she walked into his life, he was smitten. He would do anything to make her happy. She'd lost her parents very young, and then lost the baby. To make matters worse, she and Thomas were relegated to a small house, which was falling apart, on the back of the property. All because he'd been born second. Although his father had offered for Thomas to live in the main house, it was too hard to see the favoritism day in and day out. He preferred his own home.

"Your father calls out for your mother almost daily. It breaks my heart. I wish I could ease his pain."

Thomas refocused on his wife and their walk. "You've been here for him. I appreciate that, and I'm sure he does." He squeezed her hand as his childhood home came into view.

As they continued up the main road to the front steps, they were greeted with huge white pillars, a wrap-around front porch, and white siding. No expense was spared to keep up appearances. Their thirty or so slaves worked day and night to keep the house and land running. Thomas made sure they were always treated well, although he hid as much kindness as he could from his neighbors.

His mother was from the western part of North Carolina, while his father came from the east. Philosophies were very different from the coast to the mountains. His mother came from a family of generational wealth. As a young child, Thomas would hear his parents argue about the necessity of slaves and their treatment. His father always won, detailing the necessity of cheap labor, but his mother won where it mattered: she demanded the slaves be treated well. Thomas often imagined his mother smiling in Heaven, grateful her sons were being raised by Maude, a slave woman who loved them dearly.

During the years Nicholas was away at school, Thomas served as his father's closest confidant. He trusted his son with every detail about how to manage the land. Still, even then, his father never discussed financial matters with Thomas.

As he and Casey stepped onto the porch, the door swung open, and Doc Turner appeared. Thomas extended his hand to the older gentleman.

After a quick greeting, Doc offered an update. "So great that you boys could come home. I fear you won't have much time with your father. I'm surprised he's hung on this long, but I think he wanted to see you boys one last time."

One of us, anyway, Thomas thought.

"Oh, and little Missy over here is doing amazing. I hope you'll be able to come back home in about a month to meet the newest Anderson."

"Me, too. Thanks for all you're doing for my family."

"Of course. Please, take care of your brother out there. He may be the oldest, but that one was never meant for war." Doc Turner tipped his hat and continued down the porch stairs.

Was anyone meant for war? Everyone seemed to think Thomas would fair well, but was that because his life was more expendable? Before he reported for duty, his father had pulled his middle son aside.

§

"Yes, Father, you called for me?" Thomas walked into his father's office after receiving a summons from Zebadiah, one of the lead field hands.

Benjamin nodded and swept his hand toward a chair. "Sit down, boy."

Bristling at the word, Thomas glared as he took a seat.

"I just had a visit from a family friend, a man of real importance. I know you and Nicholas are heading to fight for our state rights, but I also need to protect my heir."

Thomas winced at the singular form of the word.

"Do you remember Zebulon? He's the son of a man I've known for years. Anyway, he's heading up the 26th North Carolina regiment. He's offered to take both you boys into his infantry.

You'll each be given officer titles. He knows what kind of boys I raise."

Having to stifle a laugh, Thomas simply nodded. His father had no hand in raising any of them. Maude would deserve that honor. Thomas continued to stare without offering any response except for the occasional nod. Discussion rarely worked to his advantage.

"He's promised me he'll quickly make your brother a captain and you a first lieutenant. But I have a special request of you." Benjamin paced the room, never looking his son in the eye. "We both know your brother is extremely gifted. Someday, he *will* make a name for himself as a lawyer. Matter of fact, Zebulon has big dreams himself. Did you know he also went to law school?"

Thomas shook his head, not that his father took a moment to look in his son's direction for any kind of response.

"Anyway, your brother, brilliant as he is, is not a fighter."

A pause filled the air as the man finally made eye contact with his son.

Thomas dared speak. "Yes, I remember your requests in our younger years to fight off the boys who bullied him. I took many a beating, and gave many, in the name of my brother."

"Yes, you did. And that's why I come to you again. You'll be your brother's shadow. I will *not* lose him! It's bad enough that the North won't let the South be, let us do our business, but I will *not* lose my son to their self-righteousness."

But you would lose me, Thomas thought.

Where he used to register pain at those words, he only grew in determination to prove his father wrong and someday run their family business. Thomas would not stop until he and his beautiful wife lived in the main house as the much-deserving leaders of the Anderson household.

"Understood." Thomas said what his father wanted to hear.

§

No other conversation in Thomas's life was as clear in his mind as that one, with the exception of his wife announcing her pregnancies. But those were filled with hope, whereas the one with his father left Thomas with nothing but disgust. Still, that day changed his life forever.

Such a lack of affection or concern from his own father had inspired Thomas to do whatever it would take to make a life for *his* family, Casey and their unborn child. Benji, too.

Thomas couldn't remember the last time he stepped foot into his father's bedroom. Maybe back as a child when Thomas would run in looking for his mom. Since she died, there had only been a handful of visits.

With his wife by his side, he pushed the heavy door open. A putrid blend of medicine and stale air greeted him. It was the stench of death. He knew it all too well. Even in the open air and vast space of war, death left a lingering and powerful odor.

His wife reached the bed first and took her father-in-law's hand. "Mr. Anderson, it's Cassandra. Thomas is here with me."

Slowly, as if it took every ounce of strength he had left, he turned his head to them. Thomas moved closer to the bed and met his father's cloudy and dull eyes.

"You kept my Nicholas safe." Each word came out between the exaggerated up and down movements of his chest. "Thank you."

Thomas inhaled, his hands balled into fists by his side as his father destroyed any childhood hope that death would change his perspective. "I did."

"Do you remember my last words to you?"

What son could forget such words? "Yes."

"My dying wish is that you honor them until the end of this damned war. Zebulon has been given the same instructions."

"Zebulon left our regiment quite a bit ago. You know he's set to be governor, right?"

A coughing jag erupted from his father.

Casey helped him to a more upright position and brushed stray, thinning gray hairs from his forehead. "Take it easy, please, Mr. Anderson."

"Your wife has been so good to me."

Good enough that you would give us the home that we deserve? Thomas thought the words but didn't dare speak them. "She's an amazing woman."

With a shaky hand, his father reached out. "Please, promise me again that you'll look after my son."

"You have my word."

"When will he be back?"

"I'm here, Father."

Thomas winced at his brother's voice and shifted to face him. He'd brought Benji along.

"We're all here," Nicholas stated.

Moving aside to make room for him, Thomas put an arm around his wife.

Benji came up to the bed and stood beside her also.

"I love you all." Although the patriarch included everyone, Thomas noticed his father's eyes focused only on Nicholas. "I wish... I wish..." Another coughing jag erupted before he could finish. Then, he seemed to struggle as his breaths became shallow. His eyes widened, and he tried one more time. "I wish..."

Casey's gasp filled the room as tears poured down her cheeks, and Benji stiffened and took one step backward.

Thomas strengthened his hold on Casey, afraid she might collapse, and looked to Nicholas, who stood stoic, his eyes fixed on their father. With that last breath, Thomas could have sworn his and his father's eyes connected. But no one would ever know his final wish.

"He's gone," Nicholas said as he pushed the old man's eyelids closed. "I'll have Zebadiah call for Doc Turner to make arrangements."

Even in death, he was all business. With a slight tilt of the head, Thomas indicated for everyone to step outside. "Let's talk in the hall." He lingered, gazing at his father's lifeless body. Sadness penetrated every pore, but not because Thomas would miss the man; instead, it was mourning the loss of what could have been. Children deserved love, especially from their parents. Death had robbed Thomas of a mother and torn a permanent hole in his heart. But his father had chosen to put his love in only one place.

"Are you coming?" Casey's soft voice pierced his thoughts.

There's nothing for me in this room, never was, Thomas thought as he joined her, taking her hand.

Once out in the hall, the business of planning began.

Greed ~ III ~ Greed

"We should get back to Virginia. General Lee is expecting us," Nicholas said, his voice devoid of any emotion. It was flat, with no inflection or wavering.

"*The* General Lee? How cool is that?" Benji stated, wide-eyed.

Thomas thanked the good Lord Benji was too young to join. Turning to Nicholas, Thomas stated, "I'm going to spend some time with my wife before we leave. We'll head out first thing in the morning, I presume."

"Yes. I'll meet you at the main stable around five. We'll want to be ready to go as soon as there's some light." Nicholas turned on his heel and marched out of the room with Benji close behind asking a series of excited questions about Robert E. Lee, guns, and fighting.

Casey took her husband's hand into her own. "I'm glad we'll get a little time before you have to leave. There are a couple of things I wanted to show you."

Thomas noticed his wife's cheeks were stained with tears, and her eyes were blood red. He led her to the front of the house and out onto the porch, into some sunshine and fresh air. "Thank you for all you did for my father. And for looking out for Benji."

"Your family is the only family I've had for years. I love them. I can't wait for little Tommy to meet you and your brothers."

"What if it's a girl?" Thomas asked.

"It's not. A woman knows these things." Casey smiled and patted her stomach.

"I'll be happy either way. I just want you and the baby to be okay." Thomas knew the odds of him getting back home in time for his first child's birth were nonexistent. He remembered the day his own mother died, and he couldn't bear the thought of losing his wife and another baby.

"I'm going to be okay, you know."

He pulled her close, and then they began the walk back to their place. "I pray every day for that very outcome."

"I miss you. I understand you have responsibility, more than should be placed on your shoulders, but I'm so looking forward to the day when I can wake up to you every morning."

Once again reminded of his blessings, Thomas pushed his other feelings aside so he could enjoy his limited time with her. She brought happiness and love back to his life; two emotions ripped from him the day his mother died.

"I love you. Every day away from you is agony, but I hope to be home soon. Things aren't looking good for the South, and I doubt this war will last much longer."

He hoped the end of the war wouldn't decimate everything his family had built over the years. Maude had told him the majority of their slaves would most likely stay with the family. She credited Thomas for the way he dealt with all the field hands and staff. Technically, Abraham Lincoln had declared all slaves free with the Emancipation Proclamation earlier that year. Not that the South recognized such declarations.

There was a part of Thomas, buried deep, a part he rarely allowed to surface, that hoped his brother wouldn't make it. If that happened, the land would clearly belong to Thomas. Every time the thought reared its ugly head, he pushed it back down. At war, Nicholas tended to be off planning while Thomas was responsible for guiding the troops. He'd formed quite a bond with his men and stood beside them in battle.

Not Nicholas. Some of the men had complained about his cowardice, but Thomas—always remembering the promise he made to his father—defended his brother, saying his strategic planning kept them safe.

In truth, he was a coward, and he owed his life several times over to Thomas.

"Are you still with me?" Casey asked.

Mentally, he chastised himself for wasting a second with his wife. "I'm sorry. I am. I have a lot on my mind, not the least of which is having to leave you again."

"Why do you think I wanted to take you home? I thought we could enjoy each other's company for the rest of the evening. If you know what I mean?" A sly smile spread across her face, a faint, red glow spread up her cheeks, and her eyes seemed to twinkle.

With their house in sight, he took her in his arms. "I know exactly what you mean." He leaned in close and pressed his lips to hers. Soft at first, and then more insistent. He pulled back. "Have I mentioned how much I've missed you?"

"Yes, I believe you have." She giggled. "I can feel just how much."

He put her down and took her hand, leading her up the stairs and inside. During his travels back home with his brother, they talked about moving her into the main house. It was too dangerous for her to be alone with the baby coming. Benji had been staying with her, but they'd both be more comfortable where there were no drafts. Plus, Thomas knew Maude would look after Casey like a child. Maude loved to mother.

He didn't look forward to breaking the news to Casey. She loved her independence and their little home, no matter how small or dilapidated. More than anything, he wanted to show her how much he loved her. The other news could wait.

Kicking open the door, he pulled her inside and rubbed a hand on her belly. "Are you sure you're okay to, well..."

"More than okay," she said, moving his hand from her belly to her breast. "But I have a favor to ask first." She reached up and ran a hand through his beard. “Would you mind if I cut most of this off? I miss my husband’s face.”

She’d always hated his beard. He wasn’t fond of it, either—the darn thing made him itch like mad—but there was no time for personal grooming at war. Some of the men would give him grief for coming back with nothing but stubble, but he couldn’t deny her.

“Anything for you.”

Like a child with a new toy, she jumped a little and let out a small squeal. “Okay, let me get some hot water started.”

Their house was originally built for his father’s mother, who died only months after Thomas’s mother. It had some conveniences not found in the other houses on the property, those reserved for the slaves and staff. It had a cast iron heater for cold nights, and there was a small area on top for warming food or water. Usually, the couple ate in the main house, but they could make tea and other things in their own home. Casey put the silver teapot on to warm the water.

“So, why don’t you get out of these dirty traveling clothes? I’ll wash you, and then trim your beard.” She trailed a finger down the front of his shirt.

“We won’t get to the clipping if you start bathing me.”

She began to unbutton his shirt. “Bath first, clipping later. Deal?”

"No deal."

With as much control as he could muster, he took her mouth, backing her into the bedroom. After he finally managed to get her dress off, always a tedious process, they spent the next hour exploring each other, knowing it would be the last time for a while. No inch of skin was left untouched. Thomas started gentle, worried about his own need and the baby, but Casey's moans spurred him to push further, to take both of them to new heights.

They lay in each other's arms, moist with sweat and breathing a little heavier.

"Did I mention how much I've missed you?" Thomas asked.

"Maybe once or twice," she said as she scooted closer to him. "Now, about that beard." She stood, pulling the sheet with her as she left the room.

Thomas sat up, enjoying her every movement. A grin spread over his face as he imagined more ways to revel in her before he left. With mock embarrassment, and a giggle when he patted the bed, she threw a towel at his growing desire. He ripped the material away, leaving himself exposed, and wrapped it around his neck, his hands gripping each side of the fabric.

"Come here, my love."

"When the beard goes, I'll reward you with many pleasures," Casey said as she laid the wet rag, bowl with warm water, and clippers next to the bed.

She sat in front of him, with a few supplies in hand, letting the sheet fall and exposing her pale breasts. All she wore was a simple necklace adorned with two silver bars. With all the earlier rolling around, her hair was slightly tangled in the jewelry. He took the chain in one hand and used the other one to free the captured strands, knowing how much the piece meant to her. Her father had bought it the day she was born, or so the story went, and she'd worn it for as long as she could remember. When they were married, Casey told Thomas it represented the two of them and their love.

Once he freed her hair, he pushed it behind her ear. Then, caressing her skin with slow movements, he leaned into her, brushing his lips against hers. As he continued down her neck, she pulled away, giggling.

"Let me focus." She repositioned the sheet to cover herself and placed the bowl between them. After clipping away most of the hair, she wiped his face with the warm rag, mainly to get any stray hairs. "So much better." She caressed his cheek. "I love you."

"I love you, too." He leaned closer and pulled the sheet down. "And we still have some time before dinner."

An hour later, they got dressed.

"There's something I want to show you." She led him into the next room.

Rounding the corner, he saw a wooden crib with a beautiful blanket made out of varying shades of blue thread.

"It took me several months to make it. Isn't it gorgeous?" She rubbed her hands on the material. "Oh, and Zebadiah made the crib."

It was time to tell her. "I'm going to have Zebadiah move everything you need into the main house. I'll arrange for everything after dinner. You'll be safer there. Nicholas already asked Benji to stay there, too. Close by, in case you need him."

He noticed her back stiffen as she let go of the blanket.

"You do understand this is for the best, right? Just until I get home."

She faced him, her eyes locking onto his. "Then, what? We come back here?"

Not if he had anything to do with it. He suppressed the thought and focused on enjoying the dwindling time he had left with his wife.

He slipped out of their bed. When she reached for him, he reminded her again how much he loved her and that he would be back soon.

"Take care of yourself and our baby," he whispered.

He kissed her, and then made his way into the living room to grab his bag. It was still dark outside, but he knew Nicholas would be eager to leave. Thomas walked outside but hesitated. His every movement felt labored, as if he were walking through cement. If only he could stay.

He forced himself to move forward, and when he arrived at the stables, his brother was already preparing their horses.

“Did you get everything arranged for her to move into the main house?” Nicholas asked.

“Yes, I took care of that after dinner last night.”

“We have a long ride ahead of us. We’ll meet back up with our unit in Virginia.”

“I assume you made all the plans for Father’s burial,” Thomas said. Even with their acrimonious relationship, Thomas felt guilty for leaving before his father was laid in the ground. But Nicholas had insisted.

“Everything is taken care of.”

Thomas didn’t look forward to the week or so on horseback, but he knew they had to go. He allowed himself one last glance back toward the house where his wife lay sleeping.

Date: July 1-3, 1863
Location: Gettysburg, Pennsylvania

Weeks of travel and planning filled their days. First, they arrived in Richmond. They joined with several groups there, including many from their own regiment, and heard detailed new plans. General Robert E. Lee planned to march them through Maryland and into Pennsylvania. His health was bad, and several more generals became involved.

Soon, Thomas and Nicholas found themselves in Gettysburg, in a battle such as they'd never seen before. Their goal was to take the town and change the tides of the war. But the day was brutal, and many men were lost, though Thomas caught rumblings the South declared the day a victory.

Everywhere around him, he heard voices raised in concern. From the lowest-ranking man on the field to the highest-ranking one on horse, there seemed to be little agreement on how best to continue their efforts.

That evening, holed up in a tent with his men, Nicholas came by and requested an audience with his brother.

When he stepped outside, Nicholas kept walking. It was obvious Thomas was to follow, and he understood the underlying meaning.

His brother wanted Thomas out of earshot from his men.

Once they were about a quarter of a mile away, Nicholas spoke. "I wanted to let you know the plan. Major General Pickett is on his way. We have more men, so if we can break the Union, we can win."

"Nothing about today makes me think we are close to victory. I lost many of my men, and several more are wounded. How am I supposed to inspire them to get back up and put in another day of fighting tomorrow? So many of them are missing their families and wondering why they're even here, putting their lives on the line." Thomas paced. Since leaving home again, he'd been questioning a lot himself. He was a man of duty and spirit, but he had one goal: make it back home to his wife and child. It had been nearly two months since he last saw her. His son had been born a month after Thomas left, but he'd only gotten word from a courier just over a week before. Casey had named their son Thomas Samuel Anderson. A junior. Tommy for short. Or, so Thomas assumed, since she had called their little one that during Thomas's brief trip home. The day his father died.

Everything Thomas did going forward would be for them. Not for some Confederate cause. And certainly not because his brother thought it was for the best.

"Your job is to get them back to the front of that line tomorrow. Pickett isn't due to get here for another day. We need to keep fighting until he arrives. There are plans in place. General Lee believes if we win Gettysburg, this war won't go on much longer. We win. It's almost over."

"That's a huge if, especially the way things have been going. I need to give my men a reason. Hell, half of them don't have a vested interest in slavery. We lost over five hundred men today. Five hundred! And that's just our men. I don't know about other regiments."

Nicholas stepped closer to his brother, within inches of his face. "You've lost men before. Focus on your wife and son. We fight for what we've always fought for. For the Southern way. Do you think our land will be as profitable if I have to go out and pay men to work the land and hire staff?"

Of course that was all his brother cared about. After spending the last few years honoring their father's wishes, Thomas only served to protect a man obsessed with money. A man with no family; a man who only cared about himself. *If that's the Southern way, then to hell with it*, Thomas thought, anger brewing in his blood. "Most of my men don't have money. They're fighting for their families, because they feel a duty to their state. They don't fight for the right to have slaves. Hell, Lincoln freed all of them earlier this year!"

"We don't honor anything that man does! He's not our president, so I don't care what proclamations he makes. It means nothing!" The words came out of Nicholas with so much venom, spit flew into Thomas's face.

Wiping away the nasty film, he stood his ground. "Well, I don't care about profit. I have a different bottom line than you do. I know I can run the land with most of our people in place. They deserve to make some money. We've never treated them poorly. They know that. They won't leave us."

Even as he spoke the words, he prayed they were true.

"You're so naïve. You've always been stronger than you are smart. That's why I look out for you." Nicholas extended his hand and placed it on his brother's shoulder.

Thomas swatted the hand away. "*You* look out for *me*?"

Did his brother really have no cluc about everything Thomas had done? And not just back in their teenage years. Even on the way back to their regiment, he saved Nicholas on several occasions. One was during a slave riot they happened upon at the Virginia border, before arriving in Richmond.

A house was burning to the ground, and Thomas had run inside. A woman screamed about her babies from the front yard, and he didn't hesitate to help. He was able to save the toddler, but couldn't get to the infant. While he ran in and out of the house, awash in flames he had to constantly swat away, Nicholas did nothing, continuing on his way. After Thomas made sure the woman was in good hands, he tried to catch up. When he did, he found his brother on the ground. Looming over him was a black man with a knife. The two were rolling around, each trying to get the upper hand, but Nicholas ended up on the bottom.

Racing toward them, Thomas dismounted his horse before it stopped. He flung himself at the man threatening Nicholas, wresting the knife from the man and driving it deeply into his chest. After, Nicholas stood, brushed himself off, and found his horse, which had only wandered a few feet away. No thank you. Nothing. So, to have to look at him as he talked about protection almost made Thomas sick.

Nicholas didn't stop his rants. "You wouldn't be here without me. You'd have no home, no fields to manage. Nothing without me. Dad left everything to me. Everything. If you want a roof over your family's heads, you better treat me with some respect."

Why the words were shocking, Thomas wasn't sure. Of *course* their father left everything to Nicholas, the beloved heir. No matter what happened with the war, if Nicholas went back home, Thomas would be left with nothing. Slaves or no slaves; it wouldn't make a difference.

"General Lee has commanded Lieutenant General Longstreet to take out the Union left bank. You need to do what's necessary to get your men ready for the following day."

"My men will be ready." Thomas turned away, sick of his brother's smug face.

Back in the tent, Thomas told his men to fight to get back home, to fight for their loved ones. Nothing else mattered. Figuring it was the only thing that motivated *him*, he hoped it would be the spark his men needed to face the next day.

Darkness surrounded him. Nothing but shadows and varying degrees of black and gray. He blinked several times, hoping his eyes would adjust to the light, moving his hands close to his face to try to make them out. As they came into focus, he could see silver coins being poured into them.

Yet, instead of excitement at the windfall, he felt a burning sensation and a deep sense of dread. Hoping to ease the pain, he pulled his hands apart and let the coins fall to the ground. Dark figures came at him, and he reared back, afraid.

Then, another glint of silver caught his eye.

His wife's necklace came into view, and a light shone in the same direction, increasing in intensity. He squinted to make out the beacon of hope.

Jolting awake, he grabbed a nearby discarded shirt to wipe the sweat from his forehead. Clearly, stress was getting to him. Thomas slipped out of his tent and into nature, a place where he usually found peace. Back home, they had a small pond—man-made, the perfect drinking source for the horses and other animals. He would sit by it and watch the movement of the water. It soothed him. Any disturbance, a rock skipped across the surface or an animal lapping at the shore, only had a small ripple effect. Within moments, the surface settled down, and the pond returned to its glory.

Nature during war was something else entirely. Gone were the sounds of birds chirping and the smell of flowers and trees. Instead, there was a constant haze of smoke from cannon fire, the smell of wounds and rotting flesh, the lingering scent of sickness and filth, and the sounds of explosions and the wounded's wails.

Before he could find coffee and round up a small breakfast, he noticed Nicholas in conference with several high-ranking officers in an open tent. Curious about the day's plan, Thomas edged closer.

"We need you to assess the wounded in the 26th."

Thomas's ears perked up at the mention of his regiment. He focused his energy on listening to General Armistead.

"See who can fight today. We need every man we can put out there. We hope Major General Pickett will be here soon, and the plan is for him to lead a charge up Cemetery Ridge and weaken the Union defense."

Nicholas walked the fringe of the discussion, not adding anything and keeping a safe distance.

Of course, he won't stand up for anything or try to reason with the others, Thomas thought. After losing five hundred or so men the previous day, he didn't know how they were going to figure prominently in the day's battle; yet, the pressure was there to do so.

Cemetery Ridge. Not an inspiring location name for a bunch of men hoping not to die.

"Let's get through today. The 26th was hit pretty hard yesterday, so we'll give them a day of rest. They need to ready their men for tomorrow. Plus, they did all we could ask of them," said another man.

Thomas strained to make out the man's voice, but couldn't identify him.

"I have a bad feeling."

Did Thomas imagine those words? Did the man actually say them, or was it Thomas's own feelings breaking through?

"After our success yesterday, you are still reticent?" another voice asked.

Thomas wished he had a better vantage point.

"Every day of this war leaves me reticent. Every day a man dies, I am reticent. But I will follow Lee's orders, and we will continue with the plan for today and hope Pickett gets here with his men soon."

Finally, the voice formed a mental image in Thomas's mind, and he realized who the speaker was: Lieutenant General Longstreet. Of all the decision makers, he seemed the most thoughtful and conservative. Thomas liked the man.

More conversation followed, but Thomas needed to get back and check on his soldiers. He would ascertain injuries and rally those physically healthy but mentally spent. After only two steps, a hand smacked him on the shoulder. Thomas spun around, ready for anything, to find his brother standing there.

"You shouldn't sneak up on me," Thomas said.

"Don't threaten me. I outrank you in every way possible." Nicholas's nostrils flared.

Was he always such a jerk? Ever since Father died, Nicholas seemed to have an air of royalty, of superiority. He always knew he was the favorite, but power had since been bestowed upon him. He had Thomas by the balls and knew it.

"Yes, sir." Thomas flicked his hand at his temple to salute, narrowing his eyes. Mockery oozed out, and he hoped his brother picked up on it.

"You need to assess your wounded and see who can fight tomorrow. After our success yesterday—"

"Success!" Thomas spat the word, seething inside. "What fool labeled such a loss of men a success?"

Nicholas grabbed his brother's arm and dragged him several feet away from their previous location. "Keep your Goddamned voice down. Generals abound, and you want to yell out the word *fool*. What the hell is wrong with you?" With each word, Nicholas squeezed Thomas's arm harder.

With as much restraint as he could muster, while also determined to make a point, Thomas punched his brother in the stomach. When he doubled over, Thomas quickly straightened Nicholas back to standing. It wouldn't do either of them any good to draw attention to themselves.

"Don't touch me again." Thomas stepped back but never broke eye contact.

Brushing off, Nicholas continued. "General Lee's making his move at eleven. Have your men ready."

"And where will you be? Will you be on that front line with us or cowering in a corner, only protecting yourself?" Thomas asked.

Nicholas reared back, his eyes narrowed and his teeth gnashing. If pain could be inflicted from a mere stare, Thomas would've been on his knees.

"Do you think I didn't see you yesterday? I led the men while you stood behind some trees and shouted orders. You were nowhere near the action, and you never moved forward." Thomas took a step closer to his brother so their noses almost touched. "Not even as man after man fell carrying out the orders you gave."

Nicholas straightened, although his height was no match for his brother's. "You have your job, and I have mine. Now, go do yours."

Bringing up the images of his wife and son, Thomas reminded himself of his one true mission: to get home. He headed back to his men, determined to make the best out of a bad situation. Rumors spread like wildfire. If they could take Gettysburg, they could win the war. Winning the war meant going home to his family. That was all he cared about.

As he walked, his mind ran amok. A possible solution to his problems, a consideration that always seemed on the edge of his thoughts, re-emerged. When it did, he tried to shake it off like he had numerous times.

All his problems would be solved by his brother's death.

Several times during the war, opportunities had presented themselves. All Thomas would have to have done was turn a blind eye for only a moment. Left and right, men were dying. Better men than Nicholas.

But each time Thomas allowed himself to consider such a plan, a voice broke through. "Don't forget your promise." His father's words were on repeat.

Thomas reached up and rubbed the scar just above his right eye. A reminder of yet another time he had defended his brother and paid the consequences.

They'd been out drinking at the local bar, and Nicholas started spouting off about one or the other of his achievements. Some of the local boys didn't take too kindly to it, and soon, glasses and barstools were flying. A man had Nicholas by the collar, a shard of broken glass held to his throat. Thomas didn't hesitate. He jumped in and knocked the man down, only to be accosted by another. But Thomas beat them all off. One got lucky and slashed a knife at his head, cutting into his skin. A couple more inches, and he would've lost an eye. A scar remained as everlasting proof of his commitment to his promise, and his brother's failure to care about anyone but himself.

Walking home that night, he chided Thomas for his foolishness. Never once thanking him.

If he'd hesitated then, things would be so different.

"You are heading down a dangerous path. Don't forget your promise."

Thomas heard the words so clearly he spun around to see if anyone was following him. He knew nobody but his father would utter those words. Was he haunting Thomas from the other side? Even in death, the old curmudgeon took on the role of a bully.

But another thought bothered Thomas even more. Was it his father's voice? It seemed different. Maybe ghosts took on different tones.

With a shake of his head, Thomas pushed forward. It wasn't the time to go crazy. Sleep had been difficult since he left Casey behind. She brought out the best in him and kept the demons at bay. When he was around her, he rarely thought about killing his brother. She made Thomas believe everything would work out in the end.

He remembered their last night of lovemaking and pushed evil thoughts aside. Before the war, he might have had a few ominous thoughts in regards to his brother. Since, they'd increased ten fold. War desensitized a man to killing. Really, every man there killed for his own reasons, or just for the hope of getting back to his family. Why should Thomas feel guilty about the same desire? Nicholas had no family of his own to go back to.

Plus, Thomas wouldn't have to strike the final blow. All he'd have to do was let the war do it for him.

Stop! he screamed in his head. He and Casey would figure something out. What kind of man did he want to be for his son? For Casey? If only Thomas's father had been fair, had split the property between his boys, had shown affection to more than one of them. If only their mother had survived. Everything would've been different.

What ifs were a fool's fantasy, and Thomas knew he had to get off that path of thinking. It wasn't as if he wanted the land just for himself. No, his brother held that dubious distinction. Thomas wanted it so his family would flourish, so he could provide.

"Lieutenant Anderson."

A voice broke through. A much-needed voice. Thomas was grateful. He turned to find a young private wringing his hat in his hands. "Sir. What are the orders for today?"

"I need to check on the wounded. Have all the healthy men meet me in that small area over there after lunch for further instructions." Thomas pointed to a clearing not far from them.

"Yes, sir."

Although he didn't want to see any more of his men wounded or killed, he hated a day of rest. He'd much rather be in the thick of the fight than in his own head.

Most of his men with minor injuries had been patched up and sent back to camp. Field hospitals overflowed with the wounded. Any available building in the area—from private homes to barns—had been set up for medical care. But they were at capacity. Unsure which infirmary his men were in, or how many different ones they might be spread out in, he went to ready his horse. Some of the hospitals were up to ten miles away.

Good. His day would be full.

Within an hour, he was on his way. Cannon blasts and gunfire filled the air. He wondered how many more men would be lost. When he arrived at the first hospital, he tied up his horse and went inside.

A stench—a mixture of feces, blood, urine, and antiseptic—greeted him at the door. Body after body lay in rows, resting on cots. Moans and groans filled the room. *God, if I must go, please, take me quickly. I don't want to languish in some place like this,* Thomas prayed.

How could he be expected to find his men amongst all the wounded? Thanks to wrappings and covers, few discernable features stood out.

"Thomas..."

He spun around toward the muffled voice to find Andrew lying in a bed not three feet away. He'd fallen to the ground near Thomas, from a bullet wound to the thigh, the day before. Although the boy was probably eighteen or nineteen, he didn't look a day over fourteen, which reminded Thomas of Benji. Refusing to lose another man, Thomas had scooped Andrew up and taken him over to where Nicholas stood, well hidden from any action. By the end of the day, Thomas had laid ten to fifteen men in the same spot. At least his brother had managed to keep them safe in his little hiding spot.

Taking the boy's hand, Thomas asked, "How are you doing, Andrew?"

"I'm grateful for what you did yesterday. If you hadn't..." Andrew turned his head to the side. After a few sniffles, he turned back. "Well, just thank you. I'm the last of my brothers. My mother would've been devastated."

"Glad I could help. I have a son of my own, you know. He's a little fellow. Haven't even met him yet."

"You'll make a great father."

After getting some information from Andrew about the other wounded in the building, Thomas went around and visited them all. Then, he chased down a doctor to get updates on everyone's condition. Some patients were expected to make it, but others—including Andrew—weren't. None would be able to fight the next day.

A few more hours and several more hospital sites later, Thomas returned to camp with little time to spare and no new men. They were definitely facing an uphill battle the next day.

Upon his return, Nicholas approached. It was as if he had a homing device tracking his brother. "So?"

"Most of the men in those hospitals are fighting for their lives. They won't be helping us tomorrow. Any word on Pickett?"

Nicholas shook his head. "It sounds like the 26th will be towards the front of the attack."

Wherever will you hide? Thomas thought. A sinking feeling hit him in the gut. Something in Longstreet's voice—the obvious sound of doubt—played over and over again. Something in his tone was foreboding.

Morning came too soon. Most of the men had been up all night. Pickett had only arrived with his troops the previous evening, and strategizing went late into the night. That day had been more about waiting than fighting.

As Thomas readied his troops, he saw another meeting of the minds and sought a spot to hear their plans. Again, he stayed on the periphery. Nicholas was nowhere to be seen.

General Lee discussed details with Pickett and Longstreet. While Pickett seemed raring to go, Longstreet appeared apprehensive, both in his body language and his tone of voice.

"No 15,000 men who ever lived could take that position," Longstreet said during the discussion.

Thomas backed away upon hearing the words. Rumors had spread among the men that the general thought the upcoming attack was a suicide mission. Not what Thomas wanted replaying in his mind as they headed into battle. *No 15,000 men.* Quite the statement. Thomas could imagine packing the field with highly trained assassins and still failing, and his men weren't dedicated killers.

Many of the men had been discussing their fear that General Lee was over-confident thanks to recent wins. Cockiness and war didn't mix, and Thomas feared the possible repercussions.

With mounting concerns pressing down on him, he brought out a picture of Casey from their wedding day. It was bent at the corners and cracked in places, but it stayed in his shirt pocket, close to his heart. Although the photo was black and white, Thomas saw vivid colors in his mind: the beautiful purple flowers in her bouquet, her red-stained lips, pink cheeks, sparkling eyes the color of the sea. He could feel her love, even hundreds of miles away.

"Everyone ready their troops!" The command came from several different directions.

Thomas carefully tucked the photo back in his pocket and hoofed it back to camp to rally his men. They would need to head over to their designated area: at the southern point, near Cemetery Ridge, along with Pickett's forces.

Preparation for battle always had a lot of wait time, yet everyone hurried. They were in place long before they needed to be, which only raised the men's anxiety as they stared across the open field.

Open.

No cover.

Still, no Nicholas.

Thomas figured his brother was scoping out a good hiding place and focused on bigger concerns.

"Today, we fight for our wives, our children, and our families. Today, we honor the Confederacy," one of the high-ranking officers said as he sat on his horse and trotted back and forth in front of the men.

Nicholas, as the higher-ranking officer, should've been there. But the men didn't respect him. As the time to march closed in on them, each man lined up, his rifle in position.

An eerie quiet settled for a brief moment.

Then, Thomas saw Nicholas, far in the back, and ran over.

"You need to come up front with us," Thomas said.

"We aren't going to win here today. Why stay?" Nicholas's eyes were wide, and his voice was shaky.

"We stay for our men. We stay because it's our duty," Thomas said.

But Nicholas started backing up, his eyes cast down at the ground.

7

Grabbing his arm, Thomas pulled his brother close. "Where do you think you're going?"

"I'm leaving. Who'll stop me? They'll think I just disappeared or died. I can't be here. I wasn't meant for battle."

"And bring dishonor to our family!" Thomas saw red. Here he was fighting for his wife and child, and his brother would bring shame to all of them. "Over my dead body." Pulling him by the arm, Thomas forced his brother to the front of the line.

As soon as they were in position, the sound of drums filled the stale air. They waited. Then, they heard the command. It seemed to echo throughout the valley, coming from both sides of them.

"Forward!"

In step with each other, the troops moved toward their fate. They had some ground to cover, but the first cannon blast rocked the ground within minutes, followed by gunfire and screams.

Still, the line advanced. Left. Right. Left. Right. Around them, men fell. But the line kept moving.

Suddenly, a cannon exploded, throwing Thomas, Nicholas, and a few others to the ground. They scrambled to their feet and continued their march.

All except Nicholas.

Thomas scanned the area. Blue and gray filled his vision, as body after body marched the field. Then, his eye caught a familiar gait, facing the wrong direction. Only Nicholas would retreat at such a time. His body language was frantic, confused, as he turned his head side to side. Thomas knew panic when he saw it.

Afraid the no-good coward would escape, Thomas circled around behind his brother and blocked his path, forcing him forward. After a few feet, they came upon a long wooden fence barricading their path.

Once Nicholas was over, he'd have no option but to move forward, at least not easily. At the fence, he hesitated.

He grabbed Thomas by the shoulders and shook him. "Brother, don't make me go. You promised Father you'd look out for me."

"I'm here with you, am I not?" They were in a precarious position, and Thomas knew they had to keep moving. "You two!" Thomas yelled to two privates standing on the other side of the fence. "Please, help Captain Anderson over."

The men grabbed Nicholas and hoisted him to the top of the fence.

Thomas couldn't help but smirk as his brother stared, unmoving, still atop the fence.

Putting one foot on a rung to catapult over, Thomas noticed a man in dark blue not too far away, his rifle trained in their direction.

Nicholas hadn't moved.

Thomas reached forward, planning to knock his brother to the other side.

But hesitation caused Thomas's hand to still.

Such a simple ending to all his problems. He could stand back while the war gave him everything he'd ever wanted. It wouldn't be his fault. In the precarious position, up above the others, Nicholas was an easy target.

A flash of silver—coins and the necklace from the dream—sent Thomas into action.

In two movements, he threw himself over the fence, taking his brother down, too. As they fell, gunfire rang out. He screamed, and Thomas saw a dark red spot spread throughout his brother's white shirt at the bottom of his ribs.

A new plan formed in Thomas's head. He could drag his brother back to camp. Odds were he'd die before they could get to help, but Nicholas would be out of harm's way, allowing Thomas to technically honor his promise.

Nicholas explored his torso and drew back a blood-soaked hand. As he brought it up, it shook. "Take me to the hospital. They'll understand you saving your brother. I can sign over a parcel of land and build a better house for you and—" He couldn't finish as coughs wracked his body.

Thomas drew in a breath. His brother's wound looked serious. Would he make it either way?

"Don't forget your promise."

Looking around for help, Thomas noticed one of his men still on the other side of the fence.

"What do we do, sir?" the private yelled. "It's not looking good."

Wide eyes stared at Thomas, and he could see the boy's fear. Another man's son.

Instincts kicked in. "This officer is wounded. I'm going to get him over to you, and I want you to get him to safety. Do you understand?" Thomas asked.

The private nodded.

Summoning every ounce of available strength, Thomas lifted his brother, easing him over the fence and into the waiting arms of the private and another man who'd come over to help.

"We've got him, sir," the young boy said.

For a moment, a numb feeling spread through Thomas as he watched the private put Nicholas on a blanket and begin to drag him away. Turning back toward the ridge, Thomas saw several of his men staring. Waiting for an order. Waiting for him.

He imagined his son's face, warm and safe in his mother's arms. Both of them waiting for Thomas. So much depended on him. He stood, straightening to his full height, and grabbed his gun from the ground.

All he had to do was survive. Stay focused and claim victory. "Forward!" he yelled to his men.

Two steps in, he heard the unmistakable whistle of a cannon. One that was too close. In front of him, the ground erupted, and he felt the earth shake just as he registered stabs of searing pain all over his body.

He felt himself falling.

Fighting the sensation, he forced his legs to stiffen, trying to stay upright. Casey. His memory held close every detail of his wife's face, and her image, much like the photo he carried, became crystal clear in his mind. Tommy had likely already changed. Tommy. Images of the child Thomas longed to hold flashed before his eyes, from infant to a grown man, Thomas's mind projecting hope. Then, one leg buckled, followed by the second.

Slamming into the ground, Thomas's head lolled to one side. His breathing came in short gasps. Tommy. Casey. Their names formed on Thomas's lips.

A bright white glow appeared and grew in intensity. He saw a hand being extended toward him.

A woman's hand.

Then, everything went black.

Kelly Risser

Part Four

January 3, 1930 ~ 7:00 p.m.
Chicago, Illinois near McKinley Park

The hairs on Nichole's arm rose as she stared into the dark alley. The part of her job she hated the most was getting to and from work. Unfortunately, the pitch-black path led to the club's only entrance. It was used by employees, customers, and thugs alike.

Rubbing her gloved hands up and down her arms in a fruitless attempt to warm up from the biting cold of winter, she hurried forward. The sooner she got inside, the better. January in Chicago was cruel, and the wind nipped at her exposed skin. She needed a new coat. The one she had on was so well worn it was threadbare in places, making frostbite a real possibility as she walked her five-block commute. But money was tight, and Frankie had needed a new coat before she did. The boy was growing like a weed, and the one from the year prior barely fit. She used her savings from the previous two months to buy him a fine, wool jacket.

Thinking of her son brought a smile to her face. He was only five, but such a little gentleman. She loved him more than anything and would stop at nothing to ensure he was safe, loved, and cared for. Mabel, their landlady and downstairs neighbor, was an elderly woman who enjoyed babysitting Frankie for company. She watched him whenever Nichole worked, which was often. Not that she was complaining;

she was grateful to have a job. After the stock market crashed in the fall of 1929, business was dropping. The constant worry Nichole felt as a mother was compounded by a new fear: what if she lost her job?

Lost in thoughts of Frankie and her troubles, she walked quickly through the darkness, her eyes trained on the white door in the distance. There were no lights to greet employees or patrons, and had the door been any other color, Nichole doubted she would see it. Then there were the smells, foul and sour, a mix of old garbage and body odor. The path was by far the least pleasant in all of western Chicago, and yet it was well traveled. Everyone loved the speakeasy.

A beefy arm wrapped around her, and a gloved hand firmly covered her mouth. Nichole's scream of surprise drowned in the leather. A deep, husky voice whispered, "Not a sound, see? We'll do this nice and easy, won't we, doll?"

"I ain't your doll!" she tried to shout, but all that came out were a few garbled squeaks. The brute dragged her backward down the alley, and as she clawed at his hand and arm, it took the rest of her strength to maintain her balance.

Her mind whirled with fear and her eyes darted in the blackness, looking for escape or at least an ally. Who could help her? No one would find her there. God, who would care for Frankie? She wasn't a crier, but hot tears slid down her face. *Hail Mary, full of grace. The Lord is with Thee.* Although not particularly religious, Nichole was raised Roman Catholic. If anyone would come to her rescue, it would be the Virgin Mother.

"What's a pretty dame like you doing in a place like this?" The man's voice was thick and slurred. Old Ed, the Green Door's bartender, had probably served the thug all afternoon. His other hand slid up and under her modest dress. He'd removed his glove, and his rough, icy cold palm sent a shiver through her body. Repulsed, she renewed her efforts to free herself. He ignored her and continued. "Unless you're one of them dames that work here?" His chuckle was low and evil while he placed a wet, sloppy kiss on her cheek. "You wouldn't mind giving me a taste of the goods for free, would ya? Consider it a sample."

His hand slid higher, and she reacted, stomping her sturdy heel on his left instep. He yelped in pain and released her. Turning, she kneed him in the groin before scrambling to get away. She didn't get far before he caught a fistful of her long blonde hair and yanked. Pain seared her scalp, and she cried out. He quickly covered her mouth, firmer than before. His large hand pressed against her nose, too. She fought his thick fingers to drag in air, feeling weak and lightheaded.

"You like it rough, do ya?" His quiet laugh sounded menacing. "My kind of gal."

His free hand grabbed the silver necklace hanging around her neck and pulled. She waited for the chain to bite into her skin, but it never came. The raspy voice of an old woman whispered “be brave” from the shadows, but when Nichole turned her gaze toward the source, no one was there.

Closing her eyes, she resigned herself to fate. No one was going to save her, especially not an old woman who would be no match for Nichole’s assailant. When she had turned to assault him, she’d assessed his size. Surprise had been her only element of defense. He was a bulk of a man and recovered lightning fast from the attack. Plus, he would be twice as cautious going forward. All she could do was pray he left her alive afterward. She’d heard horror stories from the other girls of these things happening to dancers; she didn’t think it would ever happen to her.

She wanted to plead with him, tell him she had a child and appeal to his humanity, but with her mouth covered, she couldn’t form the words. Stumbling on a rock, her knee buckled. He didn’t even slow his pace, just gripped under her arms and dragged her toward the street.

“What’s going on here?”

The man dragging her turned sharply, giving her a view of the alley entrance. A tall, male figure stood there. Silhouetted by the street lamp, she couldn’t make out his features. He wore a long overcoat and a fedora. A gentleman, if his fashion sense said anything.

The brute ignored the newcomer, who called out, "What's the idea?"

"I had a dispute with my gal, see? We're heading home to work it out." Her assailant patted her head like one would a dog. "Domestic business. None of your concern."

While he spoke, Nichole tried to silently communicate her fear. She widened her eyes as much as she could and tried to shake her head side to side, although being constrained didn't allow for much movement.

"I think the lady begs to differ." With confidence, her rescuer stepped forward into the shadows.

When Nichole caught his face, she gasped. It was Tommy Two Guns, the Middleweight boxing champion. She'd taken Frankie to a fight once. The seats had been far from the ring; it was all she could afford, but he'd loved every second of it. He thought Tommy was a hero, and it looked like he was about to become hers.

"What do you know, pal?" growled the man from behind her. Either he didn't recognize Tommy or was too stupid to care about going up against a professional boxer.

That was all it took. One second, Nichole was caught in the brute's smelly hold, the next, the oaf was down, blood gushing from his broken nose. Her heart raced, and it took everything in her to hold her ground and not flee. Her fingers lighted gently on her bruised skin while she studied the bloodied man with dismay.

"Is he alive?" Nichole asked.

"Unfortunately, yes." Tommy kicked the man in disgust before dragging him to the side and throwing him on a pile of refuse as if the large thug weighed next to nothing. Tommy turned back to Nichole, brushing off his hands. The dim lighting reflected the burning anger in his eyes, which quickly melted to concern. "Are you hurt?"

"I'll survive." She smiled wanly. "Thank you for rescuing me."

He tipped his hat and offered his arm. "Let me walk you home, Miss—?"

"Nichole," she answered, caught in his charming smile. He was an average looking man, and his face was mottled with bruises from his profession.

"Nichole," he repeated with a smile, and it lit his face. White teeth against dusky skin, he was handsome, just not conventionally so. Realizing she was staring, and he was politely waiting, she shook her head.

"I can't, I mean..." She jerked her thumb behind her. "I've got to go to work."

"You work here? It's not the place for a lady." He frowned.

A lady she wasn't, but she appreciated his assessment. "I'm a dancer, and the bills don't pay themselves." She wondered if he thought less of her.

"What do you make in a night?"

She was shocked by his forthright question and spluttered to answer him.

"That's all right. Don't answer that." He pulled out his wallet and handed her a bill. "Will that cover it?"

She stared at the twenty in her hand. Even on her best night, she never made that much. Pushing the money back at him, she said, "I can't accept this."

"You can and will." He crossed his arms, refusing to take it back. "I'm not letting you go back in tonight, see? Miss Nichole, I have a goal to escort you safely home, and you don't know me, but I always reach my goals."

"Oh, but I do know you!" Nichole replied without thinking and silently cursed as her cheeks grew hot. "I mean, you're Tommy Two Guns."

His right eyebrow, the one with a thin, horizontal scar, rose in doubt. "You're a boxing fan?"

"Not me," she said. "My son, Frankie. He's your biggest fan." She wondered why she was being so open with him. Most men turned from interest to disgust when they realized she was a mother.

To Tommy's credit, he didn't even look down and check her left hand to see if she was married. Instead, he gave her another dazzling smile. “Your son has good taste.”

Without stepping closer, he offered his elbow. “Let’s try this again. May I walk you home, Miss Nichole?”

“Yes, thank you.” She stepped forward and slid her arm through his. The wool of his coat felt plush and fine even through her gloved hand. His arm was strong.

“On second thought...” His voice was soft as he reached up and touched the back of her head, causing her to wince in pain. His gray glove came away darkened with blood. “I’m not sure you want to return to your son in your current state.”

“Oh,” she said with dismay.

“I’ve got three options for you. The gym where I practice isn’t far from here. There are probably still a few men working out.”

The thought of entering a building full of boxers scared her slightly.

“There’s the hospital.”

Her eyes widened. That would set her back months in wages.

“Or my place. I have plenty of bandages.” He pointed to his face. “And lots of practice cleaning wounds.”

The only real choice was his place, but she didn’t want to sound forward. What would he think? A woman he only met a moment before coming back to his residence unescorted. It was quite scandalous.

Bending down, he met her green eyes with his warm, brown ones. “I swear I’ll be a perfect gentleman. You’re safe with me.”

“Your place then.” They started walking, and she couldn’t help but add softly, “I can’t afford a hospital.”

Patting her hand with his free one, he said. “Don’t worry. You’ll be right as rain soon.”

He hailed a cab and guided her into the back seat. Rather than sit with her, he slid into the front next to the driver, giving an address which was farther than walking distance away. It was kind of him to give her space. He seemed to realize she was shaken from the encounter and not quite trusting of the opposite sex. And yet, she did feel she could trust him. He came to her aid when he had no reason to get involved. He was a good man.

She settled into the seat and let the car’s warm air relax her.

January 3, 1930 ~ 9:00 p.m.
Southside of Chicago, Illinois

"Wake up," Tommy's soft voice coaxed Nichole from a dreamless sleep. It wasn't like her to doze like that, especially in a taxi cab with two virtual strangers. The adrenaline fleeing her system must have impacted her more than she thought.

Blinking, she looked around. The street and buildings were unfamiliar, but that didn't surprise her. Without much excess money, she didn't own a car. It was a luxury to take a cab, and she mainly walked everywhere. A blast of cold air hit her when Tommy opened the door. She placed her hand in the one he offered and rose from the cab.

The two-story brick building was long with rows of windows. Briefly, Nichole wondered how many people lived there. He leapt up the three steps that led inside and held the door for her. The entrance was warm and clean. Jazz music played softly from down the hall, and to the left, stairs led up to the second floor.

"This way," he said, and she followed him past several doors, surprised when he opened the farthest door on the right to a staircase. "I'm on the lower level."

The bottom floor was dimly lit and smelled of cooking grease and cigarette smoke. Near the middle of the hall, Tommy stopped and unlocked a door. "It's not much, but it's home."

Nichole stepped past him into the room. Because they were on the lower level, the windows were small and sparse. The few that existed lined the top quarter of the wall. The apartment itself was scarcely furnished, but it was clean. She wouldn't admit it to him, but it was nicer than where she lived. Mabel Brown was a sweet Polish woman, but elderly with no close kin. The house had fallen to disrepair, and neither woman was skilled enough to fix it. They got by as best they could, covering bare spots with throws and cracks with Frankie's drawings. The leaky faucet was another story, but the drips were silenced by a strategically placed washcloth in the basin.

"It's very nice," she said politely, hugging her arms around her body and standing just inside the doorway.

He closed the door. "May I take your coat?"

"Oh, yes." How silly you're being, she scolded herself. She entertained men on a daily basis. Not in the base meaning of the word, but as a dancer, a companion. Sure, the boys occasionally stole a kiss or two, but someone was always there to ensure it went no further than that. She wasn't that kind of girl, and once she was a mother, she was even more cautious of the company she kept. There'd been no other man since Frank.

Removing her gloves, she tucked them in the pockets of her coat and unbuttoned it. If Tommy thought she was impoverished in her threadbare coverings, he had the decency not to comment. He took her things, motioning toward the living room. "Please, make yourself comfortable."

The room held a golden velvet couch and a curved chair in brown tweed. A coffee table and radio completed the furnishings. On the radio sat a framed photograph. Curious, she crossed the room and picked it up. The couple in the picture was handsome, but not smiling.

"Antonio and Maria." Tommy nodded toward the silver frame in her hand. "My parents."

"They're very handsome." She set the picture down carefully and smoothed her skirt, unsure of what to do next.

He was holding a washcloth in one hand and a large bowl in the other. "If you sit in the chair, I'll clean your wound and take a look at it."

"All right." She perched on the edge of the chair, back straight, waiting for the sting when the cloth met her sore scalp. He was very gentle, dabbing carefully at the injury. Several times he rinsed the washcloth and repeated the task.

While he worked, he asked her about her favorite musicians. They both loved Duke Ellington, Louis Armstrong, and Mamie Smith. "Do you want to listen to some music? It might take your mind off the pain."

"That would be nice," she said, adding, "But it's not painful. You're very gentle."

He made a face while he fiddled with the large dials on the radio. "For a boxer."

"For a human being." She corrected. "For a man who didn't have to step in and save a stranger, but who did." When he looked at her, slowly blinking and not speaking, she added, "Thank you again."

"You're welcome." They stared at each other for a moment before he cleared his throat and hurried to his spot behind her chair. "I'm almost done cleaning the wound. You'll have a nice scab, and you'll need to be careful when brushing your hair. It's not deep enough to stitch."

"Thank goodness for that!" Ever since she was a child, she hated needles. One time, while running through a field, she fell and tore her leg on a barbed wire fence. The cut had required ten stiches, and her mama, who was never complimentary, had told Nichole how brave she was.

"All done." Tommy stepped around and looked at her. "It's clean, but I'd like to apply some ointment. I have a tube I use on my facial cuts." He pointed to a fresh injury close to his nose. It was scabbed over, but looked like it had been painful. "Helps them heal faster and not scar."

"If you think it will help."

"I'll be right back."

He left with the bowl and washcloth, returning with a small tube. “It might feel a little strange, but it shouldn’t hurt.”

She barely felt as he applied the medicine.

“There. Give it a few days and it will be all healed.”

“I truly appreciate your kindness.” She took his hand, and he stilled. “I can never repay you for what you’ve done.”

“I don’t want repayment,” he said, sounding almost angry. “A nice lady like you should never have been put in that situation. I’m sorry it happened to you.”

“Nonsense. Nothing happened. Thanks to you.”

“Would you like something to drink?” The praise clearly made him uncomfortable.

She wished he would sit and stop waiting on her. He’d done too much already.

“Coca-Cola, water, or ginger ale?” He shrugged apologetically. “That’s about all I have at the moment.”

“Some water would be nice. Then, will you join me?” she asked and was rewarded when his cheeks turned slightly red.

“I’ll be right back.”

He brought her ice water in a tall glass and bottle of Coca-Cola for himself. While he was gone, she moved to the sofa. She watched with amusement as his eyes darted between the other end of the couch and the chair, unsure of which to pick. To help, she patted the cushion next to her. "Tell me about yourself, Tommy Mazza."

Giving her a crooked smile, he relaxed and sat down. "It's strange that you know my last name, but I don't know yours."

"I already explained that to you. You can thank my son. He tells me something about you almost every day." She returned his smile and sipped her water. "My surname is Blomgren. Nichole Blomgren."

"And you said your son's name is Frankie?"

"Good memory." She sat back and studied him. His expression was open and friendly, relaxed even. He was younger than her, hard to say by how much, maybe five years. "But I asked about you, remember?"

He chuckled, taking a swig from his soft drink. "Not much to tell. I grew up on a farm in Iowa. My parents are still there. I discovered my gift for fighting, and the rest is history."

"That's it?" His short, succinct tale surprised her. "No brothers or sisters?"

"Only child." He settled into the cushions and placed his arm along the back of the couch, not quite within touching distance of her. His hand looked strong, the knuckles scraped.

"Why do they call you 'Two Guns'?" The name sounded like a gangster's to her. Tommy guns were a favorite among the Capone brothers in the Chicago area. The *pop-pop-pop* had everyone within hearing distance diving for cover.

"Because of this." He pulled his arms back and flexed both of them.

Through his dress shirt, she could see his biceps bulging.

"I'm ambidextrous." He quickly put his arms down and shrugged as though he were uncomfortable. "I guess it gives me an advantage."

"You *are* one of the best."

He shrugged again, picking at the crease in his dress pants.

She wouldn't have figured the tough fighter to be modest, but he obviously was.

The awkward moment was saved when a favorite song came on the radio. Nichole tapped her feet and noticed Tommy's fingers were playing the same rhythm on his legs.

He caught her looking and asked, "Would you like to dance?"

It was so unexpected, she said yes before thinking of the implications of dancing with a man in his apartment. Before she could worry about it, he had her up and whirling around the living room, navigating carefully to avoid the few pieces of furniture. She laughed and went with it. He was very graceful on his feet, probably the best dance partner she'd ever encountered.

When the song ended, he flushed and released her hands. “Sometimes the music just catches me up. I apologize for my forward behavior.”

“It’s all right.” She smiled. “I feel the same way about music. You’re a very good dancer.”

Then, he did blush, but he seemed happy, too. “My mother taught me everything I know. When the farm work was done, evenings were spent learning. My mother loved to dance, my father had two left feet, so I became the substitute partner.”

“Your mother was a good teacher.”

“What about you? Where did you learn?”

She didn’t like to talk about herself. Over the years, she’d learned to keep a low profile. The less people knew about her, the better. Yet, when Tommy was studying her, with his chestnut brown eyes and open expression, she felt the need to give him something. “Like you, I grew up on a farm, only my family lived in southern Wisconsin. As a little girl, I always wanted to be a dancer.” She shrugged. “It’s pretty much all I ever did. I danced everywhere and every moment of the day, much to my parents’ chagrin.”

“We have a lot in common. Farming, music, and dancing.” His voice trailed off. They were standing so close; she could feel the heat coming off his body. He smelled nice, too, like sandalwood and leather.

As the song came to an end, the announcer said, "Eleven o'clock, folks. Still two more hours of jazz favorites."

"Eleven?" Nichole's heart fluttered. Mabel was expecting Nichole any moment, and she had at least a twenty-minute walk ahead of her. "I'm sorry, but I really must leave."

Tommy nodded. "I'll get your coat." He came back with her coat in his hand and wearing his own.

"You don't need to come with me," she said. "I'm used to walking by myself all over this city."

"But I'd like to escort you home. It's my duty. After an experience like you had, I'm afraid I can't let you go alone." He held out her coat and waited while she slid her arms inside. Only once she was fastening her own did he close his and then don his hat and gloves. Opening the door, he placed a hand lightly on her back and guided her out.

They walked to the corner where he hailed a cab. She felt bad he was spending so much money on her, but he didn't seem to mind.

"Where to?" The cabby asked, and both men turned to look at her.

"Thirty-first and Laramie," she said, not wanting to give the exact address of her house. That intersection would get them close enough. If the driver found her vague directions unusual, he didn't say anything. Neither did Tommy, but when they arrived, he spoke in a low voice to the cabby, who nodded. Tommy got out with her.

"What are you doing?" she asked, rather alarmed. If he walked her home and lost his cab, he'd have a long night ahead of him.

Tommy was unconcerned. "I asked him to wait and said I'd make it worth his while. I plan to see you to your door." He offered his arm again. "You're safe with me. I promise."

Sliding her hand through his arm, she prayed that Frankie was sound asleep. He'd love to see his hero, but Nichole worried it would be too much of a disappointment if Frankie never saw Tommy again. Besides, she didn't like anyone seeing her son. The less people who knew of his existence, the better.

"Here we are," she said, stopping outside of a modest bungalow. The soft glow from a lamp lit the downstairs window, and without seeing the woman, Nichole knew that Mabel was watching. "Thank you again, Mr. Mazza."

The smile he gave her was wry. "Let's not be formal, please. Call me Tommy. I'd like to see you again, if I may." He rushed on before she could respond. "I know the circumstances of our meeting were quite unusual, but I can't help how I'm feeling. Perhaps, next time, we can meet under better circumstances."

Nichole shook her head sadly. "You shouldn't get involved with me, Tommy. I've got a dark cloud hovering over me."

"Do you?" He glanced over her head, his lips curling up playfully. "I don't see it. Perhaps you're the rainbow distracting me."

"You're a sweet talker!" Her smile was wide and genuine. "All right. You may call on me, but not here."

"Then where?" he asked.

"Stop by the club tomorrow. I'm working an early shift. I'll be done by nine."

Reaching over, he took her hand and raised it to his lips. Although they both wore gloves, the touch was intimate, and the gesture unnerved her. "Sweet dreams, Nichole."

"Goodnight, Tommy."

Rushing up the steps and slipping inside, she didn't turn to see if he was waiting or not, but something told her he was. Something told her Tommy Mazza might just be that guardian she'd been praying for.

January 4, 1930 ~ 8:45 p.m.
The Green Door, Chicago, Illinois

The club was packed with warm bodies and lively music. Saturday nights were always busy at the Green Door. It was when Nichole made her best money. As she moved around the dance floor on the arm of an elderly gentleman, she nodded politely and smiled as he told her about his great accomplishments. He was visiting from St. Louis, a banker, and would be leaving the next morning to return home. Up to that point, his behavior was nothing but polite, and he'd paid for several dances. Her shift was about to end, though, and she told him as much.

"Come back with me," he propositioned in a loud whisper.

"No, thank you," she said in a light, friendly way. He wasn't the first to try, and he wouldn't be the last, either.

"I'll make it worth your time," he said.

She'd also heard that, or other variations, over the years. Unflustered, she opened her mouth to speak when an angry male voice beat her to it. "The lady said she's not interested."

Nichole turned in surprise to find Tommy, with his hands fisted, staring angrily at the old man. The club was no place for a fight, and no place to draw unwanted attention. She couldn't afford to lose her job. "It's all right, Tommy.

This gentleman was just leaving. Weren't you, Mr. Worthington?"

The older man nodded and scurried away, allowing Tommy's anger to deflate.

Nichole's irritation grew. She'd been expecting a nice tip. There was no chance of that after his manly stunt. She threw her hands on her hips and said, "This is my job, Tommy. You saved me yesterday, and I appreciate it, but I'm safe here. I know what I'm doing. Mr. Worthington was harmless. I had the situation under control."

Looking chastened, he mumbled an apology.

"It's fine," she said, immediately forgiving him. She knew he was only looking out for her best interest. "I'll get my coat and we can leave."

They took another taxi cab, and Nichole's jaw dropped as they exited the car. The Palace theatre stood before them, looking majestic. She loved performances, but with little money, and even less free time, she never had the opportunity to go.

"I hope you like Vaudeville," Tommy said, placing his hand gently on her back. "It's one of my favorite pastimes."

"I've never been."

They followed a small crowd into the extravagant theatre. The interiors reds and golds were breathtaking and opulent. *This must be what a real palace looks like,* Nichole thought, feeling like a princess herself. Not for the first time, she was conscious of her threadbare coat. No one paid her attention, though, as they sought their seats and waited for the show to begin.

She assumed they would sit in the back, but Tommy led her to the front row and then to the middle. They truly had front and center seats. With wide eyes, she asked, “How did you get these tickets?”

Smiling, he said, “I have season passes. Usually, I bring Mic, although sometimes I come alone.”

“Mic?” Nichole wondered if that stood for Michelle, and if that was Tommy’s girlfriend.

“Mickey Malone,” he clarified. “He’s my manager.”

“Of course.” Nichole was saved from Tommy seeing her embarrassment when the house lights dimmed and the stage lit up. She was entranced from the start of the show to the end. So many acts, and so much variety. The comedians made them laugh, while the dancers had her leaning forward in awe and envy. *How great would it be to dance on a stage such as this*, she thought. When the show was done and the performers took their bow, Nichole and Tommy were among the first to stand. Clapping, she turned to Tommy with a wide smile. “That was wonderful!”

“I’m glad you enjoyed it.” Reaching over, he tucked a few loose strands of her hair behind her ear.

When his fingers grazed her sensitive skin, she shivered.

"You have a lovely smile."

"Thank you." She placed her hand on his offered arm. Men like Tommy were hard to find. He didn't seem worried that she was a mother. Quite the opposite, because as they left, he mentioned it was getting late and he would take her home.

Walking toward the waiting taxis, the sky began to mist. She was relieved it was icy sleet and not snow, but Tommy tilted his head up and closed his eyes.

"What are you doing?" Nichole asked.

He looked at her and blinked, a sheepish smile playing across his lips. "I've always loved the rain. It's very calming, don't you think?"

"I guess I never thought about it." She pulled her collar a little tighter against her neck. "Although I might find a spring or summer storm more comfortable."

With a warm laugh, Tommy ushered her into the cab. "You're right, of course. It would be. Then again, there's nothing like the shock of cold to make you feel alive."

That time, he gave the taxi driver the intersection address to drop her off. Once again, the cabbie was offered extra money to wait while Tommy walked her home.

"You don't have to do this," she said.

"I know." Tommy took her hand and held it. "I want to. I like you, Nichole."

She inhaled deeply, feeling flustered. It had been so long since a man had been interested in her romantically. Plenty of men paid attention to her. That was her job, her charm, but those men didn't see past the physical beauty. They had no interest in knowing who she really was; they were just looking for a beautiful companion or a quick dance. Tommy seemed to genuinely care. He listened, and he wanted to know who she really was. Because that scared her, she didn't answer him. Instead, she quickened her step.

"Did I say something wrong?" His voice held confusion and concern.

"No, I..." She looked down at their joined hands and then pulled hers away, wrapping her arms around herself.

A flash of hurt crossed his face before he gave her a curt nod. "Oh, I see. There's another man. Forgive me for making a fool of myself."

He turned to go, and Nichole's heart hurt. She liked him. Two days wasn't long to get to know someone, but by his words and actions, she could tell he was a good man. A man of duty and honor. *Can I trust him? Not just with my heart, but with my son?*

"Tommy, wait." She hurried to catch up with him.

He didn't slow, and his steps were angry.

Even as she hurried, he got farther ahead. Frustrated, she cupped her hands to her mouth and yelled, "There's no one else."

He stopped instantly, his back rigid. Slowly, he turned to stare at her.

"There's no one else besides Frankie," she admitted. "I'm protective. I don't want to see him hurt."

Tommy's expression softened. He closed the distance between them, stopping an arm's length away and searching her eyes. "I'd never hurt him, Nichole, or you."

Shaking her head, she said sadly, "I don't know that. I don't know you."

He took a step closer. Then another. "But you'd like to, right?"

Biting her lip, she met his eyes, nodded, and was rewarded by the smile that lit his face. "Give me a chance," he said. "I'll be good to you both, I promise."

Taking a leap of faith, she said, "Then come over tomorrow after Sunday service. We'll have lunch, and you can meet Frankie."

"Really?"

She nodded again, hoping she was making the right choice and praying Frankie would be safe.

"That's swell!" He kissed her cheek, causing them both to blush. Then without another word, he hurried down the sidewalk, his steps seeming lighter to Nichole, whose own hand stole up to the spot where his lips had touched.

February 2, 1930 ~ 2:30 p.m.
Chicago, Illinois near McKinley Park

Show me again!" Frankie jumped excitedly around his hero. With a chuckle and an abundance of patience, Tommy showed the five-year-old another boxing move. They'd been at it for half an hour.

For her part, Nichole sat at the table with a mug of hot coffee and watched them, clapping exuberantly whenever her son managed to get a hit on the large man.

Frankie grinned widely, showing his missing front tooth, while Tommy feigned offense at her applause. "Whose side are you on, anyway?"

"Both of yours," she quipped, resting her chin on her hands and batting her eyelashes. "My boys."

She said it to be funny, and was rewarded with laughs from both of them, but she realized it was true. It was easy to think of Tommy as one of her boys. In a short time, he'd begun working his way into her heart. The attention he gave her son touched her. Most men would pat the boy on the head and move on. Not Tommy. He seemed to be having as much fun as Frankie, and she couldn't remember the last time she'd seen him so happy.

An hour later, Tommy excused himself. "I'd love to stay, but I promised Joe I'd practice today. He'll be waiting at the gym."

"Let me walk you out."

Frankie hurried over. "Me too?"

"You stay up here, Frankie Beans." She kissed his forehead. "I'll be right back. Say goodbye to Mr. Mazza."

Tommy offered his hand to the boy, but chuckled in surprise when his skinny arms wrapped around the boxer's waist. "Thank you for showing me how to box. Come back soon, okay?"

Bending down to Frankie's eye level, Tommy said, "I'll do that. In the meantime, you practice those punches. We'll see how you do next time."

He ruffled her son's hair, straightened, and then took the coat and fedora from her with a smile. "Thank you for having me."

"It was our pleasure." She opened the door and waited for Tommy to go first.

He hesitated, and she knew he wasn't used to walking in front of a lady.

"Go ahead. I'll be right behind you."

Tipping his hat, he stepped into the narrow stairwell and started down. Near the bottom, he stopped and turned abruptly. Unable to stop her momentum, she ran into him. His arms shot out to steady her, sending a shiver down her spine. Oh, yes, Tommy Mazza definitely affected her. By the way he was staring at her mouth, she had a pretty good idea that she affected him, too.

"I didn't mean to throw you off balance." Eyes still focused on her lips, his mouth slowly curved up and his hands slid down to grasp her hands. "I had a wonderful time."

Her wispy voice gave away her nerves. "Me too."

He raised his eyes to hers, and her breath caught. "I'd like to kiss you, if I may."

Please do, she thought recklessly and leaned closer. "You may."

The stairs made them almost the same height. His lips brushed hers, hesitant at first, but then with more sureness. She rested her hands on his shoulders, enjoying the contrast of the softness of his lips to the slight scratchiness of his chin. He tasted sweet from the maple syrup they'd enjoyed earlier that afternoon and smelled of that delicious sandalwood and leather combination. She wanted to curl up against him, but a soft snicker from the top of the stairs had them pulling apart.

"Mommy's got a boyfriend!" Frankie's sweet voice sang as he laughed and ran back into their apartment.

"Sorry about that," she said, referring to her son's antics.

"I'm not," Tommy said, clearly referencing the kiss.

Flustered, she said, "I didn't mean—"

He covered her lips with his fingers. "I know what you meant. May I see you again, Miss Blomgren?"

"After that kiss, I think we're on a first name basis, don't you?" She teased.

"That kiss will keep me warm for days, my dear, but you didn't answer my question."

She blushed at his compliment, pleased that he enjoyed their kiss as much as she did. "Would you like to come for dinner on Tuesday night? I'm off work."

"I'd love to." He leaned in, tucked her hair behind her ear, and kissed her chastely on the cheek. His fingers slid down along her cheek, her jaw, and the curve of her neck, coming to rest on her collarbone. He lifted the delicate chain on the necklace she always wore and studied the thin, silver bar. "Nice necklace. Unusual. Where'd you get it?"

She covered his hand with her own and stared up at him. "I don't know. I've had it since I was little girl. I always wear it."

"It's lovely," he said. "Like you."

He lowered his mouth and kissed her again. His lips lingered for a moment before he said, "Until Tuesday."

Even the bitter cold that entered the stairwell when he left couldn't kill the flames he'd ignited inside her.

April 13, 1930 ~ 6:00 p.m.
Chicago, Illinois near McKinley Park

Dinners on her day off and lunches on Sunday became their norm. As the freezing Chicago winter melted into the sloppy, warm spring, Tommy worked his way into their hearts—both hers and Frankie's, although the boy was already smitten with his hero long before he started dating Nichole. Tommy was good to them, bringing flowers for her and sweet treats for Frankie. She realized she was falling helplessly in love, and still, she worried.

Tommy often asked her to come to a match and bring Frankie. "I'll get you the best seats in the house. He'll love it."

She wanted more than anything to support Tommy, but boxing matches were high profile. Anyone who was anyone went to the arena. It was one thing for her and Frankie to sit in the nose-bleeders, unseen by the masses. It was another to be known as Tommy Two Gun's gal. The journalists would be all over it, and she couldn't risk that kind of exposure. One picture of Frankie, and her years of hiding him were through.

"I'll think about it," she always answered, and although Tommy looked forlorn, he'd let it slide.

One particular evening, though, he pressed her. "Why won't you come, Nichole? Are you embarrassed by my profession?"

"What?" She turned from the sink and stared at him.

His chin was in his hand, and he looked dejected.

"Of course not. Why would you think that?"

Running his hand through his hair, he slouched in the chair. "I can't come up with another reason why you always refuse me."

Something wasn't right. Looking closer, Nichole noticed dark smudges under his eyes and dejectedness in the way he sat. "Is everything okay? Are you feeling all right?"

He held her gaze for a moment, pursing his lips as if considering. Finally, he confessed. "I haven't been sleeping well. I've been having these strange dreams. Nightmares, really."

His words sent a chill down her spine. "What kind of nightmares?"

"That's just it." He leaned forward and grasped her hands between his own. "I don't know. I never remember them. I wake up screaming, feeling panicked and drowning in remorse, but I don't know why."

"Sounds terrible." She gently squeezed his fingers. "Is there anything I can do?"

"Not about the dreams, but would you please consider coming? Just to one match?"

"I don't know—"

"Then, at least give me a reason. Why won't you come? Why won't you bring Frankie?"

Sitting back, he released her hands and tapped his fingers against the tabletop. "I heard a rumor..."

He let his words hang, and her heart jumped. No, he couldn't possibly know. "You should know better than to trust rumors," she said carefully.

He raised his eyes and met hers. There was no judgement there, only mild curiosity. "That's why I mentioned it to you. Figured I would go right to the source and set the record straight."

Her hand fluttered to her neck as she tried to contain her nerves. "Why don't you tell me what you heard?"

Another drum of fingers, and then Tommy said, "I heard you're one of the Capone girls."

Her throat clenched in fear, but she managed to keep her voice sounding normal. "Where'd you hear that?"

He gave her a look that said he was still expecting her to answer but was giving in to her request for information first. "Some boys down at the gym were talking. A couple fellas heard the rumor at a speakeasy near Hyde Park. Is it true?"

She wanted to deny it, but she couldn't lie to him. "Clearly no longer, since I'm your girl, but yes, I dated a Capone. Frank Capone. He was Frankie's father."

Tommy's shock was evident. He paled, the horizontal scar in his eyebrow standing out in contrast to the black hairs surrounding it.

Before he could speak, she continued, "Frank wasn't like Al or Ralph. He was a good man and tried to get out. The week before he was gunned down, he'd gotten a legit job at the docks. We were going to marry."

She crossed to Tommy and knelt in front of him, taking his hands. "He didn't know I was pregnant. No one did. Al and Ralph... they don't know about Frankie, and I want to keep it that way. That's why I won't go to your match, Tommy. As much as I want to, I can't risk my son."

His pant leg was damp from her tears, and she hadn't even realized she was crying. Tommy made soothing noises, wiped her checks, and tucked the hair that had fallen in her face behind her ears. "I won't let anything happen to either of you. I promise, Nichole, and you don't have to come to my match if you don't want to."

"Why can't we go to a match? And who's Al?"

Nichole cringed at her son's voice. She thought Frankie was in his room, playing with his cars, but at some point, he'd snuck back into the kitchen.

"Mom? Please?" He begged, his brown eyes wide and pleading in a face so like his father's. Anyone who knew the Capones would have no problem connecting her child to their family.

Her heart ached with worry. She couldn't keep him hidden forever.

"I'm having a conversation with Mr. Mazza right now, Frankie. Go and play with your toys."

"Mom..."

"Go on, Frankie. Do as your mom says." Tommy's tone was mild, but Frankie immediately obeyed, scurrying out of the room. He needed a man in his life. Tommy was good for the kid, good for them both. "I know you don't want to risk it, but consider coming. I can get you seats anywhere in the house." Tommy gave her a crooked grin. "Even in the dark upper corner where no one wants to sit."

She straightened and said haughtily, "I'll have you know that's exactly where we sat the last time we saw you." She smiled to let him know she wasn't really upset and added, "I'll think about it, okay? I know Frankie won't leave it alone anyway."

"My next fight's on Saturday." He stood and pulled her up, wrapping his strong arms around her. He made her feel so safe and cherished. She loved to rest her cheek against his chest, breathe in his wonderful scent, and listen to his steady heart. That's exactly who Tommy was—steady, dependable, and hers. He lifted her chin and kissed her, sending warm shivers through her body. Tommy kissed like he fought, with focused intensity. It made her toes curl and her thoughts fly out the window. He was the perfect combination of exciting and safe. He pulled back and kissed her nose playfully. "The tickets will be waiting, middle of the house, in case you change your mind."

He donned his hat. The same black fedora he always wore, but his coat had switched to a lighter waistcoat for the warmer weather.

"Are you off to the gym?" she asked, knowing when he wasn't at her tiny upper, he was working out. His apartment was mainly neglected, a place to sleep only, and he insisted he didn't mind.

Patting his belly, he said, "I've got some meatloaf and potatoes to work off."

"You're not a pound heavier than when I met you." She laughed despite herself and saw him out, grateful he didn't pressure her to make a decision about attending a fight. Frankie would pressure her enough, and five-year-olds could be persuasive.

April 19, 1930 ~ 3:00 p.m.
Chicago Stadium

Holding tightly to Frankie's hand, Nichole navigated her way to the ticket booth. "I have two tickets on hold for Blomgren, please."

"Oh, Tommy's girl." The man behind the counter looked her over with interest. He was in his late teens with greasy black hair and small, squinty eyes. "Just a moment."

He turned and spoke quietly to another fellow in the booth, who glanced back over his shoulder at her. She wasn't sure why, but they made her uneasy. The first man, whose name tag read "Michael," turned back with tickets in hand and gave her an easy smile. She didn't care for the way his gaze bounced between her and Frankie. She could only describe it as calculating. The gnawing worry in her stomach increased, a wave of queasiness washing over her. They shouldn't have gone.

"Here ya go. Two tickets for Miss Nichole Blomgren and guest." The guy crossed his arms on the counter and leaned out to look closer at Frankie. "Why! That must be you."

Frankie giggled. "She's my mom."

"Oh!" The man faked surprise. "I thought she was your date. Are you a big fan of Tommy Two Guns?"

"Oh, yes!" her son grinned, unaware of his mother's unease. "He's the best."

"He sure is!" The man, Michael, was completely focused on Frankie, and alarms sounded in Nichole's psyche. She had to get her son out of there. "What's your name, kid?"

"Fr—"

"I taught him not to speak to strangers," Nichole interrupted in a not quite polite voice, drowning out the boy's response. She tugged his hand gently. "Come along. Let's find our seats. The fight is about to start, and we're holding up the line."

"Bye, mister!" Frankie called back.

"See ya, kid."

Nichole didn't turn to see if Michael's eyes followed them, but she made a mental note to ask Tommy about the two men later. She didn't catch the name of the short, stout one in the back, but she clearly saw Michael's name tag.

Just as Tommy promised, their seats were in the middle of the arena, centered to the ring. The view was excellent and inconspicuous. When the match started, Nichole forgot about the ticket dealer. She was fully absorbed in the fight. Tommy was magnificent—lightning fast and graceful on his feet. He easily won the match, and the crowd went wild. Fans and journalists alike flooded the floor to get a glimpse of the champion and maybe a word or two for their bylines the next day. The pop of cameras flashed around the ring, except for one that went off near her, startling and momentarily blinding her.

"Mom." Frankie tugged on her hand and pointed to a figure dressed in brown tweed hurrying away. "That man took our picture. Do ya think we'll be in the newspaper? Huh? Do ya?"

He was full of little boy excitement, but Nichole felt the blood drain from her face. Her body broke out in a cold sweat and tremors. They shouldn't have gone. She tried to clear her head and think rationally, but her mind screamed, "Run! Hide! Escape!"

She swallowed her panic and forced herself to speak calmly to Frankie. "It's time to go."

"Now?" Frankie frowned. "But Tommy's meeting us after. He promised me ice cream."

She didn't like Frankie calling Tommy by his given name, but he insisted, and her boy listened to anything Tommy said.

"He's going to meet us at home," she said, silently pleading for Frankie to cooperate. Did she have enough money to pay a taxi driver? She hoped so.

Satisfied Tommy would catch up with them later, Frankie let her lead him outside. If he was surprised when she hailed a cab instead of walking, he didn't show it. She gave the driver vague directions to an intersection five blocks away from the house. She wasn't taking any chances.

She hoped Tommy would understand when he didn't find them waiting in the lobby like they originally planned. She'd explain everything later if she had the chance. Right then, she had to get their things and go. Protecting Frankie was top priority. It was only a matter of time until they were discovered by the very people she was avoiding.

The house was dark when they arrived. At first, Nichole worried, but then she remembered Mabel complaining of a headache that afternoon. She must've gone to bed early. Flipping the switch for the stairwell, Nichole wrinkled her nose. There was an odd odor in the house, almost like rotten eggs. What had Mabel cooked for dinner?

Nichole covered her nose, knelt before Frankie, and spoke in a low voice. "You wait right here, just inside the door. I'll be right back."

He nodded and sat on the floor, eyes wide. It wasn't like him to not question her motives. Either he sensed her fear or realized on his own something was wrong.

Taking the stairs quickly, she unlocked their door. The light from the stairwell spilled into the apartment, revealing the sparkle of broken glass. The room was entirely gutted.

"Frankie, run!" she screamed before someone held a wet rag to her face and the world went dark.

§

“Nichole, baby, Nichole, wake up!”

Tommy’s face swam into focus. She gripped his arm. “Where’s Frankie? Where’s my son?”

His eyes were wide and wild. “I don’t know. I didn’t pass anyone on my way up, and Mabel’s apartment…” He stopped and swallowed. “What’s going on?”

“I don’t know. They knocked me out. I told Frankie to run.” *Where is he? Did he get away?* It was hard to think through the panic. Her mind screamed the worst, “Frankie’s gone, Frankie’s gone, Frankie’s gone.” She’d heard of people being paralyzed with fear, but she hadn’t realized it was a real thing until then. She literally could not move.

Tommy wrapped his arms around her and lifted. He held her close until her legs steadied beneath her.

When she knew she could stand on her own, she turned and fled down the stairs. “Maybe he’s with Mabel.”

“Don’t go in there!” Tommy shouted and thundered down the steps behind her, but it was too late. The scene dropped her to her knees. Destroyed, she struggled to process what she was seeing.

The kind, elderly landlady was unrecognizable. It was obvious they tortured her before killing her. Nichole had considered Mabel a friend, family even. It was hard to imagine she was gone, viciously murdered simply for being home.

Nichole turned and emptied the contents of her stomach, wiping her mouth with the back of her hand. Then, she stood on shaking legs. While the heavy nausea in her stomach was gone, the sight of Mabel's mangled body would haunt Nichole forever. "I'm checking outside."

"Nichole—"

"There's a chance he got away." She ran, hating the way hysteria made her voice shrill and fragile like broken china.

She searched the yard, behind every bush and in every shadow. There was no trace of him. Her last hope shredded, she collapsed into a boneless pile on the grass and wept.

"Who did this?" Tommy asked. "Who took Frankie?"

"Who do you think?" Nichole managed to form the words between sobs. "Capone. He's got my son. The mob has my son."

"How?" Tommy asked. "How'd they find him? You said they never knew you were pregnant with Frank's child."

"They didn't, but one look at him and anyone would know. You saw it, Tommy. He looks just like a Capone."

"He looks just like a young Italian boy." Tommy crouched down and rubbed her back, offering her the white handkerchief from his pocket. "He could be mine."

Shaking her head, she dabbed at her eyes and tried to calm down. Otherwise, she'd never manage to think straight, and she needed a cool head to get her son back. "You heard the rumor before I told you. You heard I was an item with Frank. Now, you see Frankie, five years later." She looked him straight in the eye. "Al Capone's a monster, but he isn't an idiot."

"That's true," Tommy said. "But that means someone pointed Frankie out to him."

Choking on anger, she spat. "That man at the ticket counter. Michael."

"Mikey sold you out?"

Nichole explained how the two men acted when she got the tickets, how Michael paid extra attention to Frankie, and then the photographer who snapped their picture at the end of the night. "I should've trusted my instincts and left right away."

Tommy stood and kicked the fence, breaking one of the boards. "I'll kill the rat!"

When he punched another board, scraping his already bruised knuckles, Nichole flinched.

His face fell when he noticed. "I'm sorry." Pulling her up to her feet and drawing her close, he buried his face in her hair. "Sometimes I can't control my anger, but I'd never hurt you or Frankie. Ever. I promise."

"I know." She stepped back slightly to cup his face in her hands, dismayed to see them shaking. "I know that, Tommy."

She broke down again, sobbing. Normally, she wasn't the desperate sort, but those were not normal circumstances. Al Capone had her son. She knew the gangster would never hurt Frankie. Al had a reputation of being very protective of his family. She wasn't family, though, and what would he care about the mother of his nephew. She worried that she'd lost her son forever. "What am I going to do? I have to get him back."

"We'll get him." Tommy wiped her cheeks and bent to look in her eyes. His big hands framed her face with a gentle touch, an echo of the way she'd held him earlier. His hands were much steadier than hers. "First, we need to get you out of here. Who knows if they have plans to come back."

"Should we go to the police?"

"We can't involve coppers," Tommy said. When Nichole frowned, he explained. "We don't know who's on the mob's payroll and who's clean."

"What about Mabel? We can't just leave her there."

"Do you have a telephone?"

"No, but Mabel does."

"I'll take care of it." He smoothed her hair, tucking it behind her ear. The familiar caress soothed her, providing welcome calm in a way nothing else had. "Why don't you get your things together, enough to last a few days, and meet me back downstairs?"

Nichole moved in a daze. She threw clothes and necessities in her old suitcase. She'd brought it from the farm, back when she was full of innocence and dreams of being a professional dancer. Life turned out differently than she'd expected, and she'd never complained. She was happy. Frankie was the best thing that ever happened to her. She couldn't lose him. She couldn't.

Tommy waited at the base of the stairs. His handsome face was filled with anxiety. He quickly climbed up and took the suitcase from her. "We have to move fast and quiet. The cops will be here soon, and I want to be a good distance away before we hail a taxi. Too many prying eyes might recognize you or me." With his free hand, he grasped hers. "Are you ready?"

"Let's go," she said firmly. "I'll follow you."

They crept around the back and dissolved into the shadows of the alley. Gripping Tommy's steady hand, Nichole prayed desperately. If she ever needed a miracle, it was then.

7

April 20, 1930 ~ 3:00 a.m.
Southside of Chicago, Illinois

The hour hand ticked on the clock. It was three in the morning, and Tommy hadn't returned. Before he left, he told Nichole to get some sleep and refused to let her come and help confront Michael. She tried arguing that Frankie was her son, and she had a right to be there, but Tommy was adamant. "I can't do what I need to do and worry about you, too."

She didn't like the sound of that. *What does he need to do?* She knew his anger often got the best of him and hoped he'd control it. She lay in bed, unable to sleep and staring at the clock. Blood pounded behind her eyes, the beginning of a headache. Cinching her robe, she went to the kitchen, found the hidden jar of whiskey, and poured half a glass. She downed it quickly, wincing as it burned a trail down her throat. She waited a moment, and then poured another. The second went down easier than the first. The sound of a door opening was the only thing that stopped her from pouring a third.

"Found the booze, I see." Tommy's voice was neutral. He looked almost as tired as she was, although the sight of him filled her with relief. Tired, but seeming unharmed, was a good sign.

"I couldn't sleep," she said by way of explanation. It was a sorry excuse for drowning one's grief in alcohol.

He took the bottle and nodded at the glass. "May I?" When she nodded, he poured a healthy amount and drank it. "Let's go sit, and I'll tell you what happened."

She followed him with apprehension. He didn't seem upset, but like her, exhausted. He sat and pulled her down against him, wrapping his arm around her shoulders and kissing her temple. "I'm sorry I was gone so long."

"You're here now," she said, her words slurring slightly. The whiskey and lack of sleep were equal culprits.

"Mikey confessed to everything. Turns out, he's on the mob's payroll, so is Jimmy. He was the other guy you saw. Jimmy is the one who told Capone. Mic let him go, and well, let's just say he won't be able to work for a while."

"Meaning?"

"I roughed him up a little."

"Tommy!" Even without details, Nichole felt sick. She hated violence and the thought of using it to get information. Those men were no good, but that didn't make it right.

Shrugging, Tommy looked only mildly guilty. "Jimmy wouldn't talk, and I needed answers. Capone has Frankie at the house. He's with Sonny. From what Mikey says, Frankie is scared and quiet, but safe."

Worry for her son brought fresh tears to her eyes. "How are we going to get him back?"

Squeezing her shoulder, Tommy said, "I have a plan."

While he talked, Nichole tried to listen and not judge. She didn't like the plan but couldn't think of anything better. Tommy was going to bargain with the mob boss, which was a terrible idea by itself, but when Tommy told her how he was going to do it—throw a fight in exchange for Frankie—Nichole protested. "You'll ruin your career!"

"My career for your son," he said gently. "I think it's a fair trade. Besides, plans change."

Pulling his arm back, he gave her a nervous smile. She wondered what he was up to, although her heart sped up when he shifted to kneel in front of her and take her hands in his. "My timing could be better, but I've been thinking about this for a few weeks. I love you, Nichole, and I love Frankie like my own son. More than anything, I want us to be a family. Once we get Frankie back"—she liked that he said once and not if—"we'll need to go into hiding. You know that, right?"

Staring at their joined hands, she nodded. Life would never be the same again.

Seeing that she wasn't going to say anything, Tommy continued, "We're getting a chance to start over. We'll take new identities. Start fresh."

Shaking her head, she said, "You're giving up everything."

"I'm gaining everything." He corrected gently, shifting on his knees. "Now, let me ask before my knees go numb or I lose my nerve." He grinned, and she laughed nervously. "Nichole Blomgren, will you marry me?"

She didn't even have to think about it. "Yes!" she cried, her arms flying around his neck. He was her rock through everything, and she couldn't imagine her life without him.

He stood, sweeping her up into his arms and twirling in a circle before settling back on the couch with her in his lap. She cuddled against him and closed her eyes. It was the worst day of her life, but it ended on a note of hope. The next day, they could finalize the details to rescue Frankie. At the moment, she couldn't think past the feeling of Tommy's hand slowly stroking her back. An overwhelming sense of comfort and love was Nichole's last conscious thought.

****

Nichole woke in Tommy's bed, a blanket tucked around her, enveloping her in the scent of his cologne. She stretched and smacked her lips, making a face. The residual taste of last night's whiskey made her tongue feel thick. She wasn't fond of booze, but it temporarily calmed the nerves. With its help, she managed to get a few hours of sleep. She wondered if Tommy had. There was no sign he slept in the bedroom. She checked the rest of the apartment and came to two realizations. One, Tommy wasn't there.

Two, he had terrible handwriting. In the kitchen, she found a hastily scribbled note:

N—

Went to the gym. Be back soon. Coffee is on the stove. Do not go out!

Love, T

No surprise, the coffee was cold. Nichole reheated it. There wasn't much in the icebox besides a little cream, butter, and a small block of cheese. Half a loaf of bread was on the counter, so she made a cheese sandwich. The bread tasted slightly stale, but she forced it down with the hot, strong coffee. Afterward, she washed and dressed. She'd just turned on the radio and sat down to listen when Tommy returned, an unreadable expression on his face.

"Everything okay?" she asked.

He hung his hat and ran a hand through his black hair. "The arrangements are made. All we can do is wait. I hate that my next fight isn't for two weeks."

She hated that, too. Since Frankie's birth, she hadn't spent a day apart from him before he was taken. How could she wait two weeks, knowing her boy was frightened? It broke her heart. She couldn't say that to Tommy, though. He already felt guilty. Instead, she said, "You can't help that. Two weeks gives us time to prepare."

"That it does," he agreed.

He joined her on the couch, taking her hand. Tommy had started looking for any excuse to touch her. She didn't mind. Being close to him was both comforting and exhilarating, although for the time being, romance was the furthest thing from her mind.

"Mikey's got it all worked out, and Capone agreed to it," Tommy said.

"And you trust him?" Nichole didn't.

"As much as I can." Tommy shrugged. "I don't have much of a choice."

With a sigh, she settled back into the cushion. "What's the plan?"

"Capone will bring Frankie to the fight and give him to you. I lose the fight, and Capone rakes in the bets. After that, he leaves us alone."

"And you believe that?" There was nothing to stop Capone from taking the money, taking Frankie, and blackmailing Tommy to throw more fights. Capone didn't get to be Public Enemy number one because he was nice guy.

"Not for one second." Tommy's dark eyes captured hers. "I have a favor to ask."

"Oh?"

"I don't trust Capone or his henchmen and can't have you and Frankie alone with him while I'm in the ring. As soon as you get Frankie, you need to leave."

"Where should we go?"

"Remember Mic?"

She nodded. Mic was Tommy's manager, a nice, older man with prematurely white hair, bright blue eyes, and an easy smile.

"Mic's brother, Don, works on the same farm as my parents. Don is going to meet you out front. He looks a lot like Mic, but he'll also give you a code word, 'Delilah.' Go with him, and I'll meet up with you as soon as I can."

"Where are we going?"

"Sabula, Iowa. You can stay with my parents until I get there." Tommy smoothed her hair behind her ear and gave her a fleeting smile. "They're good people. You'll be safe with them. I should be there the next day, at the latest, and then we'll go."

"Go where?" *Where will we be safe? The mob has connections across the country.*

Leaning forward, he kissed her before resting his forehead against hers. "I don't know yet. We'll drive until we find a town we like, something small and inconspicuous, off the beaten path."

"Somewhere they won't find us."

"Exactly."

She curved into his side, resting her head on his chest and listening to his steady heart. "I'm scared."

He was quiet for a moment before admitting, "So am I."

May 4, 1930 ~ 2:00 p.m.
Chicago Stadium

Straining to see through the smoke and the noise, Nichole searched the crowded arena for any sign of her son.

"Mom?"

The minute she heard his voice, she turned and found Frankie behind her, his face pale and eyes wide. She glanced around but didn't see anyone with him. Dropping to her knees, she pulled him against her and breathed in the combination of sweat and soap that was her boy. "Oh, Frankie. I missed you!"

She felt his little body shaking before she saw his tears, but he hugged her back fiercely. "I missed you, too, Mom. I didn't think I was going to see you again. Uncle Al said I had to live with him. He said you didn't want me."

Taking his tear-filled face between her hands, she kissed each of his cheeks and let him see her own tears. "That's not true, Frankie. I love you more than anything. I would never, ever let you go."

"Can we go home, Mom?" The fact that he didn't even ask about Tommy told her how shaken her son was. It would take time to heal those wounds.

Damn Al Capone! Damn him to Hell for scaring my child!

"You bet, kiddo. Let's go." Wrapping an arm securely around his narrow shoulders, she led him to the exit. To her relief, no one stopped them. Once they were outside, she looked around. A few couples lingered in the shadows, and a single man or two made his way to or from the building. No one seemed to pay particular attention to her or her son.

Once she was outside, she wasn't sure which way to head. Tommy didn't give her exact instructions. She wanted to get away from the building, though, so she started walking slowly down the sidewalk, in the direction of the train station. A moment later, she felt someone fall into step beside her. A quick glance confirmed the man had white hair and blue eyes.

When he caught her eye, he murmured, "Delilah."

She nodded, and the three of them quickened their pace. The station was only a few blocks away, and they were catching the next train. Her case was already stashed there.

§

The closest stop left them in Dubuque. Don had hidden the farm truck there. It was an old, slow vehicle, but they met no obstacles on the drive to Sabula. Frankie fell asleep, his head falling against her side, and eventually sliding down until he was slumped in her lap. Even with all the bumps in the road, her exhausted child didn't wake up.

It was after dinner and already dark outside when they arrived at the farm. Don dropped them at a small, worn, wooden cabin on the edge of the property.

"I've got to go," he said with a slight shrug and embarrassed smile. "You'll be fine. The Mazzas are good folk."

Frankie blinked sleepy eyes and crawled out of the truck cab after his mother. Taking his hand on one side and the heavy suitcase on the other, she walked slowly to the dark door-step, gathering her nerve. With a deep breath, she set the case down and knocked.

"Who's there?" A gruff voice called from the other side.

"Nichole Blomgren." Her voice wavered slightly as she raised it to be heard through the thick wood. "I'm a friend of Tommy."

The door opened, and an older version of Tommy looked at Nichole and Frankie with suspicion at first, and then concern. "Where's our son?"

"He's still in Chicago," Nichole said. "He'll be here soon."

His eyes narrowed. "You in trouble?"

"Yes, sir."

Jaw tightening, he asked, "With the law?"

"No, sir. Quite the opposite." Placing a hand on Frankie's shoulder, Nichole drew the older man's attention to her son. "Won't you please let us stay until Tommy gets here? After that, we'll leave, I promise."

With a gruff grunt, the man motioned them in. "Maria's in the kitchen. She'll see that you're fed and show you where you can rest. I'm on my way out." He took a hat off the rack near the door and placed it on his head, nodding to them both before he left, closing the door behind him.

Nichole was surprised he didn't introduce them to his wife, but he seemed like a man of few words. She placed their luggage against the wall, and called out, "Hello?"

A petite woman with graying brown hair came around the corner.

Nichole quickly explained why they were there and that Antonio let them in.

Maria was much warmer than her husband. She led them into the house, which only had two bedrooms. It was sparsely furnished, but filled with images of love and family. Pictures Tommy must have drawn as a child still hung on the walls, and brightly colored fabric was draped over the shabby chairs, giving the house an eclectic, cozy feel. She opened a door and said, "You rest here and I'll fix you a nice meal, yes?"

Her English was clear through her thick, Italian accent. Tommy's father had an accent, too.

"Thank you," Nichole said. Once they stepped into the room, Maria disappeared down the hall. The room had obviously belonged to Tommy. There was a twin-sized bed and a dresser. For a moment, Nichole considered getting their things from the front room, but decided she didn't need to unpack. With any luck, they'd leave as soon as he arrived in the morning. The quicker they got on the road, and on their way to a new life, the better.

Maria brought them a thick vegetable stew and a small loaf of crust bread. She patted Frankie on the head and gave him two cookies. "For after dinner," she said with a wink. "My Tommy, he loves cookies."

"Me too!" Frankie grinned.

It was the first time since getting him back Nichole saw him smile. She hugged Tommy's mom and tears fell.

"There, there," Maria said, patting Nichole's back. "It will be okay. My Tommy will take care of you."

They mostly ate their meal in silence. Nichole was physically and emotionally exhausted. Afterward, Frankie crawled into the bed without being told to. By the time Nichole returned from placing their empty dishes in the kitchen, he was fast asleep.

She lay down next to him and wrapped her arm around his slender frame. Grateful to have him back, she still feared for their future. Al Capone was ruthless and cunning. She only hoped Tommy was right. With their deal fulfilled, Capone would leave them alone.

After tossing and turning for hours, Nichole figured she'd never fall asleep. When the sun gleamed through the window forcing her eyes to open, she realized at some point she had. The smell of cooking made her stomach rumble and caused her to completely wake up. She panicked after realizing Frankie wasn't in the room. Throwing on a robe, she went to the kitchen and found him there, sitting with a heaping plate of pancakes.

Maria, who was standing by the sink, dried her hands and said, "I must go work. You help yourself to food, yes?"

"I will. Thank you." Nichole took in the kitchen and sitting room. They were the only three there. "You haven't heard from Tommy yet, have you?"

"Not yet." Maria gave them both a warm smile. "Soon. Do not worry."

Nichole wondered how much Don or Tommy told his parents about the situation. If they did know Al Capone was involved, they were taking it extraordinarily well. They didn't seem worried or scared.

Once Maria left, quietly shutting the front door behind her, Nichole took a plate from the cabinet and added two pancakes and a drizzle of syrup. A cup of coffee was already poured and waiting for her. She sat next to Frankie, who was already halfway through his stack.

"Are we going to live here now?" he asked around a mouthful of pancake.

"Swallow before speaking, please." Nichole's response was automatic, something her own mother had drilled into her children years ago. "We're not going to live here. When Tommy arrives, we're going somewhere new."

"Tommy is coming with us?" His voice rose with excitement.

The question made her remember Tommy on his knees proposing to her. She didn't have a ring, but he was a man of his word. "Yes, Frankie."

"Woo hoo!" Frankie grinned, and it seemed to come more naturally each time he did it. He was bouncing back quickly from the events of the previous month. "I want Tommy to be my dad."

Laughing, Nichole ruffled her son's hair. "I bet he would like that, too."

"I sure would!"

They turned to find Tommy standing in the doorway.

Frankie jumped out of his chair and ran into Tommy's arms. He smiled at Nichole over the top of the boy's head.

"It's done then?" she asked.

"Yes." Tommy made a face. "The entire auditorium stood and booed. Before the reporters could reach me, I snuck out the back and hustled to the train station. Don picked me up." He grabbed a plate and filled it with the remaining pancakes. "Why don't you two get dressed while I eat? After, we can go to town and purchase a car."

Nichole's heart skipped with excitement as she dressed, placing all their belongings back in the suitcase. She carried it out and set it back by the front door, returning to her chair by Tommy when she was done. "After we get the car, will we leave right away?"

Tommy nodded and swallowed. "I'll have to return the truck, and I'd like to say goodbye to my parents, but yes, then we'll..."

Pop! Pop! Pop!

When the unmistakable sound of gunfire filled the air, Tommy gripped Nichole's shoulder painfully. "Take Frankie and hide in the back of the house. Do *not* come out." He stood and ran for the door.

She called after him, "Tommy, don't go!"

"I need to find my parents. Please, Nichole, do as I say." He gave her one last pleading glance before slipping out the door.

She led Frankie to the bedroom.

His eyes were wide when he turned to her. "Were those gunshots?"

Nichole nodded and whispered, "We need to be quiet and hide."

They crouched on the floor between the bed and the wall. It was far away from the one window in the room, which was covered with drawn curtains. Holding Frankie against her, they listened to the sounds of men shouting. When she heard Tommy cry out in pain, she jumped up.

"Stay here." She commanded in a low voice. "I'll be back soon."

Frankie nodded, too scared to speak.

Nichole hurried out the door, took cover behind a tall oak, and listened. The usual farm noises had resumed, but between the calls of animals, she heard the fighting. Fists connected to flesh. Someone grunted, and someone else groaned. Following the noise through the field, she stepped carefully and kept herself concealed. When she reached a clearing, she found Tommy fighting what had to be one of Capone's men. Bodies surrounded them: Tommy's mom, dad, Don, and another mobster. While the two men were distracted, Nichole hurried to Maria, checking her pulse. There was none. Subsequent checks revealed they were all dead except Don, and he was losing a lot of blood. His torn pant leg bloomed with a dark stain, indicating a shot hit his leg. He also had a nasty gash on his head, but at least he was still breathing.

Nichole's attention returned to the fight.

Tommy was winning. He had the other man pinned on the ground. The gangster's lapels were crumpled in Tommy's clenched fists. "Why'd he send you? I fulfilled my end of the bargain. I made him a very rich man. Or a richer man, since he was already loaded."

"Someone else bet against you," the man garbled through his broken nose and bloody mouth. "Al only got half of his promised money."

"It wasn't me." Tommy looked confused. "No one knew except me, Nichole, and Don."

At the mention of his name, Don gave a low moan, which captured Tommy's attention. He dropped the thug and hurried over to Don, yanking him up by his shirt. The man screamed in pain, but Tommy ignored it. "Was it you?"

"I'm sorry," Don mumbled. "It was a sure bet."

"My parents are dead because of you!" Tommy spat in the man's face. "You don't deserve to live." Pulling back a fist, Tommy punched Don in the face, and then punched him again. Harder.

Nichole heard the sickening crunch when Don's nose broke. The men fell to the ground, Don's arms crossed over his head in a feeble attempt to protect himself.

Tommy pulled back his arm a third time, and it became clear he wasn't going to stop until the old farmhand was dead.

"Tommy!" She screamed his name, running to grab his arm. "Stop! You'll kill him."

"He deserves it." Tommy growled and pushed her aside. "Greedy bastard."

She stumbled over the uneven ground and fell. In his focused rage, Tommy didn't even notice. "Does he?" she cried. "Is that for you to decide?"

"He brought the mob here."

"He also brought me and Frankie." She hoped Tommy would look at her, but his jaw was clenched in fury, his eyes trained on Don.

"I'm sorry." Don started sobbing. "I'm sorry, Tommy. You're right. I got greedy."

In response to the man's confession, Tommy howled.

Nichole flinched, expecting the worst.

Tommy's fist flew forward, but instead of punching the man's face, it hit the hard dirt. Raging anger deflated like a balloon to be replaced with utter loss. Tommy crawled over and sobbed by his mom's still body.

Nichole went to him, putting her arms around his quivering shoulders, and resting her cheek on his back. She mourned, too. Tommy's parents, especially his mom, seemed to be decent, loving people.

The cock of a gun had them both looking up. The bloodied mobster was on his feet, the barrel of his gun pointed at them. "Two for one. The boss is sure to give me a raise for this one."

Before either of them could react, a gun sounded behind the gangster and blood spurted from his mouth. When he fell, he revealed the killer. The man was tall with wiry gray hair. His skin was tanned and weathered from a lifetime of working in the sun.

"Mr. Turner." Tommy's voice filled with surprise.

"Just Joe, son." Joe offered Tommy a hand, and then turned to Nichole. "This must be your lady friend."

"Nichole Blomgren." Tommy still sounded shocked when he introduced her.

She was, too, knowing Joe Turner was the owner of the farm and the reason Tommy left. He told her all about his rough childhood, mostly to blame on the man who saved them.

Joe's eyes crinkled at the corners when he smiled. "Nice to meet you, Miss. I wish it was under better circumstances." He placed a hand on Tommy's shoulder. "I'm sorry about your parents. They were good employees. Good people."

Tommy nodded, his tears falling like rain on the dirt.

Joe continued. "I heard Don's confession. Seems to me he's created quite a mess for himself. I'll be shipping him off to the hospital right soon to recover. In the meantime, he'll be giving one-third of his money to me for my troubles, and one-third of his money to you."

Looking up in surprise, Tommy stared at Joe, who added, "Hopefully, it'll give you what you need for a new start."

Don waved one hand feebly. "Take it. It's yours."

Taking Nichole's hand, Tommy turned toward his parents' house.

"Before you go, Tom." Joe looked at the bodies around them. "Will you give me a hand?"

"I can." Tommy squeezed Nichole's hand. "I'll meet you back at the house soon, okay?"

"Okay."

He bent slightly and kissed her, leaving behind the salty taste of his tears. "I'm sorry."

She gave him a faltering smile and brushed the hair off his forehead, wishing she could mend his wounds just as easily. "So am I." She kissed her fingers and pressed them to his lips. "We'll be waiting for you."

7

May 5, 1930 ~ 4:00 p.m.
Sabula, Iowa

Nichole left the men to their work and went to check on Frankie. She heard him racing back to the bedroom when she opened the front door. His curiosity may have kept him from following her exact orders, but he stayed in the house and was safe, so she couldn't be angry.

"Is everything all right, Mom?" Frankie's brown eyes were wide with concern. "Tommy's okay, isn't he?"

"He's fine." She crouched down to hug her son and kiss his cheek. Everything would be okay as soon as they left the farm.

Frankie looked over her shoulder expectantly. "Where is he?"

She decided to be honest. Frankie was young, but he could handle the truth. "Some bad men came. They killed Tommy's parents. Tommy is helping the farmer right now to bury them."

Eyes filling with tears, Frankie's bottom lip protruded. "But I liked Grandma Maria. She made good pancakes."

"I know, honey, I know." They sat on the bed, both of them lost in their own thoughts. Tommy might need a day or two to make arrangements, to mourn. She only hoped Capone didn't send more men after the first.

It was late afternoon when Tommy returned to the house. Covered in dirt and sweat, he still made her heart race.

"Everything's done?" she asked.

With a quick glance at Frankie, Tommy nodded. "I'll clean up and we can go."

"How?" Nichole asked. They'd been planning to go to town and purchase a car, but there was no way the business would open that late.

"Joe told me to take the Model T those goons drove here. He's already cleaned it out and removed the plates. When we get a few towns over, we'll trade it for something else, in case Capone is having us trailed."

Fear froze the blood in her veins. "Do you think he is?"

With a sigh, Tommy ran his hand through his hair. "Not beyond the two he sent today, but when he doesn't hear back from them, he'll be sending more soon. That's why we need to go."

"I'm sorry I got you involved in this." He wouldn't have lost his career if it weren't for her.

"Hey." He crossed the room and lifted her chin. "Don't apologize to me. I made my own choices, and I wouldn't change having you and Frankie in my life for anything." He moved to bend down, hesitated, and then straightened with a laugh. "I'll save the embrace for later. I stink right now."

"You sure do!" Frankie teased, pinching his nose.

They all laughed, and Nichole knew things would be okay. They'd get away and start new where no one would recognize them. Living in fear was no way to go through each day, and she wouldn't let it run her life. From that moment on, she traded her old dreams for new ones. Those of family, love, and hope.

N. L. GREENE

Part Five

Location: Brooklyn, New York
Date: August 12, 1995 11:23 am

Hey, baby, what'ch yo name?"

"Whatever!"

"Hey, now! Is that any way to talk to yo future man?"

"As if!"

Tia watched as Tommy was dissed by the girl walking by. Before he could open his mouth with another line, Tia saw him turn and glare at his boys who looked like they were trying to keep from laughing at him.

She cringed, knowing he wasn't going to like being ridiculed. Sure enough, seconds later, his voice rang out again.

"What the fuck you laughin' at? I don't see no hoes around either of you!" He gave them both a pointed look, which wiped the smiles off their faces. Lifting his chin toward them, he continued. "That's what I thought. Now, don't you two have shit to do?"

"Yeah." Jay grumbled as he tagged his homie, Dee, on the shoulder and stood up from the stoop they'd been sitting on. Dee shrugged but followed, and both guys headed down the street.

Tommy watched until they turned the corner. Once they were no longer in sight, he spun and sat down on the stoop his boys had just vacated, eyes narrowing as he took in what was going on around him. His eyes darted from corner to corner, as though he was expecting something to happen he'd have to handle. Tia knew him well, knew what he was thinking and why he was doing this. She did the same from her position on the fourth floor fire escape across the street where she was trying to tune in and see what he was seeing.

Most everyone on the streets around them was a neighborhood local. Not many tourists ventured into that part of the hood. It wasn't the nicest area in town. In fact, it was one of the worst, and it didn't take long for outsiders to figure it out and return to where they came from. That made it easy to spot anyone that didn't belong, especially the thugs that might try to encroach on T-Dogg's—*God, she hated that nickname*—turf. By the way his shoulders were set and his eyes were narrowed as he took everything in, she could tell he was looking for rival gang members or anyone who didn't belong. Strangers could be just as dangerous as people he knew. The general rule was if T-Dogg or his boys didn't know the newcomers, they weren't trusted and weren't welcome in the neighborhood.

Tia felt a familiar empathy for him as she watched. Setting down her sketchpad and pencils on the metal grate below her, she pulled her thighs up to her chest, wrapped her arms around her legs, and rested her cheek on her knees. As she sat on the fire escape, above the busy streets, she blocked out the noise of the honking horns and shouting people. Everything else ceased to exist as she thought about the man before her.

He might have been young, turning twenty-two only two months before, but he'd been working the streets since he was twelve. He earned his spot, not only on the streets, but also with his crew and the neighborhood residents. Growing up where they did, there were only two options: build your street cred or get out. Tommy learned long ago that running the streets was his destiny, and it filled Tia to the brim with sadness. He had so much potential. Growing up, it was clear how smart he was—not just getting-by-smart, but ridiculously smart—with mad skills in every subject. He could've gotten a scholarship to any college if he'd tried, but he hadn't.

At first, she couldn't understand why he'd made that choice, one that doomed him to a life of crime, or even worse, an early death. But as she grew up and lost that child-like naiveté most kids had, she was able to see the world around them for what it was. Tommy hadn't had a choice. Because of where he was born; his destiny was chosen for him. For that reason, Tia had chosen to distance herself, even if she was in love with him.

Releasing a deep sigh, she pushed through the heartache that came whenever she thought about it. What sucked was that not only was Tommy ridiculously smart, he was sweet, funny, talented, and fine as hell. It didn't matter though; she was going places, getting the hell out that neighborhood, and making something of herself. As much as she hated to admit it, a drug-dealing boyfriend wasn't going to help her achieve her dreams. So, she put on a good front, acted like his looks and swagger didn't affect her in the way they did, and tried to stay focused on school and art. She only had one more year.

Too bad every year made keeping her distance from him harder and harder. Thank goodness he was practically a whore, hitting on and sleeping with just about any girl that walked by him. It helped keep Tia grounded and aware of the type of man he truly was. *T-Dogg,* she thought with an inward cringe, *doesn't do emotions or relationships. He doesn't have girlfriends or even a steady girl he sees regularly.* Tia knew even if she confessed her love, it would all be in vain. So, instead, she sat back and watched him in this daily ritual, reminding herself of all the reasons why he was completely wrong for her and protecting her heart from breaking completely.

As if the world wanted to jog her memory, a low whistle sounded through the air, effectively drawing her from her thoughts. Lifting her head, she returned her gaze to the object of her daydreams to see what was happening. Her heart did the little dive it always did when she saw Tommy on the prowl.

Like always, his intense look relaxed into a sexy smile. His attention was no longer on his surroundings, and his mind no longer focused on looking for danger or threats around him. Instead, he was standing and blocking the path of a girl who was about to walk past him. The whistle apparently got her attention, and they stood face to face. He wore a charming smile, and although Tia couldn't see, she was sure the random girl had an annoyed look on her face.

"What's up, baby girl, how you doin'?" Tommy asked her, showing his perfectly white teeth.

By the girl's body language, head cocked to one side and hand planted firmly on the opposite hip, there was no doubt. She wasn't impressed. In fact, Tia would bet money the girl was rolling her eyes and blowing out an exasperated breath. She took a step to the side, and Tommy took a mirroring step and continued to block her.

The girl took a step to her left, which he took to his right, still keeping his body in front of hers, not allowing her to pass.

When she realized he wasn't going to give up, she stopped, crossed her arms over her chest, and let out a sigh. "What?" she asked, her voice loud and laced with anger.

"Aww, come on now, baby. Don't be mad," he said in a soft voice as he reached out and ran a finger down her bare arm.

She jerked her arm away, and Tia let out an unintentional chuckle. Although she knew he was bad for her, she still couldn't help the jealousy she felt whenever she saw him hitting on another girl. The feeling of relief when that girl turned him down was something else Tia couldn't help.

"Sorry," he said as he put his hands up in mock surrender. "I just couldn't let you walk by without making sure you knew that you were one of the *finest* girls I've seen in a long ass time."

The girl tilted her head, and Tia could envision the look of disbelief that was sure to be on her face. It always started that way, but he was good. Tia waited, because *T-Dogg* rarely got turned down.

"I ain't kiddin', baby. You're one fine girl, and I just thought you should know." Tommy shrugged as if he didn't care if the girl believed him or not.

"That's it?" she asked, her voice portraying the same disbelief Tia had guessed the girl's face showed.

"Yeah, baby. That's it." Then, he winked again and stepped back so she could pass.

Of course, she didn't.

The girl continued to stare at him for a moment before her hands fell to her sides and her head cocked again as if to study him better. "You aren't going to, like, ask me for my number or anything?" Her voice was slightly whiny, and Tia cringed.

And there it was! The magic of being T-Dogg, his reputation totally proved true. His charm had worked on the girl, and Tia had no doubt he'd landed his next conquest.

"Only if you want to give it me." He took a step closer to her, his finger reaching out to run down her arm as it did before, but that time, the girl didn't pull away.

Instead, her head tilted up slightly to look at him, and Tia was sure there'd be a smile on the girl's face.

She and T-Dogg stared at each other for a moment before she looked down and reached into her purse. Pulling out a pen, she reached for his arm. His large hand slid up to engulf her much smaller one, and she tugged him toward her. She pulled until his hand rested against her chest, just below her breast, before turning his palm up.

Tommy shot her a wicked grin and a wink as she scribbled her number on his hand.

When she finished, he slid his hand down her belly and squeezed her hip before he took a step back. Finally looking at what she wrote, he smiled again as he looked up at her. "Destiny." He seemed to put every ounce of game he had into saying her name as seductively as possible. "Beautiful name for a beautiful woman."

Tia rolled her eyes.

Then, she heard the girl ask in a syrupy sweet voice, "You gonna call me?"

Tia wanted to hurl something at the girl's head.

"Yeah, sweetheart. I'm gonna call you, for sure." He winked again and then took another step back to let her pass and watch the sway of her ass as she walked off.

The girl looked back once, as if to make sure he was watching.

He kissed the tips of his first two fingers and waved them at her.

She turned back around, giggling like a little schoolgirl.

"Oh, what the fuck ever!" Tia huffed out as she slammed her hands on the metal grate below her. When she did, she hit the can of Coke that had been sitting beside her, causing it to roll across the landing and toward the side. Scrambling to catch it before it went over, Tia got to her hands and knees and chased it, her knees scraping against the abrasive metal. Seconds later, she was at the side of the fire escape, gripping the railing tightly, as she watched the almost full can plunge to the ground in slow motion. It seemed to take forever, but in reality, she knew it was only moments before it landed on the sidewalk with a loud thump, exploding and spraying liquid everywhere.

Her wide eyes watched in horror as the scene unfolded. To anyone else, it wouldn't seem like such a big deal; it was just a can of soda, and no one was hit in the head with it. It was a big deal, though, because Tommy would know she'd been there watching him. Embarrassment set in before she even lifted her gaze, knowing the incident was going to give her location away, and afraid to face Tommy's laughing eyes.

Sure enough, when all the contents of the can seemed to have sprayed out, she finally looked up to find him staring at her.

Throwing a wicked smirk her way, he walked the few feet it took to put himself right next to the mess. He stared down at the busted up Coke can and brown sugar liquid all over the hot pavement for a minute before he looked back up at her.

"Yo, what's up, baby girl?"

Although it was a simple question filled with amusement, she couldn't help the little flip of her stomach when he called her *baby girl.* Yeah, he called everyone with a vagina baby girl, but it did something when he said it to her. It almost deluded her into believing he thought she was worth his time. Almost.

Not wanting to embarrass herself further by allowing him to see the way he affected her, Tia rolled her eyes, just as she always did. "Don't you fuckin' *baby girl* me, Tommy."

She loathed his nickname. *T-Dogg.* It was so thuggish, and as much as she knew what he did for a living, she didn't like acknowledging it by using the moniker his crew and customers did. She was the only one he let call him by his given name.

His back straightened slightly at the anger he heard in her voice. She hadn't meant for that to happen, but she was so tired of seeing him hit on every girl that walked past him, while never giving Tia a passing glance, and even more tired of letting it affect her.

"What's up, T?" He took a step closer. His head tilted back further, and his eyes squinted in confusion and concern as he stared up at her.

She returned his gaze for a moment, getting caught up in his chocolate brown eyes like she always did. Reaching up without thought, her fingers played with the pendant that hung just below her collarbone. The silver rod was simple and looked insignificant, but it was something that always brought her a sense of peace. She'd had it since birth, and she found herself seeking it when Tommy looked at her the way he was then.

The saying "the eyes are the windows to the soul" was a quote she'd always loved, but never believed, until she looked into Tommy's eyes. When she did, it was as if she were privy to more of him than anyone else was. It wasn't just his good looks, that cute scar in his eyebrow that he hated or his charming smile; it was as if she could feel his soul. Not only that, but it was like her own soul tried to speak to his and his responded, reaching out and trying to tell her something. The feeling was so intense. Her eyes searched his, looking for answers to questions she wasn't even aware she was asking.

And if she was reading his signals right, Tommy seemed to be doing the same thing. His gaze was equally as caught up in hers, looking for something but unsure of what.

Seconds passed while their eyes were locked and their souls called out to each other, until the booming bass of a passing car snapped them both from whatever spell they'd been under.

Wu Tang Clan's latest song filled the air, and both Tia and Tommy blinked. Tommy glanced behind him at the vehicle, offering a slight chin nod when he recognized the guy driving, before turning back to look at Tia. The moment was effectively broken, and although she cringed because she'd allowed herself to be so vulnerable, Tommy didn't seem the slightest bit affected by the moment they'd shared.

"So, yo, you comin' tonight?" He flashed a cocky grin and stuck his hands in his pockets. How he was always so cool was a mystery.

She was positive he'd felt like a raw steak in the presence of a hungry lion, because it was the same way she'd felt. Something made her want to be completely enveloped in him. It was unsettling. With a shake of her head, she came back to reality. "Yeah, I'll probably stop by for a few minutes. Is it okay if I bring someone?" Thank goodness, her voice was strong and didn't betray her nervousness.

His eyes narrowed, and his shoulders stiffened when she asked.

She glanced around to see what would cause him to suddenly seem upset, but when she didn't find anything, her gaze swiveled back to his.

"Who you bringin' around my crib, baby girl?"

"Just a friend, why? You want her number, too?" She sneered as she pulled her gaze away and reached around to gather up her sketch-pad and drawing pencils.

"Ah, so it's... one of your girls?"

Tia's head snapped up when she heard the hesitation in his voice.

His hand was rubbing the back of his neck, and his eyes were looking down at the busted up Coke can on the concrete.

Her eyes narrowed when she realized that he might actually care if she brought a guy. Interesting.

Another car passed by slowly, windows down and bass bumping, and drew Tommy's attention. She watched with a small smile on her face as he gave the driver another one of his nods and threw up deuces before he turned back to look at her.

"What?" he asked when he saw her smile.

Giving him an exaggerated eye roll, she threw her legs over the side of the fire escape to climb down the ladder. When she reached the bottom, she hopped off and faced him.

He was looking at her legs, which were bare since she was wearing super short shorts, ones she never wore out of her apartment, but she forgot she had them on when she decided to join him on the street. To distract him, she asked, "Why do you do that?"

His head snapped up. "Do what?"

"Act all thuggish and gangsta?" she said, forcing her voice to take on a slight street accent.

"Baby girl, you know why." He rolled his head and put his arms out to the side.

"Yeah, well, I can't remember, so why don't you tell me?"

He closed the distance between them and threw his arm over her shoulder.

To anyone else, the move probably looked casual, but inside, her heart rate sped up.

Touching him always did that to her. The heat from his body warmed her, and the feel of his large, callused hands on her much softer skin made her imagine what it would feel like if he ran those rough-skinned fingers all over her body. The thought made her want to shiver, but she had to fight it. It was eighty-five degrees outside; he'd know something was up if she had that type of reaction.

Instead, she prompted him and tried to distract herself. "Well?"

His soft voice so close to her ear wasn't helping. "I *am* a gangsta, baby girl." When she snorted, he gave her shoulder a small squeeze. "Tia, you know I run this neighborhood. I've got a reputation to uphold if I want everyone to stay in line and respect me the way I've earned. I got boys under me, buyers to keep an eye on, and suppliers that would put a bullet between my eyes if I fucked up or looked weak."

Her body finally gave in to the shiver she'd been fighting, but it was for a different reason. She hated the idea of him doing what he did. Even more, she hated the thought of him being harmed or killed, which she knew was a real possibility where they lived.

"I know you hate this life, baby girl, which is why I'm so happy you're getting out of this hell hole and making a life for yourself."

"Tommy, when we talked about that, we talked about *both of us* getting out of here. Not just me!" She looked up at him, imploring him with her eyes. "Remember? You always said you wanted to go live down south, by the beach. Or maybe even all the way to the west coast, Cali, or something like that. You said you didn't care as long as you were by the water. Some place peaceful and beautiful. Don't you still want to go there, live the rest of your life by the sea?"

For a brief moment, he got a wistful look in his eyes as he stared off.

Tia could see he was imaging just that. Living by the water where it was calm and peaceful. Tommy had always had a fascination with the beach and the ocean, saying the thought of the waves crashing and the sand between his toes made him feel more relaxed than anything ever had. The idea of Tommy peaceful and happy was something she'd always hoped for, especially given the life he lived.

All too quickly, the hopeful look left his eyes, and he refocused on her. "T, you know as well as I do those were just little kid dreams we shared late at night. We were like, what? Twelve and fourteen? You told me stories of how you wanted to be a famous artist, and I just told you stories about myself to encourage you."

"Why would you do that?" Tia asked in confusion.

"Well, I couldn't tell you about the nightmares."

"What are you talking about, Tommy?"

"The nightmares I had every night, the ones that reminded me that I wasn't a good person and never would be..." He hesitated, but quickly recovered, and before she could comment, he continued. "You know as well as I do that I never had a chance of leaving the hood. I was born here, and I'll die here, baby girl."

"That's not true! You could too, Tommy, you're so smart..." She trailed off when he stopped and turned to face her, both his hands on her shoulders, giving her a small squeeze to make sure he had her attention. When she looked up, his face was a mask of seriousness.

"It's too late for me, Tia, you know that. There's no going back, but I can make damn sure you and my baby sister get out of this hood alive."

Tia's eyes teared up, and she quickly blinked the moisture away. It might have been a rough way of saying it, but he was only telling her the truth.

They were both quiet for a minute, lost in the reality that was their lives. Finally, Tommy broke the silence in his usual joking way. "So, what'ch ya wearing tonight, baby girl?"

Tia rolled her eyes and elbowed him as she pulled away and turned around. "I'll see you later," she yelled over her shoulder as she walked back toward the fire escape. As she lifted her foot and placed it on the bottom rung, she looked back at him.

His eyes were intense, lacking the usual lust and flintiness they held when he looked at her or any girl. When he seemed to realize she was watching him, he shook his head slightly before moving his gaze to her ass.

"I hate to see you go, baby girl, but I sure do love to watch you leave."

Tia didn't even bother to give him a response. Instead, she made her way up the ladder, a sad smile on her lips.

Location: Brooklyn, New York
Date: August 12, 1995 9:46 pm

Ice Cube's "It was a Good Day" reached her ears as soon as the elevator doors opened onto Tommy's floor. If it were anyone else having a party, the cops would've probably been called already, but since it was T-Dogg, everyone knew to leave him alone.

As she stepped over the threshold onto the wooden floor, her heels clicked a little too loudly, and her dress rode up her thighs a little higher than she was comfortable with. Reaching down, she tugged at the hem, hoping it would somehow miraculously become longer.

"Tia, stop doing that!" Smacking her hand away from the dress, her best friend Jasmine grabbed her arm and yanked her down the hall in the direction of the loud thumping bass. "You're like a little kid. I swear, I can't take you anywhere."

"Well, you don't have to. I'm perfectly fine going right back home," Tia said as she tried to pull free from her friend's death grip.

Giving another yank, she pulled Tia close once again and gave her a dirty look. "Oh no, you don't! This is the only party I've been able to drag you to all year. You always have your nose stuck in a book or that drawing pad of yours. How you expect to get a man like that, I have no idea!"

Tia rolled her eyes at the complaining, something she'd grown accustomed to in the three years they'd been tight. "Did it ever occur to you that I might not want a man?"

Jasmine gave Tia a pointed look. "Keep telling yourself that, baby. I see how you look at T-Dogg."

"Ugh, could you *not* call him that?"

"I would stop if he'd let me, but we all know he won't let *anyone* call him anything other than that."

"He lets me," Tia said defiantly.

"Yes, he does, and you're the only one besides his family. So what does that tell you?"

"I don't know; what?" Tia asked as they reached the door that was vibrating with the music coming from the other side.

She lifted her hand to knock, but Jasmine wrapped her fingers around her friend's wrist to stop her. Tia looked at the other girl in confusion.

"Tia, girl, you need to get a clue. That boy is as into you as you are him."

"Pah-lease!" Tia laughed, even though her stomach jumped a little at the thought. "Tommy hits on every girl his eyes land on, but not once has he hit on me. Trust me, girl, he's not even the least bit interested."

"You are so clueless sometimes!" Jasmine said with a sigh.

"What? I'm right, and you know it!"

"No, girl, what I know is that *Tommy* only lets *you* call him by his real name, he watches you like a hawk when you're around, he won't let any of his boys even look at you, much less ask you out, and the only reason why he hasn't hit on you is because he cares too much about you."

"Whatever! Do you even hear yourself? That doesn't make any sense! If he liked me, he'd have no problem telling me. Lord knows he doesn't mince words with any of the other million girls he's been with."

Jasmine let out a deep sigh of resignation when she realized Tia wasn't going to give up her denial. "Look, will you just pay attention tonight? Watch the way he watches you, how he talks to you, and how he gives every other guy who checks you out the death glare. Can you do that?"

Tia rolled her eyes, but decided to concede so they could just go to the party and get it over with. "Fine, whatever."

Jasmine smiled and released Tia's wrist, giving her a mock warning glare before looking at the wooden door in front of them.

"Can I knock now?"

"Yes!"

As Tia lifted her hand, her mind quickly ran over what she'd just been told. She'd never shared her secret feelings for Tommy with

Jasmine, but she'd figured it out pretty quickly. She was perceptive like that, which made Tia wonder if her friend could be right about T-Dogg's feelings. Tia had noticed odd looks or silly comments occasionally from him, but she'd always written it off because moments later, he'd be hitting on some skanky girl that was nearby.

Before she could think about it any further, the door opened, and the loud music from before became almost unbearable. How someone even heard them knock was a complete mystery.

Jasmine was through the door first, and the guy who opened it gave her an appreciative once over as he held the door for them. When his eyes landed on Tia, he jerked them back up and gave her a respectful nod. She recognized him instantly.

"Hey, Jay!" She greeted Tommy's best friend.

He offered a small smile as he shut the door, and then leaned closer so she could hear him better. "Hey, Tia, T-Dogg's in the kitchen. He said for me to send you his way when you got here."

"Okay, thanks!" She waved, took her friend's hand, and weaved through the throng of bodies toward the kitchen.

The apartment was packed, as it always was whenever Tommy had a party. Barely dressed girls littered the middle of the room, dancing—or at least their version of dancing. Really, it was more like having sex with clothes on. Tia could never understand how those girls jumped from guy to guy, getting so close and personal with each one as if they were just shaking hands. As far as Tia was concerned, they were all sluts. The guys were no better in their jeans and white wife-beater shirts, standing around the edge of the room, beer or bottle of liquor in hand, passing joints and eyeing the grinding girls while BS'ing with the boys.

Tia shook her head, trying to avoid eye contact with everyone she passed. The girls usually sneered and made catty comments, while the guys leered and made her feel dirty. All things she tried to avoid.

Of course, Jasmine was another story. She never took shit from anyone—male or female. If they were nasty to her, she quickly put them in their place. To make matters worse, she always seemed to hunt trouble.

"What you looking at, bitch?" some girl asked loudly as Jasmine tried to come to a stop.

She cut her eyes and lifted an eyebrow. "Who you callin' bitch? Get the fuck outta my way." With a hard shove, she forced her way through the throng of bodies.

Tia held tight, tried her best to make her friend avoid being violent, and continued to guide her to the kitchen.

As they rounded the corner and moved through the entryway, Jasmine finally stopped trying to get away. Thank goodness, because

Tia wouldn't have been able to keep her grip much longer. Coming to a screeching halt, she let her friend's wrist go, transfixed by the image before them. Tia's stomach plummeted, and another fraction of her heart broke off the already damaged organ.

Tommy was in the kitchen where she was told he would be, but of course, he wasn't alone. The girl from earlier, the one Tia had watched him hit on from her perch on the fire escape, was seated firmly on his lap, arms wrapped around him, and the girl's lips were all over his neck as he played cards with the other guys surrounding the table.

Tia tried to berate herself for reacting; she knew Tommy was like that. She'd never seen him at a party without a girl, if not two, on his arm. That night was different. For some reason, the conversation she'd had with Jasmine in the hall, just before they walked in, got Tia's hopes up in a way they'd never been before.

As stupid as she knew it was, she thought maybe her friend was onto something, and that Tommy had started to see Tia as more than a friend, more than the girl in his building he looked out for like he did his kid sister. Some small part of Tia had hoped he'd be alone. That he'd be waiting for her, have *her* on his arm, and stake his claim to all his boys that she was taken and his.

How dumb could I be? I'm an honor student, for God's sake! Why did she let whimsical dreams of happily ever after even begin to seep into her brain? She knew better, and seeing Tommy with that fucking tramp was like a bucket of cold water waking Tia up from her fantasy.

Just as she was metaphorically splashed in the face and pulled out of her trance, Tommy's eyes moved away from the guy he was talking and laughing with to roam the kitchen. That chocolate brown gaze landed on her almost instantly and widened slightly before a slow grin tipped the corners of his mouth.

Then, the girl on his lap reached up and slid her palm along his jaw and cheek as she turned his face toward her.

Tia didn't need to see what happened next. She'd seen it one too many times and was tired of torturing herself. Her heart could only lose so many more pieces before it was completely shattered and irreparable. Before she could think better of her actions, or how they would look, she whirled around and fled the room. She heard Jasmine calling from behind, but Tia didn't stop. She couldn't. If she did, she'd lose it, and the last thing she needed was to allow any of those people to see her cry. Crying was an emotion she couldn't afford in a place like that, full of people that preyed on weakness and used it to their advantage. Tia had yet to show up on anyone's radar, and she'd be damned if she let that happen after so many years of keeping it at bay!

Pushing past Jay with her head down, she walked as quickly as possible toward the elevator and pressed the button with much more force than necessary, praying all the while that it would arrive before her friend caught up. Jasmine might have guessed Tia loved Tommy, but she'd never admitted it, and sure as hell wasn't going to do it while she was so upset and emotional.

Giving it about two seconds, Tia pressed the button again, leaving her finger on it while she silently cursed the old building and its slow ass equipment.

"You know holding the button doesn't make it come any faster," an amused voice said from behind her, making Tia grit her teeth.

Of course Tommy would come after her. He needed to keep an eye on her and keep her safe. She was his charity case, one of the ones he was going to help get out of that hell hole of a neighborhood. If that didn't happen, he wouldn't be able to absolve himself of the all the sins he'd committed to make sure she succeeded.

Well, she didn't need his charity, his protection, any more. *Fuck that. Fuck him.*

Whirling around, she met his amused gaze with an angry one of her own.

As soon as he saw the look, all the amusement fled his face, replaced instantly with concern. He took a step closer and reached his hand out to her. "Baby girl..." he began but stopped short when Tia moved away from his outstretched hand and raised one of her own.

"Don't. Just, don't," she said with a shake of her head as she moved her gaze to the floor, unable to look at his confused and hurt expression. *I'm the one that's hurt, damn it! Not him!*

"Tia?" he asked, not using her nickname the second time.

"I can't do this anymore, Tommy. I'm sorry," she said, her voice barely above a whisper, but she knew he heard. He was standing too close not to.

"Do what? I don't understand. Did something happen? Did someone hurt you?" His voice grew in volume, and a hint of anger tinged his words by the time he finished questioning her. The idea of her being hurt by someone obviously made him mad. If only she could tell him it wasn't any use being mad because *he* was the one who'd hurt her.

She was saved by the bell, or rather the ding, of the elevator indicating it had finally reached their floor. The doors slid open, and a few more partygoers stepped off, the girls giving Tommy a once over as they walked past him. It was odd, but finally, for the first time since she met him, he actually only had eyes for her. Eyes that were pleading with her, begging her to tell him what was going on. But she couldn't.

Shaking her head, she stepped through the open doorway onto the old metal contraption and pressed the button for the first floor.

7

Tommy stood there in silence, watching her as the doors slowly slid closed.

Only then did Tia take a much-needed breath as she leaned back against the cool wall. She knew she shouldn't have run out of there like that. It only made him more suspicious. He'd want answers and wouldn't accept no. Tommy might have let her go just then, but she knew he'd seek her out the next day, once his party was over and he was finished with his flavor of the night. Just the idea of him with that girl made Tia's stomach roll, which made her furious. The anger pushed her over the edge, and the tears finally came.

At first, it was a slow trickle, one tear then a second, but by the time the elevator reached the ground floor and the doors slid open once again, there was a steady stream. The sobs escaped her throat against all her efforts to keep them in. Knowing there would be a group of people waiting to go up, Tia fixed her gaze firmly on the floor and rushed out as soon as she could slip past the opening in the doors. Her shoulder bumped against a few people as she ran by, and she ignored the muffled curse words thrown at her. Her long hair shielded her face enough to keep from being recognized, and the short ass dress she wore would definitely throw off anyone who suspected it might be her.

Once outside, she drew in a deep breath of the cool night air. It did nothing to calm her breaking heart or the sobs that were trying to rip from her throat. She only needed a few more seconds, and then she could let it all out. Turning to her right, she ran down the sidewalk, only to stop when her ankle twisted slightly. Throwing up a hand to brace herself on the building beside her, she leaned down and ripped the stupid heels from her feet, dropping them to the ground. She had no intention of ever wearing them again, so she left them where they landed and took off as fast as she could to the end of the block. Turning, she raced through the dark alley until she reached the fire escape. Hefting herself up on the ladder, she climbed the few rungs until she reached the landing just outside her bedroom window. Only then did she finally allow her body to let go. Falling into a heap on the cold metal grate, she pulled her knees up, wrapped both arms tightly around them, and buried her face to help muffle the sobs tearing from her throat.

The amount of time that passed didn't matter. She had to finally let it all go. Her hopes that Tommy would finally see her, realize he loved her as much as she loved him, and stop lusting after every other girl in the world were over. He'd never change. Why'd it matter if he did anyway? She was leaving in less than a year. It was time to go away to college, get out of that shit hole of a neighborhood, and leave it all behind, including him.

College would give her a chance to grow, learn, and hopefully fall in love again. He wouldn't be Tommy, no one ever would be, but she could have happiness. Something she'd never have with T-Dogg. Sure, he'd made her smile and laugh, joked around with her, and teased her. He'd made her stomach flutter with hope and anticipation, her body shiver with awareness and arousal, but she'd never had happiness. Only a broken heart and shattered dreams.

So, time didn't matter. Tia didn't worry about how long she sat there and cried for all she'd never have. She didn't care who heard or saw. It was something she needed: a cleansing, ridding herself of Tommy once and for all. Once she was finished, she'd bury her feelings for him as deeply as possible and bide her time until she was free.

Location: Brooklyn, New York
Date: August 12, 1995 10:32 pm

So lost in her own sorrow, her sobs muffling any other noise in the night, Tia didn't hear the clanging of the metal ladder as someone climbed up. She didn't see the intruder move stealthily onto the landing beside her or sense his presence as he stood, watching over her. She was completely unaware of him until his hand was touching her shoulder. Scrambling back, she let out a startled scream as her head whipped up, and she tried to identify the person hovering over her. It was dark outside, the alley even more so from the lack of streetlights. The moon was the only thing to offer any sort of light, and the person before her was blocking it, leaving his face completely in shadow. But she didn't need to see him to know he was a stranger.

Unsure of what he wanted, Tia tried to remain calm. Maybe he was just another resident of the building who decided to take the fire escape up to his apartment. Which was weird, but she did it, so who was she to judge? Her heartbeat began to slow, and her breathing evened out as the idea began to take root. Placing her hands more firmly on the metal grate, she scooted back farther to allow him room to pass by and continue up the ladder. Instead, he moved closer to her, his hands extending and reaching toward her. She tried to create some distance, but soon her back was pushed firmly up against the brick wall, and she found herself cornered.

Her palms began to sweat, her breathing became labored again, and a few more tears escaped her eyes as her sorrow quickly morphed into terror.

The man crept closer until his face finally became visible. Recognition instantly dawned, causing her distress to spike. She knew him.

Shorty. He was dangerous, and he didn't belong in their neighborhood. Tommy kept a close eye out for Shorty and any of his boys. He'd been trying to encroach on Tommy's turf, dealing and causing trouble in the neighborhood. It was *so* not a good thing that the thug was standing in front of her in the middle of the night.

It was even worse that she was alone.

Tia was torn from her thoughts when his hands gripped her shoulders roughly and jerked her toward him. "Well, what do we have here?" he asked in a deep, teasing voice. The teasing didn't hide the danger behind the statement.

"What do you want?" she gritted out through the dread that consumed her.

"Well, that's not a very hospitable greeting. Here I am, visiting your neighborhood, looking for a friend, and I get a welcome like that?" His fingers dug into her shoulders as he jerked her up and into the front of his body. Meaty hands moved down quickly to wrap around her wrists, which he took firmly in one hand while the other reached around and grabbed her waist. His fingers dug into her skin so hard she was positive she'd have bruises.

Tears rolled down her face as she tried to stay quiet through it all. She knew his reputation. He liked to hurt people—especially women. The more she struggled or showed her pain, the more he'd enjoy it. As long as she could help it, she wasn't going to give him that satisfaction.

"So, Tia."

She let out an involuntary gasp at hearing her name from him.

"Ah, you didn't think I knew who I was talking to, did you?" His hand at her waist began to roam, roughly and painfully caressing her lower back down to her ass.

She had to bite her lip to keep from whimpering.

"I definitely know who you are. You're T-Dogg's bitch. Why he's so pussy whipped over a little piece of ass like yours when he can get all these other fucking sluts, I'll never know, but that's irrelevant. He is, and I plan to use it to my advantage."

"I, I think you're mistaken... Tomm...T-Dogg isn't whipped by me. We're, we're just friends." She hated the way she stuttered, showing him the fear and weakness he was sure to be craving. The way his hands roamed over her body made her skin crawl and bile rise up in her throat. He didn't have to tell her what he was going to do; it was clear in the way he touched her and in the feeling of him getting hard as he did.

Shorty started laughing, deep and hard. "Shit, he's pussy whipped over a girl that ain't even his girl? This shit keeps getting better and better. Fuck, this is going to be fun! Bet you're a virgin, too, huh?"

Then, she was shoved backward, her body hitting the abrasive wall behind her so hard that her head snapped back and slammed into the brick. Pain shot through her as white lights danced before her eyes, blinding her even further in the already dark night. Hands moved over her body again, angry and rough, lifting her clothes and pinching her skin. Tears flowed freely from her eyes as she squeezed them shut and tried to block what was happening from her mind.

Shorty wouldn't kill her; that would defeat the purpose. He was there to hurt her, bruise and rape her, and then send her back to Tommy as a warning. Tia's only saving grace was that it was happening to her and not Tommy's baby sister. It would kill her and Tommy if Chantel were ever hurt. A large, clammy hand reached under her shirt, ripped her bra away, and wrapped around her breast, squeezing hard enough to draw a whimper from her.

"You like that, baby?" Hot breath blew across her cheek as he whispered the words to her like a lover would.

It made her gag in response. *This isn't the way it's supposed to happen...*

That only fueled his assault. "That's right, you like it rough..." He trailed off as his other hand reached down past the hem of her skirt and gripped her thigh. Jerking her leg up, he dug his nails into her skin.

She tried to block him again, thinking of her parents, her best friend Jasmine, Tommy and Chantel, and going away to college, anything that would get Tia's mind off of what was about to happen. But it wasn't working; the more Shorty touched her, the more she wanted to scream. His grip on her was getting rougher and rougher, and with each movement, he seemed impossibly closer. She could feel his calloused skin, smell his hot breath, and taste her own terror as it consumed her. Finally, she couldn't hold it back any longer, and she opened her mouth, letting all her fear and anger pour into the scream she let loose.

Shorty jerked back in surprise, but recovered quickly, reaching up and smacking her in the face before covering her mouth with the palm of his hand. Slamming her head against the brick wall, he leaned in close to her ear. "Shut the fuck up, bitch! You scream like that again, and I'll kill you once I'm finished with you. Understand?"

Tia closed her eyes and nodded.

After a moment of making sure she wasn't going to scream, which she seriously considered, he resumed his assault. She was thrown to the rough metal on her back. His pants unzipped, his fingers clutched at her panties, and he thrust his pelvis forward.

Inches from her apartment, she was going to be raped, and her first time wouldn't be with the man she'd always dreamed about. Instead, it was going to be a filthy hulking piece of shit who took her most prized possession. She squeezed her eyes shut and bit her lip so hard blood pooled into her mouth.

Then, suddenly, his weight was off her.

It took a moment for his absence to register, but as soon as it did, her eyes sprang open and she was gripped by a new fear.

Tia gasped.

Tommy was there, gun drawn, touching the temple of Shorty's head. Tommy's face was difficult to see, but she could feel the anger radiating off him. "Baby girl? You okay?" He was shaking with emotion when he asked.

Unable to answer, she let out a sob as she took the few steps separating them and clung to him. He'd saved her.

Tommy gripped her tightly to his side, but not painfully, as Shorty had done. No, Tommy's touch was desperate and fearful as his hand ran up and down her back, his body vibrating with controlled rage.

"You better lower that gun, T-Dogg, if you wanna live to make sure your bitch is okay." Shorty snarled the threat as if he wasn't the one with a gun pointed at his head.

Tommy tensed before pausing the movement of his hand on Tia's back. He gave her one last squeeze before he gently pushed her away from him so he could look down into her face. He didn't address Shorty. "Here, baby, take this." Tommy reached behind his back and pulled out another gun.

"No, Tommy. I can't..." She trailed off when he pushed the gun into her hand.

"Shhh, it's all right, baby girl. I need you to help me. Can you do that?" He leaned down to look into her eyes.

When their gazes connected, she nodded her head. Decision made. He'd saved her, so she'd do whatever he needed.

"Good girl. Now, climb down and wait at the bottom. I'm going to send this piece of shit down, and I want that gun aimed at him the whole time. If he so much as sneezes, you shoot his fucking head off, you got that?"

Unwilling to believe she'd actually have to pull the trigger, she nodded her head again.

"That's my girl." He praised her, and she turned to do as he'd instructed.

7

Before she could take a step, he leaned down and brushed his lips across her mouth. It was quick and soft, nothing most would even take note of, but for her it was everything. Her heart thundered, and she prayed they'd make it out alive so she could show him how she felt.

"Go on, I'll be right behind you," he told her softly to get her moving.

She nodded, a bit dazed, but she quickly reined in her feelings.

Shorty was still standing there, gun to his head, snarling at her.

Taking a deep breath, she descended the ladder as carefully but quickly as she could while holding a gun and feeling awfully bruised and battered.

"Okay, Tommy," she called up when both feet were firmly on the ground and the gun was steady in her hands. "I'm ready."

She heard movement from above, feet stomping on metal, shuffling and grunting, and fear gripped her once again. *What if Shorty's fighting Tommy?* Unable to see them, she certainly couldn't help from down there. Just as she took a step back toward the ladder, a leg swung over the side of the fire escape, followed by another, and Shorty started to come down. Tia took a few more steps back, trying to put as much distance between them as possible while still staying close enough to hit her target if she needed to.

She'd never even held a weapon, much less used one, and she hoped the son of a bitch coming down couldn't tell. Her body shook with fear, sweat trickling down her spine, and her instinct to run and get help was almost too much. The only thing that kept her rooted in place, gun firmly in hand, was what Shorty could do to Tommy if she left.

As soon as Shorty's feet hit the hard concrete, he took a menacing step toward her.

She trembled, but her hand was steady as she gripped the gun tighter and placed her finger on the trigger. "I will fuckin' shoot you if you take one more step toward me!" she shouted, her voice firm and angry.

Shorty raised his hands in surrender, but a sly smile formed on his face.

"I sure do love a bitch with a gun," he practically purred, and Tia had to fight the keep from throwing up.

This guy is fucking sick!

Thankfully, Tommy was already making his way down. Although she knew he was still up there, waiting for Shorty to descend first, the sight of Tommy still took her breath away. His presence not only gave her a sense of calm, it also kept Shorty from saying anything further, although it didn't stop the heated looks and lip licking.

She shivered.

Tommy walked up behind Shorty and shoved the gun in his back, pushing him forward a step. "Don't look at her, don't speak to her, don't even fucking *think* about her! You feel me?" Tommy asked in a menacing voice Tia had never heard from him before.

Her Tommy was gone, and before her stood T-Dogg. The drug dealing, crew running, girl chasing thug who ran the neighborhood and did what was necessary to secure his position and keep those he loved safe. She may not have liked it, but it was keeping them both alive.

"Yeah," Shorty drawled as his eyes narrowed, and his attention turned toward Tommy. "I feel ya, homey."

Tia didn't like the sound of Shorty's voice, or the way he looked at Tommy. It immediately made her suspicious. On instinct, her gaze roamed the dark alley, trying to look into the nooks and crannies that were completely hidden by darkness. She got an uneasy feeling as she did, her mind running with the possibility of someone else lurking in those shadows. If Shorty had brought people with him, she and Tommy were in serious trouble.

As if Shorty knew exactly what she was thinking, he chuckled. "Smart bitch you got there, T-Dogg. At least one of you realized I wouldn't be stupid enough to come to your hood alone."

Then, as if on cue, two guys emerged from the shadows. They were both huge, much bigger than both Shorty and Tommy, and each man had a gun in his hand. One was pointed at Tia and the other at Tommy.

She gasped in horror.

"Now, why don't the two of you lower your guns, I'll finish what I came here for, and we can all walk away alive?"

"You think I'm going to stand here and let you hurt my girl? I'd rather die!" Tommy shouted, shoving the gun into the side of Shorty's head.

Tia's heart broke for the second time that night. Tommy was finally admitting he cared for her, calling her *his* girl and saying he was willing to die for her, but it was bittersweet. Either Tommy died, or she let Shorty have his way. The idea of him touching her again, hurting her the way he had earlier, made her sick, but it didn't destroy her the way the thought of Tommy dying did.

Taking a brave step forward, she lowered her gun and spoke to Tommy. "It's okay. I'll do what... I'll do whatever he wants, Tommy."

"Like fuckin' hell you will!" he shouted at her, his eyes bulging, and his body visibly shaking.

The other two guys took threatening steps forward, raising their guns just a bit higher, the warning clear.

"Why don't you listen to your bitch, Tommy? She's seems to know what she wants." Shorty snickered.

"Don't. You. Fucking. Call. Her. That!" Tommy bellowed and then pulled the trigger.

Shorty's body fell to the ground with a thud, and then it was silent. Everyone stared in utter disbelief. But the silence and shock only lasted a moment. Then, more shots rang out, bullets were flying, and everyone was ducking for cover.

"Tia!" Tommy shouted, running toward her while his gun was aimed at Shorty's boys, firing randomly to keep them at bay.

Just as Tommy reached her, a sharp pain pierced her stomach. Her hands flew up to help soothe the sting, but she felt a hot stickiness that wasn't there before. Looking down, she watched as the blood blossomed on her dress, quickly covering the whole top. Tommy reached her side, and she looked up to see his face etched with concern.

"Baby girl," he whispered, followed by a choked sob. His arms went around her just as her legs failed. He helped her to the ground even as shots still sounded through the night.

"Tommy, go!" she told him desperately. He was paying too much attention to her and not the other two guys that were still a threat. "Get out of here!"

"No, baby girl, I'm not leaving you!"

"Tommy." She pleaded, her body turning cold.

"Never," he whispered as he leaned down and touched his forehead to hers. "I love you, Tia," he said fiercely, and then his body jerked.

She couldn't think straight for some reason but she knew something was off. "Tommy?" she asked, confused and tired.

"Shhh, baby girl," he whispered as he lay down beside her. He pulled her close, his bloody hand moving up to run over her face and through her hair. His voice was choked, his words seeming difficult to form as he continued to soothe her. "I've got you, baby. I'll always have you."

As they lay there in each other's arms, the night became silent around them, their attackers having fled. It began to rain. The light mist usually wouldn't have been enough to bother either of them, but the cool water soaked into Tia's clothes, making her even colder. Her teeth chattered and her body shook.

"It...it's s...s...so c...cold," she whispered between shivers.

Tommy pulled her more tightly against his body, his arms wrapped snugly around her. "I know, baby girl, I know. I lied to you before, you know, when I said I didn't have dreams. I did. I do. The water, the rain, it's usually so soothing. Calms me down and makes me dream of things I don't deserve. But now, it's not working. It's only reminding me that those dreams'll never come true."

"I... I... love you, T... Tommy," she whispered, relishing the feel of his body wrapped around hers, his lips brushing against hers, and the sound of his voice telling her how much he loved her. *If only we'd come to this place sooner,* she thought. She'd never get to show him all the things she felt. Even worse, she'd never have the chance to truly share love with him the way they deserved. It was over as quickly as it began.

Everything began to fade. Tommy's voice grew faint and fainter still, the heat of his body turned cold beside her, and the grip he had on her slipped away. As light turned to darkness, she held on to the fact that he loved her, and she loved him.

Part Six

"We are given the gift of choice during creation, but it is not a present if we are not allowed to make mistakes—to be human."

The White Place

He pried his eyes open and instantly shut them again. It was so bright, so white, it hurt. Like he had been sleeping for months, his muscles screamed at him to stop moving when he stretched out a leg. Pins and needles ricocheted through his limbs, making him groan and grab at them.

Voices floated to his ears, the sweet melodies sounding as though they were being filtered through something, softening the impact on his sore eardrums. Definitely women.

One of them said, "There he is."

"He looks like he is in pain," another, deeper voice, said.

A laugh from the first. "He will be fine. Many years have passed. His body is acclimating."

It took effort, but he peeled back his lids. First one, and then the other. Five blurry figures stood before him. From his position on the floor, they seemed impossibly tall. His sight sharpened, and he took in the beautiful females. Each looked distinctly different, but all had pale silver irises, wore similar expressions, and were garbed in flowing white robes.

As his eyes met theirs, visions flashed in his mind: a senator, a knight, a soldier, a boxer, and a gangster. *What does that mean? For that matter, who am I? Where am I?* His memory was blank, but he clung to the faded images like chalk marks hold onto a blackboard recently wiped clean. He voiced the latter question once the tingling of his body receded and his tongue recalled how to function.

One woman stepped forward. She was lithe and blonde, her light hair giving her a more angelic appearance than the rest. She tilted her head and studied him with open curiosity. “Do you not recognize us, dear husband?”

Husband? Confusion tied his lips together as he strained to remember. *I am married to this ethereal creature?* Wary, his eyes darted from one woman to the other. Given the matching eyes, he assumed the ladies were sisters. And yet, they were so different in every other way. He did not recognize the one speaking. Not surprising, since he did not even know his own name. But her question gave him hope that *she* might.

Frowning slightly, he rasped. “I do not. I am not even sure who I am.” He tried to push up with shaking arms. His body was so weak. “You know me?”

All the women laughed, the sound light and musical. The one before him hushed the others before bending forward and offering her hand. A necklace hung around her slender neck.

From it dangled a silver bar etched with one word: Wrath.

An unusual choice of jewelry, he thought.

"We know you quite well, Thomas," the woman said with a sweet smile. "I go by many names, but you may call me Nichole, as that is the name you knew me by."

Thomas. So that is my name.

When he swayed on his feet, she braced his arm, providing subtle support. She was surprisingly strong given her slender form. He met her eyes with what he knew was a wavering smile of nerves and fear. Her returning grin was steady. "Be brave," she whispered before stepping back into line with the others.

He looked down at the dark leather binding his feet, shifted to one side, and twitched. Wiggling his toes still hurt. A long, scratchy, light brown tunic with sleeves that reached his wrists covered him, and he turned his hands this way and that, examining the fingers and short, clean nails.

The women stood back, smiling, their eyes following his every movement. It was that way for a long while as Thomas surveyed his surroundings. Not one of the ladies spoke.

Nichole. The name seemed so familiar. If he could only remember. Each time he thought he grasped how he knew her, it flitted away like a fly avoiding being smashed. He grew increasingly annoyed at the buzzing.

Here it is!

No! Wait! Try over there.

Sorry, still not the answer!

Frustrated, he sat down and stared at her. Neither spoke; all she did was smile.

Another woman came forward, same silver eyes, but with long, brown hair so dark it was almost black. She extended her hand and waited with a welcoming smile. "It is okay. You knew me well at one time. I am Josephine. Sometimes, you called me Jo."

Standing, he placed his hand in hers and gripped her fingers, afraid he might fall back to the floor if he did not hold on tightly. *Josephine. Jo.* A flash of a memory entered his mind. A dark-haired beauty writhing in ecstasy beneath his strong, young body. He jerked his hand away. It was as if he had been burned with the touch, the recollection.

Josephine smiled. "You remember me."

Finding his voice again, he answered, "I remember something. Yes."

As she clapped her hands in front of her, the memories came. All of them at once. Josephine in the gardens, head tilted back, laughing at something he said to her. His hand in hers. The scent of her hair, and the silken feel of it. Her stolas. A golden laurel leaf comb. A battlefield. The stench of death and coppery blood around him. The weight of a sword in his hand, and a shield tethered to his arm. The hard planes of the helmet on his head.

Smoke.

Pain.

Screams.

He shook his head to chase away the visions of bloodied women and children, but more rushed in as replacements: A toga, a small house filled with sunlight and laughter, a rich palace, an evil man who was as disgusting on the outside as he was within.

Emperor Nero.

"No!" Thomas screamed, grabbing his temples, willing it to stop.

The painful recollections tore at him, the threats against his wife, his love for her that filled him so much it hurt, and the men who said they would find her.

"Ahhh!" He sank to his knees, still clutching his head as if to squeeze the memories from it. "Stop. Please, stop." If those men had located Thomas's wife, it would not have ended well. Never had they respected a woman, and she was beautiful beyond compare. Sorrow rose in him so profoundly, he lost his breath. With blurry vision, he gazed at her.

Josephine's smile had faded. She turned to the others. "Now, he remembers everything of our life together. Let us begin."

A long, marble table with four chairs behind it appeared before the women, and they took seats. All but Jo. She stood before him like a statue of Justice, beautiful but cold, her expression as set as stone. The other women kept their gazes trained on Jo.

“Sit down.” She gestured to a chair on a raised platform that had materialized in front of the table.

They seemed to be waiting for something... *What can it be?* He wondered, although he complied with the request.

As soon as he was seated, shackles bound him hand and foot, light filled the room, and a memory flooded into him. Just one. Something from before. Winding roads that stretched for miles, and a man with long, brown, wavy hair. He had eyes the color of a clear sky, and they were filled with tears. Fear lit in Thomas’s belly as the sorrowful expression struck him. “Why is this happening to me?”

Jo laughed and threw her head back. “I can see by your face that you remember the mortal sin you committed, your betrayal of a friend. Because of that error, you have been tested.”

“Tested? Mortal sin?”

“Yes.” She nodded, and her expression fell. “There are seven deadly sins, Thomas: sloth, gluttony, pride, greed, envy, wrath, and lust. We have accompanied you through five lives, each testing your character on one or more.”

A chill passed through him, and he shivered.

"It is time for your judgment," Nichole said.

"How do you five have this power?" he asked.

One of the women rose. Her short, reddish brown hair billowing in a phantom wind. "I am Kelly. You and I strode through one of your lives as partners. You will remember me in time. We five have the power of judgment as passed to us by our mothers: Clotho, Lachesis, and Atropos. You may know them as the three fates."

All four of the others nodded and whispered, "Bless our mothers."

So they are *sisters.* Terror rode through him like a kicking mule, tearing down all resolve. He felt the urge to run, but his bindings held him tightly. All he could do was clench his fists.

"While the ultimate decision as to whether you passed or failed lies in their hands, placed there by another whose reasons are not to be questioned and whose identity shall be revealed in due time, we are the ones who will hear your pleas, consider what we witnessed while watching you, and take our final word to them for your sentencing. That is all you need to know."

"But—"

She held up her hand. "You will have a time to speak, but that time is not now. Jo has bestowed upon you your memories from your time with her. It shall begin with her retelling of the moments where she found you lackadaisical in your test. We shall ask her questions. You shall remain silent until your chance to defend yourself is presented. Do you understand?"

He shrank back from her blazing eyes and nodded, pressing his lips together for fear she may lash out at him physically.

Another one of the women stood. She was smaller and had hair similar in color to Kelly's. "It is time to begin. We cannot wait any longer."

They both lowered to their seats. Kelly lifted a gavel and pounded it twice on a wooden sound block, the last thrum vibrating through the air, wrapping a blanket of impending doom over Thomas's shoulders. She turned toward Jo. "Let us begin."

"We belong to one another. As long as we hold tightly to that, we will remain at peace."

Trial for Thomitus Caelius
Sloth and Gluttony

Nichole laced her fingers together and leaned forward. "What is the first thing you remember, sister?"

Jo paced and sucked her bottom lip in, worrying it with her teeth. "I met Thomas when we were young. About seven, I believe, but we did not join until we were nearly sixteen. His Roman name was Thomitus Caelius. He eventually became a brave soldier for Rome. I thought it very grand, and I saw in him a passion and verve for life that was unrivalled."

"Did you fall in love?"

"I did. Instantly. I now know it was the draw the mothers placed upon our souls, but back then all I saw was that he was hardworking, honest, and driven." She blushed and put her fingertips on her cheek as though remembering a caress.

Smiling, Nichole leaned back and crossed her arms over her chest.

Her body language made Thomas wonder if she had already judged him—and not in a positive way. He shrank farther back in his chair, shoulders pulled to his ears. The women were beautiful, yes, but they were also terrifying in the way their eyes swirled when pensive.

Another of the women, the one who had spoken to Kelly before, asked, "And did he uphold those values throughout life?"

"Until the end." Jo nodded and looked down. "Until..." Tears rolled off the tip of her nose and splashed on the floor, leaving a rainbow of watery colors swirling together. "Oh, Tia, I cannot bear to think of it!" She buried her face in her hands and sobbed.

Tears threatened at the inner corners of his eyes as he thought once again about the brutality he witnessed the soldiers dole out on frail, young creatures. Those same men who had promised to find her. He squeezed his hands into fists. *Jo was mine, and I failed to protect her. Perhaps I do deserve harsh judgment.*

"Take a deep breath, and try to forget the horrors that followed your separation. What we need to know right now is how Thomas changed over time. Do you believe he gave in to sloth or gluttony?" Tia prodded.

Alarm raced through his veins. He knew the answer.

Jo lifted her head and nodded. "Near the end, I believe he did. But I am not sure he is wholly guilty."

"How can that be?"

"Because, when we became separated by Nero's guards, Thomas was writing something, and he apologized to me for his laziness during his time with the senate. I believe he was repentant. But I have no way of knowing without hearing his defense." She sniffled.

Her sisters put their heads together and whispered. When they parted, Kelly nodded. "Very well. We understand, and approve of, your decision to not hasten to judgment. We, also, are baffled by this revelation. While the information and decision brought to the mothers belongs to you, we would like the opportunity to ask him about these things." She gestured to her right, and another chair appeared. "Please, sit while we hear his tale."

Tia glared at Thomas. "This is your chance. We will ask, and you are to answer to the best of your ability. I will begin.

"You are charged with the sin of gluttony, among many others. Did you ever partake in excess food or drink? Beyond that, and what interests me more, did you have an excessive desire to consume more than you required for life and happiness?"

Thomas steeled his spine. "While I was young when elected to the Senate, I had seen far more battles than a person my age should have, atrocities the average citizen hopefully never would. My eyes were wide open when I agreed to spy on the Emperor. A large part of the city had burned, and rumors swirled that Nero had set the blaze himself to clear land for a palace richer than anyone could imagine. I was to get close to him, to see if that rumor, and others, were true before reporting back to the Senate. The members were trying to unseat him. My mission was clear. Getting close to Nero was not easy. I had to do things, partake in things, I normally would not have. So, yes, I was gluttonous. I had way too much to drink, ate too much, and became lazy and complacent."

Her stare bore into him. "You did these things only to achieve your goals?"

Thomas swallowed. "At first, yes. Then, I will admit, it grew easy to have people wait on me, to eat the rich food, to taste the finest wines in the Empire. I lost my way. I am humble enough to say it. I am guilty of gluttony, and not just because it was part of my mission to rid Rome of the tyrant Nero."

The hard expression on Tia's face softened to a slight scowl. "Humility will behoove you in this trial, Thomas. Continue to possess it." She adjusted her robe, clasped her hands, and rested them on the table before looking at him with one eyebrow lifted. "You are also accused of the sin of sloth. While there are many facets to this sin, there is one of which I most wish to hear your defense. Too many think sloth is only about work ethic. It is not. It is about not tackling the difficult situations to attain something good, something valuable to our lives and to those we love. So, I ask you, did you give what you believe was necessary to attain that which would have made your life complete?"

"I failed. Completely and utterly. Josephine was my life. In losing sight of what I was doing in the palace, I lost sight of everything that was truly important. My association with Nero put her in danger, and I fear that she—" Thomas's voice broke "—was hurt because of me." Scalding tears carved paths down his cheeks. "For that, I cannot forgive myself. Nor can I ask you to have mercy on me."

Turning her head left and right, she glanced at her sisters. "He faces many judgments here today. Shall we debate each one and pass judgment sin by sin, or shall we hear him out on each and deliberate, holding our final recommendation until the very end?"

Nichole answered, "I believe we should reserve our judgments, even if made, until the end. Otherwise, we may dishearten him from answering to the best of his ability in the further trials. A man who believes himself to be condemned is a man who will not care if he is caught in a lie."

They all agreed.

Thomas let out a breath before looking at each of the other women, trying to gauge their facial expressions. They were stoic unless reliving their lives with him. His fate rested in their hands, and he prayed they would be careful in the handling of his soul. *Should I dare hope? I deserve every ounce of their scorn.*

Jo rose and paced, worrying her lips with her fingers, everyone's eyes following her. She had the most intimate knowledge of those particular sins because she lived through them, and he knew her words would hold tremendous weight.

"What say you, Jo? Do you have anything to add about your Thomitus? Any questions you suggest we ask so we fully understand how he fared with gluttony and sloth?" Tia asked.

Studying Jo's face, his eyes had never left her even when Tia was speaking, he steadied his breathing and prepared for the disdain he knew was coming.

"We should query him on the tome he penned while imprisoned." Jo faced him. "What was its purpose? How many days and nights did you spend writing it? Was it done in repentance or for a more selfish reason?"

Shock hit him like a thousand lightning bolts when she asked that question. It was his last chance to save himself, and he dare not lie.

All eyes turned to him.

He inhaled, hoping his last action would be enough to negate the damage done. "I wrote to my fellow Senators, begged their forgiveness, and provided them details about Nero's corruption. I also asked for them to come and get Josephine and me. I wanted out." His voice shook while his gaze held Jo's, captivated. "I wanted to get her out of there before Nero made good on his threats against her. I was focused in my desire to free her. During the day, I fulfilled the

Emperor's duties, but I spent every evening documenting my findings."

"And, did they reply to you?" Kelly asked.

With some effort, he tore his eyes away from Jo to look at the sister who spoke. "I did pen the document but cannot be sure it was delivered. The palace was overtaken soon after I gave it to a servant who promised to deliver it to the Senate right away. I am not sure that he actually had time to do so."

Kelly nodded once. "I see. That is enough for me. Jo?"

Eyes cast down, Jo nodded and took her seat. She pulled at her lip with her teeth, and when she glanced up at him, her brows were drawn toward the center of her face, creating a wrinkle on the bridge of her nose.

Silently, he begged for her forgiveness and understanding.

"One who is wisest is often the first to admit he knows nothing."

Trial of Sir Thomas Russell
Pride

Kelly approached Thomas next. Though he could not read her cool eyes, a slight smile played on her lips. Placing a hand on his shoulder, she leaned forward, kissed his forehead, and straightened. "In our life together, you knew me as—"

"Kelleigh." He gasped. Regret tore through him, its blade sharp and merciless. What had he done? His love for her had also been great, but it had not been enough to save him from pride. Though she had given him counsel, he had ultimately allowed the voice of his desire to drown her out. He swallowed hard and found he could not meet her gaze. "Proceed with your testimony, my lady."

Her sigh was soft as she turned from him to face her sisters. The sound's meaning was lost on him. *Is she disappointed in my reaction to her or burdened by the story she must tell her sisters?*

Casey smiled at her sister encouragingly. "Tell us your tale, when you are ready."

With a lift of her head and a straightening of her shoulders, Kelly began. "Sir Thomas, as I knew him, was an artist, a man who could form any metal into the finest of jewelry. He could create such fine settings they were barely noticed other than as an adornment to exquisite gems. When we met, he worked that same magic with my heart." Her lips twitched in memory. "We married after a brief courtship, and we had a daughter, Marian. She brought light and joy to our lives."

Kelly paced, her eyes distant with memories. "Thomas worked hard and won the favor of our sovereign Queen, Elizabeth. He became the royal goldsmith, and we moved to the palace. For a while, life was as sweet as it was grand."

"But what of his sin?" Casey interrupted, leaning forward. "Did he succumb to pride?"

The brief joy that lit Kelly's face darkened. Her scowl was one of confusion and guilt. "That is not an easy question to answer, I am afraid. Life in Elizabethan England was harsh. Disease ran rampant, and our little family was not immune to it. Marian grew ill with ague. As I held her listless form in my arms, something broke inside me. Though she recovered, and I tried to as well, my fear for her never quite subsided." Tears filled Kelly's eyes, and she stole a quick glance at the man behind her. "Because I failed in my role as wife, I did not offer Thomas the support he needed. It is, in many ways, my fault that he failed this test."

"No, my love!" Thomas surged to his feet, the shackles making it difficult for him to maintain his balance. His weight drove him to his knees, though he clasped his hands before him. "The fault is all mine. You tried to warn me."

"You will get your turn to speak, Thomas," Tia said, not unkindly. Sympathy and concern filled her eyes as she looked upon her sister. "Describe this failure, so we may understand your angst."

Wrapping her arms around her middle protectively, Kelly focused on her sisters and continued. "Thankfully, Marian recovered, but I did not. I fretted she would grow ill again. My world revolved around my daughter, and for that, I often missed attending royal events with my husband or giving him much of my time and love."

She wrung her hands, her eyes studiously trained to the floor. "The incident Thomas spoke of occurred before Marian got sick. We had traveled to his boyhood home to make final arrangements for his father. It was then Thomas confided in me that he sought fame for his work, his art."

Once again, Kelly glanced at Thomas. The man, still on his knees, hung his head shamefully. She could not seem to break herself from the sight until she heard Jo's urging voice. "Go on."

Turning back, Kelly took a fortifying breath and visibly fought back tears threatening to fall. "I warned him pride was a mortal sin, and no good would come of it. I thought my words got through, but then Marian grew ill…" The tears she had tried so hard to contain made rivers down her pale cheeks, staining her toga in a myriad of colors. "I distanced myself from Thomas, my focus solely on our only child, and it seemed his pride grew in my absence. To add further insult, there was a man by the name of Lord Hale who I allowed to flirt shamelessly with me." She chuffed. "I was away from my husband, I had just given birth, and I wanted the compliments he gave me so freely. He would commandeer my attention at most every event, and people talked.

"It was so prevalent and obvious, Thomas became worried enough to ask me if I had closeted with the man. I had not, but his concern made me realize my actions were not harmless. I did my best to shun Lord Hale after the warning, but I fear the competition was too much for my husband to handle. He became unstable."

"And did his actions give way to pride?" Casey asked.

Tilting her head in a slight nod, Kelly said, "Yes. He paid the ultimate price for it, losing his position at the palace."

"That was not the ultimate price," Thomas whispered behind her. His voice broke on each word, his ears catching how tortured he sounded.

Kelly gasped at his softly spoken words, but did not reply. Wiping her eyes, she said, "That is the entirety of my testimony as I know it."

"Thank you, sister," Nichole said. "Please, take your seat and gather your emotions while we hear Thomas's side of the story."

"I..." He shook his head, regret for what his wife missed filled him. "It is best if I tell you of the time after she passed." After scrambling back into his seat, he hung his head.

All the women nodded and leaned forward on their arms, gazing at him without blinking, their molten, metal-colored irises swirling.

Again, he hesitated, feeling as though he was defending something he should not be. If they had never been forced to return to the place where his father died, Kelleigh would have never been taken by disease. It was his fault she was exposed to the illness a second time.

"Go on, Thomas," Nichole said.

His heart sank. "Our daughter became the loveliest creature. I married her to a commoner, so in love were they. I could see, when they looked at one another, they were the ideal match. He treated her with love and respect, and they had three children who all married well. The youngest became a duke."

Tears continued to stream down Kelly's face, but she was smiling.

"Please, do not smile. It was my fault you missed it all. Something I was only able to realize after your death." Sadness enveloped him like the shroud he had tucked his wife into when she passed. "I begged God for forgiveness every Sunday." He locked eyes with her. "My ambitions exposed you to the disease that killed you, but I was determined to live a life free of sin afterward."

Wondering if it would even matter, he groaned and confessed something else. "I never even bedded another, so fearful was I that Marian would be taken as revenge, as you were."

"The Christian God is not a vengeful being. He allows humans to have lessons they may accept or reject. It is mostly the same with the Pagan gods. Kelleigh's death was by circumstance only." Tia narrowed her eyes. "But, if you learned something from it, Thomas, then she did not die in vain."

He nodded. "I learned much."

Pressing dainty fingers to swollen lips, Kelly nodded at the man before them. "Thank you for raising our daughter into a strong woman. My heart is lightened in hearing your tale." She sobered, straightened her shoulders, and banged the gavel once. "Now, we shall hear from Casey."

7

"To be flawed is to be human, and to be humble is to admit your flaws."

Trial of First Lt. Thomas Anderson
Greed and Envy

Thomas watched as the woman known as Casey approached. The tiny dimple in her left cheek and the way she carried herself immediately flooded his mind with memories of her. He remembered her happiness when they were married, her determination in cleaning up the old shack they had lived in on the back of his father's property, and the overwhelming anguish Thomas cloaked from her after they lost their first child during pregnancy. He could remember seeing her on the porch swing, belly protruding as she gently rubbed it and sang sweetly. Thomas had been gone too long, but any time away from her was an eternity.

"Casey." The name tumbled from his lips.

Casey smiled. "He remembers me. He always called me that, while most everyone else called me Cassandra."

One side of his lips pulled up in a return half grin, but it quickly faded. A few times, his brother had used the nickname, and it made Thomas cringe. Her allure had always taken his breath away, but seeing her swollen with his child transcended his ideas of beauty. She was ethereal. "How could I forget you?"

Immediately, her mouth turned down. “It seems it was not so hard a chore for you back then.” Her frown softened. “At least, in the end. In the early days, you were so good to me. Gentle, loving, kind. When we lost our first baby...” She turned away and swiped at her face before facing him again. “You were always there for me. But you did not come home much after I conceived the second, and you were gone most of the time I carried our child. You chased your father’s acceptance, but you denied your own son a father.”

He hung his head. Her life had been so full of loss. First her parents, and then her first child. Yet nobody would have called her sullen. She never raised her voice against any unfairness; instead, she found the light in everything. Not once had she envied his brother the inheritance of the farm.

Jo’s voice broke through Thomas’s thoughts. “Throughout the lifetime you spent with Cassandra, the very short lifetime, you were tested for the sins of greed and envy. Do you feel that you succumbed to those sins or overcame them?”

Thomas swallowed. The women knew everything, so it would do him no good to lie, though he was sure there was no point in continuing. “I am guilty of both sins. It is what ultimately killed me and left Casey a widow. She had to raise our son alone.” His voice wobbled. He had not once set eyes on his namesake.

"How did it kill you? And who were you envious of?" Jo asked.

"My actions killed me, and my brother was the unfortunate victim of my sin."

"Explain."

"It was simple jealousy, present from birth. I was the middle child, and my older brother, Nicholas, was the favorite. In life, my father gave Nicholas everything and promised him the entire estate upon death.

"Nicholas was a coward. He did not care for anyone but himself and was never made to do anything that would get his hands dirty. Father would tell me to watch out for him. Me! Even though I was younger. Made me promise, never concerned with my needs or safety. Nicholas was the priority. He needed to be defended at all times, against neighborhood boys that were twice my size and in war. His life was the one that needed preserving. Not mine. I was expendable. After a lifetime of feeling the stabs of my father's favoritism, I cracked. And it was Cassandra who paid the price."

He dared a quick look at her, but he was unable to read anything from her stoic face. It saddened him, because she always wore a smile in his memories.

"I wanted Nicholas, for one time in his life, to stop hiding behind men like me. I wanted him to march to the front line and fight bravely, so I dragged him there. After he got hit by enemy fire and was injured, I got caught up in a cannon blast myself."

Nichole asked, "What of Nicholas's possessions were you envious of?"

"Our family estate. Nicholas never wanted it except to make a profit. I loved to work the land and wanted to preserve our family's legacy. My heart was in that soil. He only saw dollar signs, and Father only recognized the value of his firstborn. When I was young, I envied Father's love for Nicholas. As I grew older, I desired to gain the same respect from Father that he had for my brother." Thomas cleared his throat. "However, what I wanted more than anything was to secure my child's future."

He slammed his fist against his thigh. "But all I did was take my little boy's father away and leave my wife with no husband. She had already lost so much, and I took away more." Memories of his last day on the battlefield surfaced, the moments of indecision, the wavering.

"In the end, I sent Nicholas, albeit wounded and barely holding on, to the hospital, and I led my men. I hope someone told my son, told Casey. Maybe, if nothing else, they were proud of me. Can any of you answer a question for me?" He looked around the room, trying to make eye contact with each of the women. "Can you tell me how it turned out for Casey and my son?"

Casey stepped forward. “In good time. You will have a chance for questions of your own. But we must move along now.”

"Regret is a disease that will consume the human soul, but if mistakes are applied as lessons, one will grow instead of shrivel."

Trial of Tommy Two Guns
Wrath

It was time for him to face the fourth sister. She was the most terrifying because of her angelic appearance. He could feel something lurking beneath the surface, waiting to emerge and pull him under.

"Hello, Tommy," Nichole whispered as she reached up to caress the side of his face, sweeping her thumb gently across his cheekbone. At the feel of her warm, soft skin against his, he closed his eyes, and the memories flooded his mind.

The first time he laid eyes on her, there was no mistaking the look in her eyes as she stared up at him. Wide with terror, they screamed for help as a man's hand lay across her lips, squeezing, preventing her from speaking the words she desperately needed to say. She had not needed a voice, though. As soon as their eyes had connected, he had felt something deep in his soul; he could hear her pleas just as clearly as if she had spoken them aloud. Those feelings, as well as the scene before him, had caused intense anger to swell inside him. Seeing that man's hands on her, roughly forcing her to do things she did not want to, had snapped something Tommy had always kept tight reins on. He may have been a fighter, but ever since the one incident on the farm, he had always had control. He made a point of it, but that night in the alley, he lost it. Had he not heard her whimper of fear as he pounded the flesh of her assailant, Tommy would have killed the man.

The vision of her helpless and terrified was one that had haunted Tommy for many nights after. It fueled his anger, spiked his rage, and had his hands balling into tight fists as he stood before the woman he had grown to love so fiercely.

A look of sympathy flashed in her eyes, as if she could sense exactly what it was he was remembering. He did not want her to feel sorry for *him.* It was she who needed the sympathy, comfort, and reassurance. Reaching out a hand, he took hers lightly in his own, intent on doing just that, but a throat clearing from his left had them both turning. As they did, Nichole gently pulled her hand away.

Jo leaned forward slightly more than the others with a knowing grin on her face. "We must continue with the judgment." She reminded them softly. His gaze slid to the other sisters, *his past wives,* who all sat and watched the exchange just as intently as they had done with each telling previously.

Nichole's delicate hand, running whisper soft across his shoulder, brought his attention back to her. “I am okay, Tommy, there is no need to comfort me,” she said with a calming smile before nodding her head encouragingly at him. “Now, think of the rest so we may continue.”

Thomas closed his eyes for a moment, trying to rein in his anger once again. As he did, an image of a little boy danced before him.

Frankie.

One of the most amazing kids Tommy had ever met. The boy was full of life, spunk, and determination, reminding Tommy of himself at that age. He had loved being around Frankie, teaching him to fight while making his mother laugh at their antics. The fact that he was not Tommy’s son was not something ever dwelt on. When Tommy fell in love with Nichole, Frankie was one of those reasons. A woman that could raise such an amazing boy, all on her own, was one Tommy planned on keeping.

He remembered the moment he decided he wanted them both to be his. Plans had been quickly made in his head, how she and Frankie would meet his family, where they would live, what life would be like, but then Capone’s men intervened.

Fear, anger, and pain swelled in Thomas again as the memories ripped him apart like fresh knife wounds. Not being able to find Nichole and Frankie after the fight, Frankie missing, the sight of poor Mabel’s body... and then later, the sight of Thomas’s own parents, shot and killed for protecting the woman and child he loved.

The pain was so raw, the anger so intense, he could not stand up against it any longer. Thomas fell to his knees, pulling the shackles tight, and cried.

Nichole was at his side instantly, her hand gently rubbing circles over his back as she murmured soothing words to him. No one interrupted, each of the sisters remained sober and quiet as they allowed him the time he needed to grieve over the pain, suffering, and loss he had encountered.

Once he had calmed, Nichole lifted his face and wiped the tears away. "Are you ready now?" she asked softly.

He nodded, ready to tell his story and plead his case yet again.

Tia leaned forward. "Do you feel you gave in to wrath? If so, under what circumstances?"

With a wry twist of his lips, Thomas answered, "Wrath, it seems, was a companion throughout my life. As a child, I was physically abused by Joseph Turner, the man who owned the farm and employed my family. I hated feeling helpless and vowed to change that. Years of physical labor made my muscles big, and sneaking off to watch fights taught me how to move. I was seventeen the first time I fought back when Joe hit me. I knocked him out cold and broke his jaw."

In response to the memory, Thomas rubbed his face. "That was the last straw. I could not stay and work for him, but I would not jeopardize my parents' livelihood either. Luckily, one of the farmhands, Don, saw me throw that punch. His brother was a boxing manager in Chicago, and Don took me to him that night."

"And, after that?" Tia asked. "Were there other times?"

"Many." Thomas barked a laugh full of self-depreciation as he reseated himself. "Nichole witnessed several of my struggles, though the worst she never saw."

The women waited in silence while Thomas and Nichole exchanged a meaningful expression. The tightening around her eyes was barely visible, but it was there. For her sisters' benefit, most likely, she said, "Mikey and Jimmy."

Thomas nodded at her before addressing the other women. "Mikey and Jimmy worked the ticket booth at the arena. We were unaware at the time, but they were also on Capone's payroll." His voice shook as he tried to keep from screaming. "Those rats sold out Nichole and Frankie. I almost lost them! Why? So, those two scumbags could make a lousy buck."

"You told me you left those men alive!" Nichole pointed her finger at him accusingly.

"I did! I swear!" His eyes grew wide. "I beat them up to get them to talk, and yes, I can admit it to you here, I bloodied them more than I needed to, because I was angry and vengeful, but I promise you, I did not kill either of those men."

"Violence is not an answer to our problems," Jo said with a frown. "But I can see how your emotional state contributed to your actions. Are there any more instances you need to confess?"

"Yes." His voice cracked, and Nichole held a glass of water to his dry lips while he took several long drinks. He smiled at her gratefully before continuing. "We formulated a plan to get Frankie back and get away from Capone. I threw my fight..." His voice trailed off and he grew contemplative.

"Yes?" Tia asked, leaning forward with her eyes wide and her eyebrows raised.

"I was just thinking how much my priorities changed. There was a time when winning the boxing championship was everything, but I learned all that mattered was keeping my loved ones safe."

She smiled. "A good lesson. Please, continue."

"Unfortunately, it was easier said than done. Don, the same farmhand who helped me escape as a teenager, agreed to take Nichole and Frankie to my parents while I was preoccupied in the ring, and I planned to meet up with them as soon as I could." He tapped his fingers on his legs while his eyes filled with tears. "I did not know I was being followed by two of Capone's men. While I went and found Nichole, they killed my parents. And Don—" Thomas's muscles grew tense as he remembered "—it was Don's fault. He got greedy and made a bet. If he had left it alone, my parents would not have died."

"You cannot know that, Tommy." Nichole chastised.

At the same time, Casey asked, "Is there any way you could have repented for your sin, and did you turn your back on it or take it?"

Staring at his clenched fists, Thomas slowly relaxed his hands until they were resting on his knees. He took a deep breath, lifted his head, and met their inquiring eyes with an earnest expression. "I wanted to kill him. I felt justified in that moment. For a few seconds, I allowed wrath to embrace me like a warm cloak." His gaze landed on Nichole, and he held his hands out to her.

She stepped forward and took them in her own.

"But, through my haze of pain, I heard an angel's voice. Nichole helped me remember who I was, and I was not a man who murdered for revenge. I was not a man eaten by anger. I let him go, let wrath go, and we were able to move on with our lives. That was the last time I struggled with that sin."

Nicole's smile reached her eyes as she squeezed his hands. "He speaks the truth. We lived a long and happy life together, and even gave Frankie two younger sisters to adore. Our dreams changed when we met, fame and notoriety slipping from our grasp, but our simple life together was more than we ever hoped for."

"Thank you," Thomas said. She embraced him and stepped away, rejoining her sisters. He looked at Jo. "May I ask you a question?"

"You may," she replied, straightening herself.

"What happened to you?"

"You feared that I would be harmed?" she asked sternly.

"I died screaming out for you. The last thing I wanted was for you to pay for what I had done, or failed to do, Josephine. I loved you, even through my selfishness."

"Exactly what you feared happened, though I will spare you the details. Take the worst thing you can imagine the soldiers who took over the palace doing and increase it tenfold. That is what happened to me."

Thomas hung his head. An apology would never atone for the horrors she had endured. He had seen the extent to which those men plied their power. The soldiers were high on revenge, and everyone in their paths would have suffered in the extreme.

Josephine stepped back among her sisters where they consoled her. Even the angelic being was affected by the horrors of Jo's life, the horrors that were entirely his fault. As the women convened, guilt pulled Thomas into a state of despair. He wept openly, each sob violently shaking his body.

"Lead others as you would like to be led."

The Grove

Perhaps it is time for a break," Kelly suggested quietly to her sisters. "Clearly, Thomas needs one."

The women held hands and surrounded the weeping Thomas. The air stirred, and his vision swam. When his surroundings fell back into focus, he found himself in a small grove. The women leaned him against a sturdy olive tree, and Jo waved a hand to release his shackles. "Do not try and escape, Thomas."

The thought had not crossed his mind, but he nodded. In the tree's shade, he was cool and comfortable, and his angst slowly slid away.

Casey waved her hand, and a table appeared, laden with fruits; fragrant baked goods; and a pitcher of lemonade. "Please, join us for a snack."

They ate in companionable silence, and he remembered why he loved each of the women. They were his partners and his equal in every sense of the word. Although many of his memories were cruel and tormented him, in each life, he could find quiet moments where his heart had filled with love and joy for a particular sister.

As if sensing his thoughts, Jo smiled. "They are not all bad memories, are they?"

"I would say many of them are good." His eyes met each of theirs in turn. "I loved you each very much in the life I had with you."

Casey sat on the grass, a bunch of grapes clutched in her hand. As she picked them off and ate them, she talked to him. "Our son grew up proud and strong. After your brother and you were killed, your youngest brother took over the family property. He was good to us, and when he died way too young, he left the property to Tommy. He learned to work the land at the knee of my new husband and grew to think of him as a father."

Thomas watched the light come into her face as she spoke about her new husband, and curiosity tickled. "Who did you marry? Anyone I knew?"

She nodded. "It was Henry Smith."

"Our neighbor?"

"Yes. His wife died in childbirth, and we were very much alone on our farms after the passing of your father and brother. Of course, you know how brutal running a homestead can be when there is just one pair of hands to do the work."

"I do. I remember my father struggling, even with the hired help, until my brother and I were old enough to work. I still wear the guilt of sending Nicholas to his doom. I had hoped, in that last moment, he might survive after all." Thomas chuffed as his emotions swirled. "I suppose it was too little, too late."

While he was happy she had moved on and had a full life, he was not enjoying the idea of her with Henry. He was an impressive man with a large holding, and there were not many others around she could have done better with. Having a mild temper, and being a devout churchgoer, he always had the women swooning for him. “Henry was so big he could have pulled the plow.” Thomas chuckled.

“Yes, he could have.” Tilting her head back, she gazed at the branches overhead as though lost in thought. Her voice was soft when she spoke. “We joined the farms, and Thomas had quite the inheritance when we died. Benji left it all to our son.”

“I wish the old man had done more for my family.” A deep sigh escaped. “Did you love Henry?” He felt his face turn red, but he had to know.

“While our partnership was initially a necessity, I did grow to love him.” She closed her eyes and took a deep breath. “But never as much as I loved you.” A rogue tear slipped down her face.

“I am sorry, you know.”

As she brushed her fingertips across her chin, she nodded and turned her head away. “I do.”

Thomas’s heart broke. He hoped Tia had fared as well as Casey. Jo, Nichole, and Kelly were foregone conclusions. A shudder ripped through him as images of the soldiers’ brutality invaded his mind once again. With a shake of his head, he cleared away the thoughts and leaned toward Nichole. “Our life together was such a blessing.”

She smiled and caressed his fingers. “Yes, it was.”

He wished he already had the memories of his life with the fifth sister bestowed upon him. “How many times have you done this?” he asked.

“I have been sent as a guide to at least twenty. My sisters have had more. You are not the first. Nor will you be the last.”

“And have you always been sent to—” he gulped “—men?”

She smiled and chuckled. “No. I have guided men, women, and children. You see, my inherent nature is that of peace. I teach others how to be kind, let go of anger and regret, find forgiveness, and regard one another with love and trust.” Nichole’s eyes glazed over as though she were reliving some memory of a past life.

All the women sat, joining them on the grass.

Casey nudged him. “Would you like to hear a tale or two?”

Unsure, he nodded slightly, kind of hoping she might not notice. He was torn between wanting to know more and feeling the jealousy he knew would come from hearing tales of other men. To prevent the latter, he made a quick decision. "Could I hear the tale of a child?"

Kelly shouted and clapped her hands. "Yes! We do so love the stories of the children. Many of them are light and happy, and the little ones were able to pass on with no stains on their souls."

Tia's face softened, and she nodded. "Kelly has some wonderful tales. Since her gift is modesty, she often guides a soul through that crux in life called adolescence. It is a turning point for many a mortal." After a moment, she snapped her fingers. "Tell us of Rebecca."

"All right." Kelly's expression grew wistful. "Rebecca was a beautiful child with a voice like an angel. Her parents were wealthy and pampered her. Spoiled children often grow prideful, and Rebecca was no exception. Between her talent and her looks, she drew the attention of many men and the resentment of the women. I came into her life as a classmate. Disguised as a plain, uninteresting girl—"

"I cannot imagine that." Thomas interrupted and was rewarded with sweet, musical laughter.

"Well, it is true." Kelly smiled. "I became a target of teasing from the other children, but I gave Rebecca something to focus on besides herself. She never teased. Beneath the tarnish her soul received from mistreatment, she was a good person. She took me under her wing, and in doing so, found her own modesty. We became lifelong friends, and although she did find a career in music, it never owned her."

Thomas realized just how important these women were. Not only to him, but to mankind. "Can you share another?" he asked.

"Kelly's not the only one who works with children," Jo said. "Nichole often does, too, since she offers the gift of peace."

Casey tapped Nichole's hand. "Tell him about the little boy named Zane."

"Zane? Seems like an odd name," Thomas said.

"Yes, but it means God is gracious, so it was fitting. He was in such a need for peace. His entire life had been one struggle after another, and he was battling extreme anger with his parents over their divorce. Every time you turned around, they were squabbling over money or visitation. Zane was having several impure thoughts about harming small animals and other children. I had to do something." Nichole picked at the grass.

Thomas asked, "What happened? How did you get close to the child?"

"His father put out an ad for a nanny—with a little suggestion sent to him in a dream." She winked. "I am the one who answered, and I was hired immediately. Zane and I used to play games all day, talk about everything that was bothering him, and I even taught him how to cook!

"There was nothing in the world I would not do for that sweet child. Cooking gave him something to focus on besides his anger, and he ended up becoming a world-renowned chef with a beautiful little family he adored until he took his last breath." Rainbow tears ran down her face, and she swiped them away. "I miss him so much."

"Are you not allowed to visit those you help once your task is complete?"

"No. It would be too painful. Along with our gifts, our mothers endowed us with the ability to love with the passion of an inspired artisan. Once our heart breaks and the trials are complete, we simply cannot bear to see the subjects of our adoration again."

Rolling the idea around in his head, he became mortified at the thought of the five suffering so much heartache. It made him sick to think of them being used that way. "Who decided you ladies have to do all this? Why would anyone force you to suffer?"

"We do not suffer; we are allowed to love. Freely, with no restrictions but the assignment," Tia answered.

"How can you shoulder so much loss?" he asked.

Jo narrowed her eyes and shook her head. "It is what we were created to do. It is in our nature to be what we are. Would you ask a tree to do something other than reach for the sun or bury roots in the ground day after day? Do you think it is sad doing what it was created to do? Would you lament its inability to move around freely?"

"No."

"Then do not assume we are in misery because we are doing something you find difficult." She widened her eyes.

"Point taken. But you never answered my first question." For some reason he could not fathom, he felt like he needed to know who cast the women's lots.

"Our mothers."

"Why can they not do it? You said they are the three fates, right? Does that not give them the power to fulfill the assignments?"

She sighed. "Yes, but they grew tired of laboring over guiding each human on the path they were meant to follow, so they created us from their lifelines. Atropos chose to cut three, and her sisters, Lachesis and Clotho—my mother—each cut one. They dropped the five segments into a cauldron, and we arose, draped in beauty—even as infants—and endowed with gifts."

"Gifts?" Thomas was intrigued beyond his wildest imagination.

"You already know of two: peace, which belongs to Nichole, and modesty, which is Kelly's gift. Tia was given faithfulness, Casey generosity, and I was given the gift of self-control. As my sister stated before, we are the antithesis of the seven mortal sins. Therefore, we are sent to guide humans in need of direction." Jo smiled. "Do you understand?"

"So, how was I brought into all this?" His nerves were frayed as he wondered what path he was supposed to have taken in life. "Did I complete my path?"

Tia said, "Your case was a special one, for it was not judged on one life, but six."

"Six!" Shock caused him to yell the word, and the women flinched. "Sorry. Six?"

"You have seen a bit of your first life, the one that held such an egregious error, and you were returned to be tested five times. While we were able to guide you and help you right the wrongs committed by living five, pure lives, we were not allowed to interfere with your decisions once made." She turned her mouth down.

"Can you tell me more, or give me more memories, of my first life?" While he was terrified to learn what kind of sin could have landed him in what was really a prison, his heart ached to know. He clutched the hem of his tunic between his fingers and pulled the fabric taught time and again over the atrocity that had been only hinted at.

Putting her hand on his, she gave him a small smile. "No. I am sorry. We cannot speak of it yet. You are to receive those memories last, before your judgment is delivered."

"I see. But why was my trial handed to your mothers?"

"That is something you will learn in time."

Their vague answers were annoying him, but he pressed on. "And what of your necklaces? I noticed they have words on them when I first saw Nichole's. Now that I see the rest, I find myself a bit confused. If I am remembering correctly, they were blank in your lives with me."

Jo answered, "They are gifts from our mothers, created to tie us to this realm and guide us on our journeys through yours."

Leaning forward, he paused. "May I?"

She leaned toward him. "Of course."

Carefully, he fingered the cool metal bars, turning them over as he examined them. "Sloth and gluttony?"

"They are the sins I am responsible for guiding man away from."

"I see." Clarity sank in, and he released his hold on the necklace to scratch his chin. "You have wise mothers."

Laughing, Jo said, "Yes. They are wise indeed."

He opened his mouth to ask another question, but Nichole interrupted, "I want another story! Casey, tell us of the time you were sent to Cleopatra!"

The mood was considerably lightened as Casey told her story, and they chatted amicably for a few more minutes before Jo announced it was time to return to the trial.

Everyone stood and brushed the grass from their clothing.

With a sweep of an arm, Casey made the table and its remnants disappear. Then the grove faded out, and they were once again in the white place.

“Please, return to your chair,” Tia said.

Once he sat, the shackles bound him as though manipulated by invisible hands. “I will not run. On my honor,” he said.

“You could not get out if you tried,” Kelly replied with a small smile. “Do you see a door?”

He did not. It was not something he had noticed before she called it to his attention. The room was both confining and seemed to go on forever.

“It is mandated,” Nichole explained. “We do not set the rules. We just follow them.”

As the women sat, he tracked them with his eyes.

“Are we ready to proceed, sisters?” Jo asked before he could question who did set the rules. Not that he minded the interruption; he had a pretty good idea of the responsible parties already.

"Every time you cast judgment, another piece of your character is revealed."

Trial of T-Dogg
Lust

"My apologies. I should not have taken my seat." Tia stood and approached him. Rather than the gentle brush of a hand, she gazed into his eyes.

Pain flashed through him, stealing his sight and causing his stomach to cramp. Wrapping both arms around his middle, he leaned over as the memories slammed into him.

"What is happening? Is it too much?"

He could hear her questions, but the bile in his mouth and rising nausea were causing his ears to ring. She sounded so far away. Gasping, he tried to hear the answer.

Not sounding the least bit alarmed, one of the ladies responded, "This is the fifth life of memories. It is normal. Just wait until he gets the rest of the ones from his first life. That will be agony. You have souls experience this before. Do not fret."

Panic mixed with the searing pain, and he dry heaved until his sides ached. It felt like ages until the sensation passed. When it did, he sat up and took a deep breath as he accessed the memories he had been given.

"Perhaps, while he is recovering, sister," Kelly spoke to Tia. "You can describe the events to us from your point of view. How did you come to know him in this lifetime?"

He studied her movements as she glided closer to him. Something on the edge of his memory begged for recognition.

"I called you Tommy, but you were T-Dogg to your friends," Tia said.

As soon as the words left her lips, an avalanche of the crispest memories assaulted him. They came so fast and clear, his head ached with the jarring images. Guns, drugs, and sex. Over and over again. Something about that life felt dark and cold.

"Do you remember?" she asked.

He nodded. "You were so beautiful. Although every part of me wanted you, I knew you were safer without me as your lover."

"I almost cannot remember a time when I did not love him. We lived in a very unsafe part of town, and he had to do what was necessary to survive and keep those he loved safe. It was never easy. Many a night I sat in bed, clutching the covers, as the sound of gunfire ricocheted through the air outside. I would whisper a prayer that I would see him again the next day. Drugs and gangs permeated our neighborhood."

Squeezing his eyes shut, he recalled more than one occasion of taking a man's life over some turf issue or drug deal gone bad.

Guns.

Drugs.

Sex.

Little else filled his mind. A cacophony of orgasmic responses, moans, grunts, gunfire, screams, and intense music left him feeling sick, and he put a hand on either side of his head, hoping he could squeeze hard enough to drown it out.

"This lifetime challenged T-Dogg with lust. On this sin, how do you believe he fared?" Jo asked.

Tia seemed lost in thought for a moment, and he wondered if she would even answer.

Jo cleared her throat.

Tia shot a glance her sister's way. "To put it more in the terms of the time... he screwed everything that walked."

He gulped. There was no denying her words. In a time filled with constant danger and loss, sex became an escape.

"So, then, how do you respond to the allegation of lust?" Jo asked him.

Thomas bowed his head, shame taking root deep in his gut. It was the fifth time he had gone through the pain, reliving and rehashing a life that was less than perfect. Admitting his faults and begging forgiveness was the only thing to do, but it was not easy. In fact, having the woman he loved in that life stand before him as he admitted his faults was killing him. The fact that he slept with more women than most in his short life, but never truly appreciated the one that mattered, made him regret his actions and despise having to voice them aloud.

Inhaling deeply, his chest expanded with the action. His lungs filled then emptied, but the weight of what he was doing did not leave him as his breath did. So, he did the only thing he could to help relieve some of the weight that lay upon his shoulders. He braced himself as he looked up and met the eyes of the one he loved in that life. "There is no denying that I am guilty of this sin."

Once the words had left his mouth, the room remained eerily silent. His eyes met that of each sister, but when they came to rest once again on Tia, his heart broke as a lone tear slid down her cheek. On instinct, he tried to lift his hand, intent on wiping the tear from her soft skin, but he was reminded of his restraints when he was unable to reach her.

Tia held her hand up. "No, I am fine."

"But you are crying," Thomas stated, confusion flowing through him like a fountain.

Tia shook her head as she wiped the tear away and blinked the unshed ones back as well. "Do not mistake my tears. I am not crying because I am ashamed, or hurt, by your admission. In fact, it is just the opposite. The memory I have of you and our life together is very vivid and fresh because it is the last life I lived as well. Although my heart still aches for the love we were denied, I am also proud. You were not a man known for admitting when he was wrong. So, for you to admit your faults, and own them in the way you are, is very unlike the Tommy I knew. It makes me proud to see you as this man."

Thomas shook his head. "I am not a man to be proud of. The life we shared together was one I am ashamed of. I was a kid from the hood that grew up to be a drug dealer. I threatened and killed anyone that questioned my authority or tried to move in on my turf. And just as you have said, I had sex with anything that walked and was willing. I am not even sure how it was that you came to love me."

Tia stood and swiftly moved across the room until she was standing just before Thomas. Kneeling, she gripped his biceps tightly, her eyes boring into his. "Yes, you are correct."

Thomas's eyes widened with disappointment.

Tia's fingers increased pressure like a vice, slowly, painfully. "But..." she said in a voice that commanded he give her his attention. "You were also much more than that. You were exceptionally smart and an extraordinary musician. To your friends, you were loyal to a fault, but more importantly, you loved your family fiercely and selflessly. You loved them so much you sacrificed yourself, your dreams, and ultimately, your life, so your parents would be safe and your sister could have a future. You may have committed many sins, but the good you did, the sacrifices you made, far outweighed the bad. At the core, you were a very good man. A man I loved easily."

Thomas shook his head, still not agreeing with the words Tia spoke. "You should never have fallen for me. Had you not, you would still be alive as we speak, living the rest of your life. I am sure you would have graduated college, probably with an art degree, met a man, and fallen in love. All the sacrifices you speak of would have paid off. All the reasons I tried so hard to stay away from you would have afforded you the life I always knew you deserved, the life you were meant to have."

"The life I was meant to have was the one I did have. I—"

Before Tia could continue to try and convince him of his worth, she was interrupted by Nichole. "Tia, I think we have heard enough."

Tia looked back at her sisters, each of them giving her a stern, yet understanding, look. The time had come. Giving a slight nod, Tia turned back to Thomas.

Recognition was clear in his eyes. He knew the time for pleading his case was over. All his lives with the sisters had been revealed, and the sins he committed within each lifeline divulged. The women would convene and discuss if his excuses and reasons for such sins were justified. They would determine his fate.

"A man can only walk so far in one pair of shoes; after that, he must find new soles, stop his journey, or be brave enough to continue barefoot."

The Judgments

The five sisters held hands, a chain of blinding beauty mixed with fury, love, and grief. He felt the same emotions roiling through him, bubbling just beneath the surface of his skin, and he ached. His head, his heart, his hands—how they longed to reach out for the women he had loved. Others had gone through the trials before, had lived lives at an attempt at... *What? Redemption?* Thomas was not sure he deserved the chance at all, let alone the blessing of having such amazing women in his lives. *Had the other people been confused or ashamed at having loved so fully, so incredibly, in each life? Had they been able to compartmentalize it all as he was doing?*

His love for Tia was different from that of her sisters, for instance, but no less. He loved them each for reasons only they knew, for traits only they owned. Whatever the women were—harbingers, fates, angels—they were part his. They held his heart as much as memories of them and their lives together were etched upon his own.

"It is time," Kelly said. "To remind you of your original life."

7

She snapped her fingers, and every detail of that first existence flooded his mind.

Twelve. He was one of the twelve.

His name was...

"Judas," Kelly murmured.

Like lightning, the pain and shame of what he had done lanced his heart. As it continued to assault him, all the memories of his first life blasted his insides to pieces. He writhed in the chair, straining the chains to their fullest length, wishing he would die rather than have to endure a moment more.

Leaning over, he retched several times, the small meal he had shared with the women presenting itself and splashing over the pristine floor. He coughed and wheezed as the wind was stolen from his lungs. Still, the memories came.

Twelve. There were a dozen pieces of the abhorrent metal given to him for the information he provided. They burned as they lay in his hand; just as the words he spoke in exchange peeled back the flesh as they passed his lips.

His friend and companion, made to walk on the hard roads in nothing but a shabby pair of sandals as he was humiliated. Items thrown at his head. Taunts screamed at him by women and children lining the streets.

I did that.

Greed had owned Judas's heart when he gave over the one man who had always been gentle, kind, and compassionate. All with a kiss. Such a simple gesture revealed his savior and damned the man to his accusers' wrath. The ultimate betrayal resulted in more guilt than one man could bear.

"I am not worthy of your justness!" Judas cried as tears streamed down his face.

Nichole smiled. "If you were not worthy, you would not have been given this opportunity."

Tears clogged his throat, gagging him on the truth he was trying to swallow. "But I betrayed him... and you. I was not good enough in my first life. I certainly did not improve in the others afforded to me."

"I wish I could have known you before, to see what was truly in your heart at the time of your betrayal," Kelly whispered. "Though I am happy to see you as you looked in your first life."

Judas stared at his calloused, olive-toned hands and long arms. From his eyes, he brushed away strands of the wavy, dark hair that hung to his shoulders. While he appeared different in each of the trial lives, he had returned to his original form.

All at once, it came together; the dreams haunting him nightly, reminding him of the betrayal, trying to break through and be known.

He looked at each face, weighed down with sadness and heaviness, and he knew. He knew he wanted it to end for them. It was too much.

7

Panting, he managed to ask, “May I say something before you begin?”

“You may,” answered Jo.

“I don’t deserve this. After my first life... the things I did, the betrayal of someone so pure and perfect. I did not deserve a second chance at all, let alone five of them. And I do not deserve redemption or mercy from you. I put each of you through hell. Each of you suffered because of me.” He looked at Jo. “Some worse than others, but all equally heartbreaking. Just send me where I deserve to go. Know I truly loved each of you.”

A second question caused his brows to knit, but he had to ask. “Have you all always looked so beautiful? Do you change with each person you guide, with each life you lead?”

Casey giggled, the dimple flashing at him. “Our appearance never changes, only our circumstances.”

“But I remember you so differently.”

She brushed his long hair back. “You see what you wish to see. It is that way with all humans.”

“And sometimes, we add a little persuasion to see us in a certain light, as was the case with Rebecca,” Kelly said with a laugh.

“What of my name? Why was I Thomas when I arrived?”

Tia tilted her head to one side. “Judas is the original form of Thomas, of course, but we could not have you using such an obvious moniker. As Judas, you were infamously known as the betrayer, and someone would have told you that. If you think the reinstatement of your memories was a painful experience now… Just be happy we changed it."

His mouth went dry.

Jo beckoned Casey back. "It is time."

Judas gulped as he watched them gather once again. When they leaned toward one another, the table and chairs disappeared, and their voices were amplified as they discussed his fate.

With an upward sweep of her hand, Jo took the lead. "I was prepared to damn him to fail. In light of the evidence he presented, I am not sure I can do that. I suffered greatly, yes, but it was not by his hand. He tried to rectify the wrongdoings and atone for his mistakes. I blamed him. I thought he betrayed me. Here, I have discovered I was mistaken on all counts."

Tia interjected. "All humans sin. It is part of their humanity. I think we must judge how he chose to react to each sin. What he did to overcome it. Or, when time ran out or was limited, what paths he took to rectify his wrongs. He has freely admitted to committing most of these sins. But I want to discuss how he tried to amend them."

"I agree," Jo said. "What he did was not as important as what he learned from his mistakes, and how he tried to correct them after the fact should hold heavy weight on our considerations." She sighed. "Which makes this all the more difficult. I cannot damn him to repeat life when he risked life and limb to save us both. What say you?"

Nichole nodded, agreeing with her sisters. "He may have committed many sins, but he made up for them in many of his lives. Risking his own life, and sometimes even sacrificing it, to protect the ones he loved."

"We must also keep in mind, that although he was judged for a particular sin in a given lifetime, how he handled the other aspects of his life and faced the other sins not being judged. It is those acts that show his true self," Kelly added, her brows drawn.

The women are as fair as they are beautiful, Judas thought.

Jo moved her head up and down slowly. "You are all wise in your suggestions. We must also not be blinded by our love, or the sin we were to judge. All facets must be brought to attention." She panned her eyes around the circle, stopping on Kelly. "How did Sir Thomas fare in the six other sins?"

Smiling first at Judas, Kelly said, "Sir Thomas was a pious man. He loved his family and his Lord. He was faithful to me, although in his prominent position, he surely had offers from ladies of the court. When my own reputation was questioned, he trusted me and remained by my side. He held no hatred, even for those who sought to destroy his career." She paused and considered, nodding as she added, "Yes, in all aspects but pride, my Thomas was a very good man."

Judas's heart ached. Her words were full of truth. He was devoted to her and their daughter throughout his life, but his wife grew ill and died because he gambled his position on pride and lost. No matter how devout he became, no matter how well he lived his life, it would never make up for destroying hers.

"It was the same in Rome. He was kind, faithful, loving, and a hard worker until he fell in with Nero." Jo spun around suddenly. "Judas, was there a time when you lent yourself to the lust the other men had for concubines?"

"That was a temptation ever-present in the palace, anywhere Nero was, really. And there were times when I *did* look at the women presented to the inner circle. But, Josephine, I swear to you, I remained faithful. It was only you for me. I lost myself inside that place, but I never lost you. You were always with me, in here," he said, placing a hand over his chest. "That said, I was not a good man. I became what I swore I would never be. I let Rome down. I let you down, and I will forever be sorry for that."

"There is no shame in repentance. Thank you." She turned back to her sisters and addressed the next in the circle.

Judas noticed her hand, daintily covering her heart, shook slightly as though his admission had affected her more than she realized.

"Casey, how did your Thomas fare?"

With her shoulders back, Casey stepped away from her sisters toward Judas once more. "My Thomas was a good man. He was wholesome, loving, and hardworking. I wish you all could have seen him. Where Nicholas was concerned, he was envious, but if I am being honest, I understood it. It ate away at him, and I hated that it hurt him so much. Those types of sins, the ones that crawl beneath the skin and eat away at a person slowly, are the worst, I think." She watched him nod, barely perceptible. "Are there any other sins you'd like to speak about during your life with me, Judas?"

"Although greed and envy ruled many of my days during that time, my greatest sin was placing those feelings above my love for you. For not being able to see past what I did not have to what I had. On the battlefield, I realized I wanted nothing more than to come home to you. But it was too late. I only had one choice at that point: whether to save my brother or not. I chose to do what I could to save him, hoping it would lead me back to you, but I waited too long." He hung his head, shaking it back and forth, his eyes never leaving the ground. "If only I had made the decision sooner. If only I had put our love first."

"Every human takes the ones they love for granted," Casey whispered so only he could hear.

Judas looked up and shook his head. "You did not."

"I was not human," she argued.

"Were you not? In your lives, you lived as a human. You made mistakes, fought to live and survive like everyone else. You were not infallible. Yet you did not fail. Not like me."

Casey gasped and put her hand over her heart. It was as if the memories and emotions were invisible threads linking her heart and life with his own.

Her reaction brought a smile forth on his lips. She certainly seemed human in that moment. *Perhaps there is hope for me after all.*

Giving an upward movement with her head, Casey gazed at Nichole. "It is your turn, sister. What say you?"

"Tommy saved me. The first time I ever met him, he rescued me from a fate that was sure to be painful and deadly." Nichole whispered, her eyes staring off in the distance at the memory. "I had a son, one that I worked hard to take care of on my own. Had Thomas not been there that night..." she shook her head and focused on her sisters once again.

"A man that steps in and saves a stranger is a good man. I knew that the moment I laid eyes on him. After that night, I trusted him not only with myself, but with the one thing I held closest to my heart, my son. He treated us as if we were the most precious things in the world to him. He loved my son as if he were his own. That takes a special kind of person. And then, when my son was threatened, Tommy took care of us again. He protected us and did what he had to do to keep us safe. To make sure we stayed a family. He not only put himself in danger, but he lost his parents in doing so." Nichole looked each one of her sisters in the eye. "I do not condone the sins he has committed, but I do feel he has more than made up for them."

"Thank you for your kind words," Judas said. "Do you have any questions for me?" Hot tears carved paths down his face, flowing rivers of relief, love, and sadness.

"In our life together, you were often my savior. Mine and Frankie's. You gave up your family to save us. Do you regret it?"

Judas lowered his head for a moment. When he looked up, his eyes were fierce. "Losing my parents was hard. They were the source of my only good memories from childhood, and they loved me very much. I wished I had more time with them, but I never blamed you or Frankie. I blamed Capone, but at that point, I only wanted to get away and start a new life with you."

Nichole reached up and wiped the tear from her cheek. "How could you not have blamed me? From the moment we met, your life was turned upside down. Because of me, your parents died."

"I could never blame you. I was a broken man when I met you, scarred from abuse, scarred from fights, lost in my own anger. You gave me something real to fight for. A family of my own. Love. My career was nothing compared to the light that you and Frankie brought into my life. I lost my parents, but I found myself in my time with you. We truly *lived.*"

Nichole smiled softly at him, tears still streaming down her face, and then she turned to her sisters. "This is why I loved this man and why I cannot condemn him to relive yet another trial. He may not have been perfect, but he did the best he could given the circumstances."

Judas scanned each face before him, and his eyes landed on Tia's. He knew she had yet to speak her mind on his fate. Of the five, the time with her was filled with the most sin.

Wringing her hands, she paced in a small circle before turning her attention to him. "Our life together was marked by violence, yet I knew you loved me. I understood your lack of choice in our surroundings, in the constant peril we found ourselves in. You sacrificed a life of your own to keep me safe, to provide a possible future where there was none. Yet, I often wondered if you ever considered leaving it all behind, running away with me so that we could make a new life together. I knew you had your sister to protect, but did it ever cross your mind to get your loved ones to safety? Including me?"

"No," Judas shook his head, eyes determined like Tia remembered from her life with him. "I had no way to take care of you all, protect you, or provide for you if we left. I was a kid born to run the streets. Had we left, no one would have given me the time of day, much less a chance to actually make something of myself. I knew my parents would not leave, so my only option was to protect you and Chantel, make sure you had everything I could give you, and get the two of you out of there."

Tia's gaze never left Judas, and she began nodding about halfway through his response. "Life on the streets was tough. I know. Without you, I would have had no opportunity to leave. For that, I was always grateful. But, I did struggle during our life together. Every time I saw you with another woman, I questioned what I thought we had. I wondered why I put my faith in you. What can you say to me now about your lustful ways? About all the women? How could you love me and do that?"

Judas looked up and took a deep breath. When his gaze dropped back to Tia's, some of the determination had dimmed. "Like I said before, I am guilty of that sin. My only excuse is that I was selfish. I loved you so much, and although I wanted nothing but the best for you, I also did not want to lose you. Those girls, they were merely a distraction, a way to keep me from thinking about the day you would leave me, and I would never see you again."

With glistening eyes, Tia whispered her next question. "Did you ever consider coming to me? Letting me love you? You took so many women to your bed, but never me. Never me." A sob tore through her last word.

"I could never do that to you. You were more than that. You *deserved* more than that. I may have committed many sins, but allowing you to commit them as well was not something I was willing to do. You were all that was good in the hell that I lived in."

"I appreciate you looking out for me. In that capacity, you never failed. Deep down, I knew sex never equated love for you. In a way, I always knew by not asking me for sex, something I would have freely given, you were showing me how much you did love me." Tia knelt down on one knee, a hand outstretched to Judas. "Although you are guilty of lust, you never let it ruin what *we* had. And in the end, you died protecting me."

"I only wish I had saved you," Judas bowed his head in defeat.

"During our life in Rome, you were my everything: my soldier, savior, lover, and friend. I want you to know how much I loved you, and I know how much you loved me in return." With a kind smile, Jo looked into Judas's eyes, certainly bloodshot from the tears he had shed. His lip quivered as he knelt in submission, in surrender. "The most important thing, as we have finally learned, sisters, is that the man Judas was when he betrayed the one he pledged his life to protect, is not the man he is now. It is because of the journey, because of the five lives and seven sin trials, that he has become the man kneeling before us. He is repentant. He is redeemable. Every soul is. Some just take longer to realize it."

Tia stepped forward. "You do realize it, do you not?"

Judas nodded. "I have learned so much from each of you. The gifts of wisdom you have bestowed enriched my soul."

Casey smiled, looking up toward a bright light filling the space from above. "I vote for redemption. You are deserving, Judas, not because of the mistakes you have made, but because you realize them and are repentant, because of the love that fills every part of you and makes you more than you were before you had it." Light radiated from her skin, from her hair and eyes. Every part of her shone as though the heavens were trapped beneath her skin, trying to escape their confines.

As one, the women joined hands and formed a circle, lifting their voices. "Mothers, we have judged. Come forth and hear our pleas!"

Judas's chair disappeared, and he rose to his full height, not daring to move.

In a flash of light, three haggard old women appeared in the center of the ring the sisters made with their clasped hands. They bowed deeply.

Jo's voice rang out. "Welcome, mothers."

They broke the circle, and one of the old ones stepped forward. She had a silvery white streak in her hair, and her voice sounded like a thousand viper hisses when she spoke. "Tell us."

"Atropos, I believe I should go first, as I spent the first lifetime with Judas. Allow me to show you."

Nodding, Atropos wheezed and held out her hand. Jo took it and gazed into the eyes of the eldest mother. Lights flashed between their palms, and Jo seemed to fall into a trance. Rainbows scattered the room and fell in pools of swirling color. In them was the entire story of Thomitus's life in Rome. One ghosted image after another played out across the colors, Nero, war, sweaty men raping innocent women.

Judas gasped when he saw a flash of Jo in the vineyard with lips stained from the grapes she had teased him with by eating one after another. Then, a brief moment of his lips on her neck as she sat at her mirror. It was too much, but it was over far too soon for his liking. He yearned to see more, be reminded of more, go back and taste the wine once again. As the colors faded to silver and dissipated, he groaned.

In a voice that sounded hollow, devoid of emotion, and deeper than her usual tone, she said, "I find the betrayer, Judas, to be forgiven for his crimes against the one known as Jesus."

Sparks flew between the two women, and Jo collapsed on the ground.

Alarmed, Judas let out a cry.

"It is okay, Judas. That is part of the process. Jo will recover shortly." Kelly stepped forward to take her mother's hand. When their palms touched, an aura of silver glowed around their bodies and a breeze lifted strands of their long hair. An old melody, long forgotten, played through the room, and in it, the details of Sir Thomas's life were shared. When the song ended, Kelly spoke in a similarly hollow voice. "I find the betrayer, Judas, to be absolved from the sins of his betrayal."

The colors and wind died when the connection broke, and Kelly slipped to the floor in a heap.

Casey approached Atropos with caution, stepping over her sisters' prone bodies. She glanced at Judas. The old woman's wrinkled hands enveloped Casey's youthful ones, and a gasp tore from her throat. An impenetrable beam of shimmering white light spilled from her lips. The old woman watched as the scenes, one after another, flashed onto the light beam. Lieutenant Thomas, as he had been known, had been quite the life lesson, it turned out. His hands on Casey's pregnant stomach, her lips pressing softly upon his, anger furrowing his brow when his brother approached on a stallion that should have belonged to Thomas. Judas couldn't tamp down the emotions that threatened to reignite.

His heart beat erratically, and he couldn't catch his breath. More scenes filtered from Casey's mouth. His father sitting behind a desk. It was the moment he told Thomas his life meant nothing, that his brother would inherit Thomas's childhood home, would go to college, would always be more, and he would be less. Casey's sobbing form when she lost their first child. It was too much.

"Stop!" he cried. "Please, stop."

But, Judas's pleas were ignored. Atropos watched, her eyes taking in everything, sharp as the eye of a hawk despite her age. Then came the images of their son, of their son with another man as his father, and Casey as another man's wife. It damn near killed Judas to behold.

With a loud boom, Casey's mouth snapped shut, and the light show was over. The images were burnt into his mind, and his body shook from the visual assault. Sure, she had told him about marrying their neighbor, but seeing it was more than Judas could bear.

Atropos squeezed Casey's hand as if awakening her. Instead of coming back to life, she fell into a similar trance, her voice ringing out strong and sure, nothing like the sweet voice he was used to. "I find the betrayer, Judas Iscariot, redeemed." Casey collapsed immediately next to her sisters. Before she fell, Judas lunged forward to try to catch her, but an invisible force pinned him against an equally invisible wall.

"Do not move!" said another of the old women. She was taller than the other two and very thin, missing the fingernail on the digit she extended. "I am Clotho, and you will show my sister respect!"

His upper lip shook with exertion. It was as if his body was being crushed, and he couldn't lift the weight off it. "I am sorry." It rasped out between difficult breaths.

"Release him," Atropos ordered quietly, and Clotho waved her hand toward Judas. He fell to his knees, gasping for air. The skin at his neck felt hot, as though hands had choked him. Those three wrinkled hags were perhaps more powerful than their daughters. *I would be wise to be cautious.*

The third of the elderly women spoke. "We have a majority, but would like to hear from our final two daughters."

"I agree, Lachesis." Atropos motioned to Nichole. "It is your turn."

She stepped forward, placing her hand within the woman's. "Mother," Nichole said with a smile.

As soon as their hands connected, the light show began, bouncing off each other and creating a screen effect where they crossed. Images of Nichole in the dark alley, a brute's arms roughly forcing her farther back. The bruises Tommy tended, the dance they shared, and the quiet cab ride home. Then Frankie, a boy so filled with life he was impossible not to love. Images of the family they would become, the love they shared, and how happy they were together made Judas smile, but it didn't last long. The wonders they shared passed all too quickly to reveal the horrors.

His stomach tightened with anger and sadness at the image of Capone and his men. What they had done to Nichole's landlady—that poor woman—and how they had taken Frankie. Then later, what they had driven Tommy to do, and the loss he had suffered because of them. It ripped through him as if it were happening all over again.

While still holding Nichole's hands, Atropos watched him closely, as did the other elders. He refrained from lashing out again, knowing it would be in vain. Bile rose in his throat, but he held it in, waiting to see what would happen next. Just as with her sisters before her, Nichole was awakened from the trance, her voice strong when she stated, "I find the betrayer, Judas, absolved of his sins." Then, like the other three, she slipped into unconsciousness and melted to the floor.

Only one daughter was left standing, but she did not appear afraid. In fact, her expression was almost eager.

"Come here, child," Atropos wheezed to the final sister.

When Tia stepped forward, she almost tripped over the pile of her sisters.

Atropos caught her daughter's hands, with more strength than the old woman should have possessed, and held her child up. Although the smallest of the three mothers, not a single muscle bulged at the effort of lifting Tia.

Judas flinched, and a ribbon of awe tied itself around his middle at the herculean display.

"I am sorry, Mother."

Again, the raspy snake voice issued forth. "I hope you are over your clumsiness."

Like a scolded child, Tia nodded and stared at the floor while she grasped her mother's hands, and the exchange began.

Tia's head jerked back, her mouth fell agape, and dark scenes of alleys and poorly lit street corners flew from her as life regurgitated. Everything was so dark in comparison to the others' memories, Judas struggled to see detailed images. Then, one flash of bright white followed by another gradually illuminated a particular scene, and it crept to the forefront.

Judas remembered it all too well. Cradling Tia in his arms, clutching her as she professed her love, he watched the light drain from her eyes and felt her body go limp. Then, a rage of loss erupted from T-Dogg as a guttural scream and reverberated throughout the space. Judas watched as his body jerked with the force of bullets ripping through his chest. Dark red liquid oozed down his shirt as he fell next to the lifeless form of his beloved.

Judas's nails pierced the rugged skin of his palm, his fists clenched from the moment the image came forth, and a thin line of blood trickled past his wrists and around to his forearm. His hands shook as he unfurled his fingers. Deep creases—lifelines he was once told—were etched in crimson blood. He squeezed his eyes shut, unable to witness another devastating moment from his lives. His heart constricted with pain and loss.

An eerie silence came over the room, and he lifted his lids with hesitation.

"You have come this far, do not succumb to your feelings now," Atropos said, her voice an octave lower than the last time she spoke.

He knew what would come next as he saw Tia's eyes flutter and the light within them begin to shine again. Her words would bring absolution or condemnation.

"What say you?" Atropos prodded when Tia hesitated, her eyes glued to Judas. Their connection seized his breathing as he awaited her judgment.

"I stand with my sisters and find the betrayer, Judas, absolved of his sins. "As she uttered the final word, her body collapsed onto another.

Judas pulsed with the need to take Tia into his arms and cradle her as he had done before, to gather each of his loves into his embrace, but Atropos waved her finger back and forth in front of him while clicking her tongue. “No, no, no. She will return to us. They all will. Do not fear. Do not lose your focus.

“All the judgments have been heard,” she said, her voice like a thousand knives drilling into his head. “Our daughters have found you to be redeemed. Do you have final words, betrayer?”

He paled as her eyes pierced through him. All he could do was shake his head and tremble in fear. Five women lay on the floor in a heap, and he could do nothing to help them or himself. Gathering all his courage, he voiced the question that had been nagging at him since the memories of his first life were returned. “W... Why were you three charged with my fate? I held belief in the Christian God in my first life, and thought you three to be the creation of Pagan lunatics. Should it not have been His task to decide what should happen with my soul?”

Chuckling, Atropos turned the corners of her mouth up into a sneer. “Would you prefer the one who fathered the man you condemned to death to have the ultimate decision in your fate?”

Judas’s blood drained to his feet, and he felt his cheeks grow cold.

"He propositioned us to find another way, believing as He always does that His creations are redeemable. While you were the catalyst in His son's demise, you were also one of the twelve, a recipient of Jesus's teachings. You were, and are, a special case."

Clotho and Lachesis cackled.

"Do you understand now, betrayer?"

He nodded and swallowed around a tongue that felt as though it had been dipped in sand.

"Then be silent, and let us complete our task." Atropos turned back to her sisters. "We have seen and heard all there is. Do we give the power of the judgment over to our daughters in this most important trial?"

Lachesis was the one who answered. "This is what they were created to do. We do not have time to tend every life. I say, let it be as they deem. They are as wise as they are beautiful and terrible."

Clotho nodded.

"You, Judas Iscariot, the betrayer, have been found redeemed." Atropos clapped her hands, and the three old women disappeared.

As the light from the old ones' exit faded, the five sisters awakened.

Judas rushed to them, helping them to their feet, embracing each one in turn. Once they were all standing, and he was assured they were fully recovered, he spoke. "Thank you for having forgiveness in your hearts. A man like me, who erred so egregiously, does not deserve your love. But I am grateful for it. Your mothers have accepted your council, and my soul has been freed. Because of all of you."

Jo hugged him. "You are a good man. Everyone errs, but those with a pure heart find their way to redemption. Go, Judas, and let it end with peace."

He embraced each of the remaining sisters one last time and turned in a circle, seeking an exit.

A path, full of light, with a riot of colors bouncing in circles, opened in the middle of the room and floated there. The scent of flowers filled the air, along with a sense of joy. Judas found himself being pulled toward the opening.

Casey blew him a kiss. "Goodbye, Judas."

One foot in front of the other, he slowly walked into the spiraling mass of luminescence. As his body was consumed, he sighed. He was finally free.

The End

Turn the page for part seven, an exciting bonus short story:

Fate of the Fates

Part Seven

Fate of the Fates

"Perhaps a mother's greatest gift to the world is her offspring. Hope for the next generation."

Fate of the Fates

The Fates, known to most as Clotho, Lachesis, and Atropos, controlled the lives and destinies of mortals. Although the goddesses had a most important job, they grew weary of it and each other. What they longed for most was to give life from their own flesh and blood. Atropos, especially, longed for this, for she was the one to take it from mankind.

On a particularly cold and bleak evening, the goddesses huddled near the hearth, rubbing their arms to find warmth and discussing their bleak lives.

Clotho, tired of always complaining about things and not taking action, rose and paced while she chastised her sisters. "Why can we not control our own fate? What is stopping us from creating daughters of our own? On this eve, we shall do just that."

She crossed to the mantle and brought down a beautiful box, carved from ivory and accented with gold. With a gentle caress of the cover, she lifted the lid and pulled out three golden strings.

Lachesis gasped. "We must use our lifelines?"

With a gentle smile, Clotho nodded at her sister. “How else can we give life except through our own? Giving over a piece of one’s body is how the mortals do it, though their process is a lot messier. We shall do the same.”

Atropos, eager to bring forth hope rather than instill fear, took her lifeline from her sister and cut three even pieces. While the other two watched, a ribbon of Atropos’s silky raven hair turned white, and she winced. Unbothered beyond the spark of pain, she clutched the three segments to her heart and handed the remainder of the string back to her sister to place in the box.

Encouraged by their sister’s brave act, Clotho and Lachesis each cut a segment from their lines, similar in length to the ones Atropos cuddled.

Clotho cried out when she cut her line and a fingernail fell off her left hand.

“There must be pain in order for us to feel indebted to our creations, as you mentioned,” Atropos said. “Lachesis, are you well?”

Lachesis’s arms were wrapped tightly around her abdomen, but she nodded.

“Then, let us proceed.”

The sisters dropped the five segments in a boiling pot, and Lachesis stirred.

The liquid changed from black tar to shimmery, silvery ichor, and a scent filled the air that was both floral and joyful. Music, encapsulating all the orchestral instruments, flowed from an unknown source and filled the room.

"You first," Clotho whispered to Atropos. "You were the bravest one."

Atropos rested her hands on the side of the cauldron and peered in. The heat did not scald her; as a goddess, she was immune to such mortal dangers. "My daughters." She spoke in hushed tones. "You will be fair and wise. Mankind accuses me of being unjust, not allowing them to choose their own destiny. I give you as a gift to them, to guide them, and to help them make wise decisions."

In response, the liquid bubbled and sizzled. Three silver spheres rose and floated into the waiting arms of their mother. With a gentle *pop*, the globes morphed into three beautiful baby girls.

Holding up the first baby with downy, white blonde hair, Atropos said, "I name you Nichole, and you will be the harbinger of peace. When mortal souls tremble with bitterness and rage, you will bring them the gift to forgive and let go of resentment and regret."

She held up the second baby, whose head was adorned with bountiful curls, and kissed her plump, rosy cheeks. "You, my darling, I name Casey, and your gift is generosity. When man finds himself laden with greed and envy, you will encourage him to share what he has, celebrate the success of others, and be richer for it."

The last baby she cuddled close, breathing in her sweet scent. "Darling daughter, I name you Kelly. Modesty will be your path. When talents grow and hearts boast with pride, you will be the whisper in the wind that keeps man true."

A large wooden crib shimmered into existence, and Atropos gently laid her daughters inside. The babies cooed and squirmed before settling into sleep, their arms wound tightly around one another. Their mother beamed. "They are already so graceful and loving."

"I am next!" Lachesis called with glee. She gripped the pot in excitement and anticipation. "My job is to determine a soul's worth, its length in the mortal world. For my daughter, I grant her faithfulness to guide mankind through the journey, no matter how long or short."

Another bubble rose from the cauldron. Like before, this one landed gently in the arms of its mother. This time, revealing a cherubic girl with soft, dark wisps upon her head. Placing a gentle kiss on the baby's forehead, Lachesis pronounced, "I name you Tia. Your steadfast ways will help those who struggle with commitment stay the course and find their dedication. You shall be the savior of so many souls."

The baby gurgled as if to agree, and the sisters gasped in response. The two new mothers turned their expectant eyes to Clotho, who trembled as she stepped up to the large kettle.

"It is my joy and burden to spin the threads of human life. I do this knowing, at some point, the spool holding that existence will run out of room. This job requires discipline and strength of heart, the same qualities I wish for in my offspring. To you, my daughter, I request self-control, that you may know your role in this world and adhere to it."

On a light sigh, the liquid released its final gift. As the sphere floated to Clotho's waiting arms, the women watched the silver mixture dull to a sickly gray. It would give no more life.

And yet, as the last bubble popped and the baby gave a healthy cry, the sisters laughed.

"Jo," Clotho declared. "You will be strong when the mortals you assist are weak. Your self-control will allow you to encourage them to work hard, becoming their backbones when they feel they cannot continue, and never to partake in more than they need to sustain life."

As the newest babies settled in with their sisters, the women sighed with satisfaction. Their wish had been fulfilled. They were now mothers, and their daughters would grow to help mankind.

Clotho stared at the infants. “We need a way to draw them back once we have put them on one path or another. Something that will keep them rooted in their true selves and remind them of their tasks.”

The women sat around the fire and discussed what gift they could bestow.

Lachesis snapped her bony fingers. “Silver. We should bestow upon them necklaces, made from the purest silver, with their antitheses etched on small bars. While the charms will appear blank when in the human realm, their reminders will burn brightly. Once the girls return home, the words will become visible.”

“Silver is perfect. It will match their eyes when they are in goddess form. I will conjure the metal,” Atropos said.

“I will enchant them so they grow as our daughters do and always remain the perfect size,” Clotho said.

Lachesis felt she needed to add her contribution. “I will infuse the metal with our blood, so the girls always feel us close by.”

All the women nodded and set to work.

“I call thee forth from the grounds of Bolivia. Come to us, so we may craft our charms.” Atropos waved her hands over the cauldron, and five large pieces of silver floated out, moved to hover over a nearby table, and dropped softly to the worn wood. "That is from the purest source."

"Give me your fingers, sisters." Lachesis took three vials and collected a drop of blood from her own finger, one from Clotho, and three from Atropos. After settling in front of the silver blobs, Lachesis waved her hands. Steam issued from the ore, and it grew so white-hot, it melted into puddles, leaving scorch marks on the table. "Now, it is pure as freshly fallen snow." Once the impurities burned away, she dribbled the blood over the molten metal, ordering it to swirl and combine in an unbreakable bond.

Once cooled, each sister dropped hers in the cauldron. It hissed and sparked, tiny flecks of multicolored flame scattering in every direction.

They lifted their hands and chanted, "These gifts we create for our daughters, imbued with our blood, so they shall always feel a part of who they truly are. May these charms protect them from ever becoming lost on their paths."

Five tiny necklaces rose from the liquid; each with one or more silver bars dangling from the fine chain.

Clotho snatched them out of the air and hurried to the workbench. After placing them carefully, evenly spaced, she removed a bit of powder from a pouch at her waist and sprinkled it liberally over the jewelry. "I give thee power to transform as our daughters grow and hide your messages when not in this realm of existence. You shall also be our line to call them home."

Words flared, appearing like fiery ink, on the metal bars: Lust, Pride, Greed, Envy, Sloth, and Gluttony—the sins the newly born goddesses would help humanity resist.

She blew across the metal, and the words dimmed.

Atropos came and gathered three, fastening them around her daughters' necks. Once it was done, she kissed the top of each infant's head. "May the power of the Fates be with you."

Clotho and Lachesis repeated the ritual, and the women stood back to admire their offspring.

These five babies were the Fates' gifts to the world, guides for humanity, created to assist struggling humans on the paths to redemption the old women set.

About the Authors

If you review this book, please send an e-mail to:

SevenAuthors@yahoo.com

With the subject line:

7 Review

Include the perma-link for your review in the e-mail, and get a response with a surprise from the authors!

For your reference, following the author bio, you'll get a list of all the signings they'll be at in 2016 and some of the ones in 2017 (so you can get your book signed and more)!

Thank you for reading our novel. We appreciate it more than you know!

Casey L. Bond

Award-winning author Casey Bond resides in West Virginia with her husband and their two beautiful daughters. They have two fur-babies, a cat named Nefertiti and an enormous puppy named Benson. Casey loves to read almost as much as she enjoys writing young adult and new adult fiction. Dystopian is her favorite, but all of her works include a romantic element.

Casey's books:
Harvest Saga (set):
Reap (FREE – Winner Best World Building award in 2014 from IABB)
Resist
Reclaim
Catalyst

Sin (Winner 2015 Utopia Award for Best Serial Series)
Temptation
Dark Bishop
Prep for Doom (anthology)
Liquid
Winter Shadows
Shady Bay
Crazy Love
Light in the Darkness (anthology)
Fractured Glass: A Novel Anthology (Finalist – IBA/Fiction: Cross Genre & Finalist – Reader's Favorite 2015/Young Adult Sci-Fi)
Chasing Wishes
Devil Creek
Prisoner of Prophecy

More at: http://authorcaseybond.com

Casey will appear at the following signings:
2016:
RAI—April 2, 2016—Roanoke, VA
UtopiaCon—June 22-26, 2016—Nashville, TN
R&R—November 4-6—Huntington, WV

Jo Michaels

Jo Michaels is...

Hi, I'm Jo. Let's forget all the "Jo Michaels is blah, blah, blah" stuff and just go with it. I'm a voracious reader (often reading more than one book at a time), a writer, a book reviewer, a mom, a wife, and one of the EICs at INDIE Books Gone Wild. I have an almost photographic memory and tend to make people cringe at the number of details I can recall about them and/or their book(s). My imagination follows me around like a conjoined twin and causes me to space out pretty often or laugh out loud randomly in completely inappropriate situations.

<u>Jo's Books</u>:

<u>Mystic series</u>:
Bronya
Lily
Shelia
Melody
Coralie
Markaza

<u>Abigale Chronicles</u>:
Book 1
Book 2
Book 3

M
The Frivoloity Fairies: A Christmas Short Story
I, Zombie
The Bird
Yassa: Genghis Khan's coming-of-age tale
Fractured Glass: A Novel Anthology (Finalist – IBA/Fiction: Cross Genre & Finalist – Reader's Favorite 2015/Young Adult Sci-Fi)
The Indie Author's Guide to: Building a Great Book
Emancipation
Utterances

More at: http://writejomichaels.com

Jo will appear at the following signings:
<u>2016</u>:
RAI—April 2, 2016—Roanoke, VA
UTOPiAcon—June 22-26, 2016—Nashville, TN
<u>2017</u>:
UTOPiAcon—Unknown dates—Nashville, TN
Chapter.con—August 24-27, 2017—London, UK

Tia Silverthorne Bach

Tia Silverthorne Bach has been married to her college sweetheart for twenty years, has three beautiful girls, and adores living in sunny California. Her daughters were born in Chicago, San Diego, and Baltimore; and she feels fortunate to have called many places home. She believes in fairy tales and happy endings and is an avid reader and rabid grammar hound.

She is an award-winning, multi-genre author and an Editor for Indie Books Gone Wild. From an early age, she escaped into books and believes they can be the source of healing and strength. If she's not writing, you can find her on the tennis court, at the movies, reading a good book, or spooning Jif peanut butter right out of the jar.

Tia's Books:

Tala Prophecy series:
Chasing Memories
Chasing Shadows (Finalist – Reader's Favorite 2014/Young Adult Paranormal)
Chasing Forgiveness (novella)
Chasing Destiny

Depression Cookies (Winner – Reader's Favorite 2011 Silver/Realistic Fiction, Finalist – Reader's Favorite 2011/Chick Lit & Finalist – 2011 Next Gen Indie Book Awards/Chick Lit)
Fractured Glass: A Novel Anthology (Finalist – IBA/Fiction: Cross Genre & Finalist – Reader's Favorite 2015/Young Adult Sci-Fi)

More at: http://tiabach.com

Tia will appear at the following signings:
2016:
RAI—April 2, 2016—Roanoke, VA
UTOPiAcon—June 22-26, 2016—Nashville, TN
Penned Con—September 23-24—St. Louis, MO
2017:
Chapter.con—August 24-27, 2017—London, UK

Kelly Risser

Dreamer. Writer. Wanna-be Princess. Kelly works full time as an eLearning Instructional Designer, fitting her creative writing into the evenings and weekends. She's often found lamenting, "It's hard to write when there are so many good books to read!" So, when she's not immersed in the middle of someone else's fantasy world, she's busy creating one of her own.

Kelly's books include the Never Forgotten series (Never Forgotten, Current Impressions, and Always Remembered); Sea of Memories, a novella collection set in the Never Forgotten world; Twists in Time, an anthology on time travel; and Fractured Glass, an anthology that is one continuous story written by five authors.

Kelly lives in Wisconsin with her husband and two children. They share their home with Clyde the Whoodle and a school of fish.

Kelly's books:

Never Forgotten Series:

Never Forgotten (FREE – Finalist - International Best Book Awards 2015/Fantasy & Finalist USA Best Book Awards 2014/Sci-Fi)

Current Impressions (Winner - Reader's Favorite Silver 2015/Young Adult Fantasy)

Always Remembered

Sea of Memories

Certain (anthology)

Twists in Time (anthology)

Fractured Glass: A Novel Anthology (Finalist – IBA/Fiction: Cross Genre & Finalist – Reader's Favorite 2015/Young Adult Sci-Fi)

More at: http://kellyrisser.com

Kelly will appear at the following signings:

2016:

UTOPiAcon—June 22-26, 2016—Nashville, TN

Once Upon a Book—August 12-13—Frankenmuth, MI

Penned Con—September 23-24—St. Louis, MO

N. L. Greene

Author N. L. Greene is a writer of YA and NA Contemporary and Paranormal Romances. She currently lives in Florida with her husband and two beautiful daughters. When she isn't writing or reading, she enjoys traveling around the world with her family, shopping and doing other girly things with her girls, or playing video games with her husband. She is a lover of dogs, chocolate, and anything pink!

N. L.'s Books:
MysticSeeker Series:
Illusions Begin
Magic Unfolds

Twisted
Fractured Glass: A Novel Anthology (Finalist – IBA/Fiction: Cross Genre & Finalist – Reader's Favorite 2015/Young Adult Sci-Fi)

As author Riana Lucas:
The Deadly Flower Series:
Poppy
Poppy: Awake
Poppy: Revealed

More at: http://nlgreene.com

N. L. will appear at the following signings:
2016:
AITC—March 12, 2016—Kissimmee, FL
UTOPiAcon—June 22-26, 2016—Nashville, TN
Penned Con—Sept 23 & 24, 2016—St. Louis, MO
Indie BookFest 2016—October 7, 8, & 9—Orlando, FL